E.C. MADRID

The Flickers of Fall

Book One of The Aazar Series

First published by Tiger House Publications 2023

Copyright © 2023 by E.C. Madrid

This novel is entirely a work of fiction. The names, characters, and incidents portrayed in it are the work of the author's imagination. Any resemblance to actual persons, living or dead, events, or localities is entirely coincidental.

First edition

ISBN: 9798987500910

This book was professionally typeset on Reedsy.
Find out more at reedsy.com

Contents

Dedication

I dedicate this novel to all those in the Johnson family who we've lost: My mother, Una, my grandmother, Celestene, my Uncle Butch, and my Aunt Barb. We miss you all.

Special Thank You

A special thank you to Jamie Davis and Pamela Madrid. Without them, this book would still be rotting away on my computer. Thank you for believing in me before I did.

Chapter One: Choices

Norma stared into the darkness with no hope of rescue. Her head throbbed with pain. She felt cold pavement against her cheek as sweat dripped down her face. She was lying flat on her stomach on a dirty cement floor. Norma's hands were tied behind her back with a coarse piece of what felt like a rope. She winced as another piece tied her feet and dug into her ankles. She couldn't move. There was only one thing Norma knew for sure: She would die in this place. Fresh panic gripped her all of a sudden, and her heart pounded with fury in her chest.

She tried to calm herself. Panic wasn't going to help. What was the last thing she could remember? She wrinkled her eyebrows and bit her lip as she tried to think. She couldn't see anything. If she held her palm to her face, she wouldn't be able to see her hand. Her last memory came back and gripped Norma with terror: she was in an attic of a house outside town, where she held hands with Adam. A shaman said they'd be safe there. She remembered the crash as the floor broke from under them, and they fell into the debris. A dark boot covered in grime moved toward her face before blackness settled in front of her eyes.

The silence was deafening. She couldn't hear water dripping or wind blowing. She knew that wherever she was, she was alone. Norma heard no breathing or shuffling from anyone other than herself. Her stomach growled with demand against the pavement, breaking the silence. Her head throbbed in pain as she shifted into a seated position. That's when Norma realized the wet substance on her head wasn't sweat: it was blood. Blood from a head wound, no doubt given to her by the owner of the black boot.

She almost laughed, but instead, it came out a whimper.

They had been so careful. Norma paid the shaman well, and he swore his 'shield' would protect them. But The Order swarmed them as if they had been standing in an empty field. The shaman probably sold them out the moment they left.

She couldn't stand the Variants or the war. Why was she alive during this time in history? Her parents never stopped talking about the last recession before the war. Norma wished she could go through that instead. Her mind snapped to them. What happened to her parents? She tried to remain calm. Norma would be fine. She was innocent. She wasn't part of the war and hadn't chosen sides. That had to count for something. Maybe she could cut a deal, and they would let her go. She tried not to think about the mass grave sites found a few weeks ago across town. All those people couldn't have been soldiers.

She shivered with cold and fright, realizing she was almost naked. Norma wore what felt like a worn-out hospital gown or a thin potato sack with holes to put her arms through. She wore jeans and a T-shirt when she was captured. Thankfully, the sack went down over her knees. She was glad they hadn't left her naked, however filthy and horrible the thing smelled. Maybe it wasn't the rag that smelled horrible.

Perhaps it was her.

She scooted back until she felt cold brick against her back. Her head throbbed as she rested it on the wall, and the coolness seemed to numb the pain. She felt dizzy. The room smelled stale of something she couldn't put her finger on. Something metallic. More blood, she realized. Norma had never smelled so much in her life. She leaned to the side as she threw up bile, adding a new smell to her surroundings. She wondered how many prisoners had been locked in this place. How many spent their last moments alive here? How many bled to death on the floors?

She sat up as straight as possible, wishing she could wipe her mouth and head. Or at least be able to push her hair out of her face. She also wished she could've said goodbye to her family. They had gone into hiding in haste. She and Adam just grabbed a couple of backpacks and left. She ached for him and hoped he was okay. She hoped he was thinking of a way out of this. Adam had always been good at coming up with ideas. Then again, maybe it was better they finally got caught. It would end the running, the hiding in basements and living in barns. Norma tired of traveling during the night and sleeping during the day. Maybe being caught would be for the better. Life on the run was no life for her.

Then, light blinded her as a door opened. It materialized from nowhere. She blinked her eyes, trying to force them to adjust as a silhouette in the doorway began gliding toward her. She couldn't hear its footsteps and before she could look around, the light disappeared, and the door closed. She heard it shut behind the figure, bringing her back into darkness. The figure was inside, waiting.

She sat for a moment, waiting for the person to say something. It seemed like an eternity. What were they waiting for, and why would they stand there, torturing her in this way? Wouldn't taking her life be enough?

"Who are you?" Her voice cracked and she realized how thirsty she was. How long had she been there? Had it been days? Hours? Had she been lying there for even longer than that?

The figure stood silently. She couldn't see, but Norma knew it was staring at her. She could feel its eyes. She couldn't stand the silence, but she wasn't going to beg for her life. Norma would take whatever they did to her, but she wouldn't beg. She owed her family that. She waited for a response, realizing the figure had ignored her.

"WHO ARE YOU!" she screamed with all the rage she could muster. It came out as a whisper.

A soft light floated from the figure to the ceiling and hovered there. Norma could finally see the walls of the square room. It was bigger than she anticipated. It was a black box theater, and all the doors were cemented shut. What was she doing there? The black walls and floor were covered in grime and a dark liquid. She could see a faint outline of where the sound and light studio used to be. The door the figure came through was the only entrance into the room unblocked. She noticed it had a small slit in the bottom to give food to prisoners, yet she knew she hadn't received any. Then she noticed a small dirty mat lying a few feet away. It was barely more than a towel. She looked for a toilet of some sort but saw none. The sack she wore was filthy and blood splattered. Some of it was hers; some were someone else's. It took everything for her not to throw up again at the sight of it.

In front of her stood a tall woman wearing the uniform of The Order: black boots that went up to her knees, dark charcoal cargo pants, and a tight red T-shirt under a worn brown leather jacket. "S.O." was sewn on the left shoulder in scarlet. She had brown skin and dark brown eyes that saw everything. Her chestnut hair sat in soft curls on her shoulders. Her plump lips wore a solemn expression that seemed permanent. She looked as though she had never smiled a day in her life. It may have been true. She stood straight as her arms hung loose by her tiny hips. She was gorgeous. She was also someone Norma knew.

Norma felt a wave of relief. She had been preparing to die all this time, but she had been delivered. She had lost hope too soon. No one knew what happened to her savior last year, but Norma was happy to see her now. She was glad that she came to free her from certain death. She couldn't have picked anyone better.

"It's so good to see you, Aazar," Norma croaked with joy, wishing she could hug her.

Aazar looked Norma up and down, appraising the situation. The pain of watching a friend suffer was evident.

Aazar glanced around the dreary room. "Such a strange place for us to meet again, wouldn't you say?"

"No kidding," Norma said with a quick smile, although she was uncomfortable with Aazar's tone.

"How did they catch you?" Aazar asked. "I figured they'd be years before finding someone as esteemed as you. With all your friends and influence…" She trailed off.

Aazar seemed different to her. She couldn't figure out what it was. She appeared calm, yet malice dripped from every word she spoke. Norma didn't understand how someone could change so drastically.

"Trusted a Shaman," Norma said as she sucked her teeth disapprovingly.

"A horrible mistake."

"A mistake indeed," Aazar said in a soft tone.

Norma tried to wriggle free. "Come on, untie me, and let's get out of here."

Aazar blinked. "Leave?" Her head cocked to the left. "Norma, you can't leave. You are a prisoner. Surely, you've gathered that?"

Norma stared at her from the floor. She glanced at the floating light on the ceiling: it was a ball of fire. It was strange how accustomed Norma became to witnessing these abilities. She hadn't even registered that Aazar used them. Norma glanced at the uniform again. Of course, she wasn't here to help her. She must have lost more blood than she had thought.

"You're one of them? A...Variant?" Norma's face flushed with rage. She calmed herself again and tried to reason with Aazar, "You can't possibly be saying you won't help me. We're friends."

"The time for 'help' is long gone," Aazar said, waving the statement away as she pushed some thick brown hair away from her face. "You knew your choices." Aazar smiled in humor. "But friends...are we, really?"

Norma's ties were so tight they were cutting off the circulation in her wrists. She could feel them chaffing. "What choices are you talking about?" she spat as her eyes flickered. "To live underneath the rule of monsters and freaks? To fight on the losing side of a war?"

Aazar threw her head back and laughed. Then her eyes narrowed dangerously as she hissed, "You chose to live a lie!"

Norma blinked, surprised. What was she talking about?

"To live a lie?" she repeated with her eyebrows furrowed.

Aazar's eyes softened again as she bent down to her. She pushed the matted blonde hair from Norma's face and looked into her eyes. She put a knowing smile on her lips.

"It's not your fault, really," Aazar said in a soft tone. "Just about everyone believed the same. When you're raised to hate, you will hate." Her eyes narrowed again. "Until someone teaches you differently."

Norma felt as though someone had poured ice water down her back. As Aazar stood, she looked off into a distance, much farther than the black box walls. "I know why you chose what you did. I remember the day. It was the funeral. I know you don't realize that was when you chose at all, but nevertheless, you did."

Norma couldn't understand what that had to do with anything. Why she would bring up such a hurtful topic made Norma even more furious.

Aazar turned her back to Norma as she went on. "You were upset that day," she said softly, remembering. "So was I…"

Her voice trailed off as silence filled the room with shared grief.

Aazar gathered herself, and when she turned around, a menacing air came from her, overriding her pain. The violence was evident in her eyes. "And I stood next to Adam."

Cold fear swiped through Norma at the mention of her boyfriend. Aazar had always loathed Adam for no reason. Norma knew that Adam wouldn't last very long under the care of this new Aazar. "Where is Adam, Aazar? Where is he?"

She stared at her. "I've been to better funerals," Aazar said in a mocking and flippant tone.

Appalled and confused, Norma gulped. "Excuse me?"

"That's what he said while he was at the funeral," Aazar said, remembering, "'I've been to better funerals. Much bigger, many more people. I mean, this is nice, but I've been to better.' So disrespectful. So disgusting." Aazar glared at Norma. "Not that this was different behavior for someone so self-absorbed. Why would he show respect? He had never shown respect to anyone before. It was his nature. But you sided with him anyway." Aazar's eyes narrowed even more. "You slept with him anyway."

"At least he was there for the wake. You disappeared. He held me when I cried in his arms," Norma said as she tried to push out her chest in defiance. "He cared for me."

"He cared about looking good to the public," Aazar said. "Tell me, did he still marry you after the money was gone? Or were you still waiting for him to love you?"

Norma was silent, so Aazar continued, "He wanted the title of 'nurturer' that day, so he nurtured when he knew it was opportune. He didn't care about you. He cared about his self-image."

"I don't believe you."

"Of course not, and so," Aazar said and gestured around the room. "Here we are."

Norma stared in stunned silence. She couldn't believe how angry Aazar was. The woman had always been so kind to Norma. How could she have thought so ill of her and never shown it? To let Norma be a prisoner to these people. But Norma realized that these Variants were Aazar's people.

Aazar watched her. She tilted her head, suddenly curious, and asked, "Would you die for him?"

"What?" Norma asked, coming out of her deep thought.

"Would you be willing to die for Adam?" Aazar smirked. "Your dear, sweet Adam? Your 'nurturer'?"

Norma lowered her eyes and muttered, "What a morbid thing to ask."

Aazar almost laughed. "He wasn't willing to die for you." She allowed that thought to settle in before her eyes glazed with menace as she continued, "But he died all the same."

Alarm rang through Norma's blood vessels. Sweat poured from her head, mixing with the blood from her wound as tears sprang to her eyes. Adam was gone, and she was next.

"Are you going to kill me?"

Aazar stared at her, masking her emotions. She tilted her head again as if trying to understand.

"ANSWER ME, GOD DAMN IT," Norma hollered.

Aazar looked at her, smiling. "Finally, you show some spine. Where was this when you allowed yourself to be manipulated by liars and cheats? Where was this when you allowed yourself to be walked over by people who didn't even care about you?" Her smile melted away from her face as her eyes hardened. "You chose your side. You chose the side of your friends and family instead of the truth." She lowered her eyes to the floor. "Most do."

A deathly moment of silence passed as Aazar glanced at the ceiling lost in thought. "There was an old saying: You should never surround yourself with people you wouldn't want to die with." She turned to Norma. "Do you think you were successful in this?"

Norma blinked away tears as she closed her eyes. How could things have gone so wrong? How could all her friends and family members die? She thought about her family just then. If they were killed, she wanted death too. If Adam was gone, she wanted to join him. She hated the war, The Order, and everything else about this new world the Variants were building. Aazar was right. She had made her choice a long time ago.

"Yes," she squeaked. "Yes, I was."

Aazar offered a small smile. Norma watched as a small dagger slid from Aazar's sleeve into her open palm. "Then you are where you should be."

Two Years Earlier

Chapter Two: The Maiden Awakens

Aazar Salazar closed her eyes and cleared her mind as the wind blew through the golden leaves of the willow tree where she sat. She listened to the wind as it whistled past her ears and brushed against her skin. The sun beamed through her eyelids, and as she heard the birds chirping and the tiny creek babble in front of her, she felt at peace. An ant nibbled on the little toe that poked through her sandal, but Aazar ignored it as best she could and remained still, keeping her mind clear.

She often sat under this tree after school, clearing her mind of the day. Her mother didn't like it when she disappeared into the forest and preferred for her to come home immediately after school to do her homework. She thought Aazar had a secret cell phone she kept hidden somewhere. She didn't want Aazar to be influenced by Nomophobia. More people had been diagnosed with the inability to live without technology, and her mother, a very proud Regressor, was very concerned.

Regressors were a new religious group against all electronics. After the climate disaster in 2075 destroyed most of California, many Regressors thought cell phones and technology culture brought people to a level of insensitivity that allowed them to ignore environmental problems. Although the church said it cared about nature, it didn't do anything to help the planet and often frowned on climate refugees that came through town. Regressors spent most of their time spreading fear about Nomophobes and the mysterious Variants.

Aazar didn't know much about what was happening in the world, but it wasn't uncommon for people living in small towns to be ignorant of world events in 2078. Her family had no cell phones, televisions, or computers, which made them outsiders in an already small community. Aazar's mother was still ashamed. Aazar's father owned the only arcade in town. He'd inherited it after his father died, and since work was hard to come by, he decided he couldn't close it down. It was an indispensable source of income since her mother didn't work. Her mother kept Aazar and her father away from the church as much as possible because of her embarrassment.

Aazar paid her no mind. Her father ran the home for the most part. Her mother did her fair share of complaining, but when it came down to whether Aazar was allowed to give out their landline number to a classmate, her father had the last say. When he decided to name Aazar after a girl he'd known from Iran, she fought against it, claiming the long A sound would confuse people, but eventually relented like she always did. Aazar loved her dad. She was an only child, and since he adored her, he let Aazar do what she pleased despite her mother's worrying.

Her modest father was a hardworking man. Although he claimed to be a Regressor, he could never escape the love for video games his father instilled in him and didn't share his wife's beliefs about technology. He ran the arcade alone for the most part unless it was the summer when Aazar could help. She would hand out tickets and prizes while he maintained the games and sales. Aazar and her father sometimes watched America's Fan Pick together in the backroom of the arcade before closing on a tiny TV that he used to watch the news, even though her mother called it filth.

She heard a movement behind her, and her eyes flew open, breaking her concentration. They relaxed when she saw the rabbit hopping off in front of her into the woods. She liked rabbits. They always seemed so happy and playful. When Aazar was younger, she often imagined she was a rabbit and hopped alongside them until they realized she wasn't kin (which was quite immediate). She looked around. The sun was almost down. Grabbing her backpack, she kicked the ant off her toe, stood, and brushed off her orange skirt as she headed toward home.

Their home was one of the smaller ones in Newmalton, but not the smallest. The city had grown since the new mayor, William Kang, came three years ago. He wasn't the most pleasant man, but he won everyone over after building the town bowling alley, except for Aazar and her father. Aazar didn't like him because he smelled strange and looked at her like she was crawling with fleas. Her family was poor but not poor enough for him to smirk at her. Since her mother didn't work, the house was spotless, and she always had clean clothes.

She passed the community pool on her way home that day. She tip-toed to the gates and looked up to the chair that surveyed the water. Her face flushed with blood when her eyes landed on him. Avery Kang was sitting in the lifeguard box, watching the last swimmers as they got out of the pool. He was a Korean teen who wore a tattered green baseball hat that she'd never seen him without and a tight white T-shirt he probably wouldn't take off even if someone drowned. Although she knew rippling biceps sat comfortably underneath, Avery never walked around without a shirt. He wore brown swim trunks to his knee and brown sandals that looked like they'd been passed down from generation to generation. She looked at the dark hair on his legs and wondered if it was soft or scratchy. Staring at Avery on her way home was becoming the highlight of her weekdays.

The one thing that Mayor Kang brought to Newmalton that Aazar liked was his handsome and kind son. Even though he was the most popular guy in the city other than his father, he had a heart of gold. Avery always opened the doors for the girls, no matter who they were. He had the voice of the Jocks and the ear of the Nerds. Avery had always been able to connect with everyone in a positive way. She wished she had an ounce of his charisma.

He sat up straighter, showing off his lean yet muscular body. Aazar watched as he took his hat off and ran a hand through his dark black hair. He surveyed the pool with his intense green eyes. They were the strangest color of emerald she had ever seen. She froze as his eyes found hers and their eyes locked for a moment in an intense stare. Then he smiled his perfect smile and waved. Too shocked to wave back, she felt her face warm and walked quickly toward her house. She knew he was nice to everyone but hated it when he was nice to her. She hated how special he made her feel when she knew she wasn't.

* * *

The Regressor church was a simple one with red bricks, small windows, and a dome ceiling. The grass on the front lawn had already become brown, brittle, and crunched under the crowd's feet as they passed the large "Regressor" church sign in front of the building. Aazar and her mother stood in front of the church, which was more crowded than usual that evening. Christmas was approaching, and looking as pious as possible was essential.

Aazar tried to ignore the reproachful faces all looking in their direction. She filed in behind her mother, full of regret. Although her mother was a beautiful Black woman, her standoffish demeanor took away from her graceful figure and luscious hair. Her mother narrowed her dark brown eyes at Aazar without warning.

"Don't start," her mother hissed in Aazar's ear as they walked down the aisle. "We just got here."

"I didn't say anything," Aazar said when they reached the third pew.

Aazar's mother smiled at the woman sitting at the end of the bench, and she graciously pulled her legs in so they could get through.

Aazar's mother rounded on her as they found a seat, "You didn't have to say anything. It's written all over your face."

Aazar sighed. It was going to be one of those "Mom hates me for breathing" days.

"You could've just left me at home."

"You've missed too many days!" her mother whispered as she waved to another congregation member across the room. "I had to bring you or your father, or people will start to talk."

"They already do, Mom. Maybe we should stop coming. You don't have to come here to practice your religion. You can hate electronics from anywhere."

"That is not the point." Her mother said as they sat down, "The point is to find people in your community that believe the way we do."

"Well, I don't believe the way these people do," Aazar said with her arms crossed.

"Quiet! Someone might hear you."

Just then, a short, plump woman walked up to them with a fake grin plastered on her face, holding a cardboard fan. Aazar was sure she had practiced this expression in the mirror many times for such occasions.

"Anaya!" she bellowed at Aazar's mother in case anyone else hadn't known they were there. A few patrons glanced around. "How are you? Where's Howard?"

Anaya blanched and fiddled with her hands, "I...he had to work today."

"At the 'arcade,' right?" The rude woman shook her head, fanned herself, and continued, "Men lack the fortitude to stay on the righteous path. It's so hard to steer them in the right direction."

Anaya gaped at her while Aazar tried to pretend to be interested in the wood of the bench.

"Anyway, enjoy the service, dear. I'm sure there's still hope for Aazar. The young are often easier to mold." The woman patted her mother's arm and walked off.

Aazar looked at her mother, giving her a small, sympathetic smile.

"Hush," her mother replied, pulling out her worn bible. "It's started."

A thin, light-skinned man (who sweated like a man far larger than he was) named Pastel Flemmings sauntered up to the pulpit. He had lost most of his hair but refused to shave the remaining strands off for the sake of his pride. He reminded her of a vulture perched over the congregation, looking for the weakest prey so he could eat their remains. His eyes landed on a young couple in the back of the room. After many patrons had looked over their shoulders to see whom he'd chosen, he began opening the fairly new-looking book. The religion was very young but had grown significantly in the past few years.

"Temptation is all around us, family," he began.

A few congregation members murmured in understanding while others looked at their feet in shame. Aazar had to keep her eyes from rolling back into her skull.

He continued, "I know how difficult it is to navigate this world without a cell phone. The devil is alive and well and burrowing himself inside these small devices we carry everywhere."

The congregation was enthralled with fear, an ideal state for this type of teaching, Aazar had realized years before. She saw the church as a verbal horror movie that everyone came to listen to get their morbid addiction to fear off. If people thought they were safe, they needed someone reminding them that they weren't.

"They may seem harmless, even good at times," he stated. "But the good of these devices is nothing but a gateway to the evils of this world."

He paused for effect. "You say you will use them to study, but low and behold, you will find yourself looking at pornography! You say you will call your mother, but you will call your mistress!"

The congregations applauded, approving his message, as the young couple hung their heads in shame, clearly a part of a scandal she knew nothing about. Unlike the rest, her mother didn't look away from the priest unless she needed to write something down.

He paced back and forth to show the true urgency of his message. When Aazar was a little girl, she remembered getting wrapped up in the drama, but the older she grew, she realized the church used the same technique television executives used: staged walking, music crews, rehearsed lines, etc. The hypocrisy was unbelievable.

She looked around the crowd, noting the adults dosing against pews, other women like her mother writing down notes on the book with highlighters, and children bouncing bored in their seats. Her eyes caught an intense flicker of green from across the room, and then, her eyes were locked with Avery's. He wore a gray suit with a white dress shirt underneath. He looked back at her.

He didn't smile.

She felt a shiver go down her spine as she looked away. She felt like he could see right through her. She pulled her blouse closer to herself and unconsciously scratched her wrist. She forced herself to look away and spend the rest of the service trying not to glance in his direction. She could still feel his eyes on her, regardless of what she did, but she wasn't bold enough to let herself look over to confirm that his gaze was in her direction.

When service ended, Aazar pushed her way to the exit, getting quite a few gasps along the way. When she reached the church doors, she shoved her way through and breathed in the cool fall air. Her mother came out afterward. She thought her mother would yell at her for her abrupt exit, but instead, Anaya encouraged her to go home so she could talk to her friends. Aazar was relieved to walk home alone and skip the recap of the sermon her mother would've indeed given her.

She clutched her purse as she walked toward home and passed the market and the bowling alley before reaching the convenience store. Evenings were her favorite things about Newmalton. Everyone went home early, even for a small town, leaving the streets clean and quiet as they burned their fireplaces to combat the cold. The smell of burning ironwood filled her nostrils as the wind blew small autumn leaves into her already wild hair. She watched as the skinny stray cats and dogs sniffed trashcans for a bite to eat. Aazar had decided long ago that when she grew up and became a veterinarian, she would make sure she left food out for the animals wherever she worked. She would be eighteen soon, so she wouldn't have to wait long to start training.

Her road was on the other end of the city, and she had a long walk ahead of her. There was no bus system in Newmalton since they were seldom considered a city. They weren't even on the local news weather maps. She stopped at the convenience store to look for some gum. A small radio on the counter blared the news throughout the store.

"Billionaire Ryan Hurst has purchased the California Islands north of Mexico. The California area has been abandoned since the devastating earthquake of 2075 three years ago, but Mr. Hurst believes he can change things."

Aazar walked to the register and handed the teenage boy at the cash register her gum as the new continued.

"Officials in South Utah have declared a state of emergency. Bandits and vagrancy have overrun the new territory, and all people are warned to stay away from the area for the time being."

The teenage boy handed her the change without glancing up from his phone. She wondered if he could live without it. You could never tell a Nomophobe until they were without a cell phone. She turned back down the street, chewing her gum.

Aazar turned onto Boyd St, the street she grew up on. The lush gardens on the front lawns were full of vegetables and fruit trees. A couple of girls standing on their porch saw Aazar and began whispering. They both gave a big laugh and ran inside the house. Aazar sighed.

She wasn't favored much by the kids in the neighborhood. She wasn't sure if it was how skinny, poor, or bushy her long brown curly hair often was. She knew she was a little taller than most girls, and her brand of dark brown eyes and brown skin wasn't seen much in this part of Arizona, but Aazar knew how to keep to herself.

She was almost at her gate before she heard feet running toward her. She turned around and saw Avery sprinting down the uneven sidewalk, still in his church clothes. He flashed her a brilliant smile before doubling over to catch his breath. She was frozen, watching his back rise and fall as his hands rested on his knees. His jacket was unbuttoned and hanging loose on his shoulders. His shirt was still tucked in his pants, but some of it had come loosened. The bottom of his ironed pants had dirt on them. As he stood up, he ran a hand casually through his hair as though this was a regular thing.

"You walk fast," he said, out of breath, looking up at her with a smile.

She couldn't understand why he was grinning so much or why he was here at all. Avery Kang had never been down her street before. Not that he should have, since he lived in a big house with all the other rich people a mile in the opposite direction. She looked around at the homes around her. She saw a few blinds close as her eyes landed on them. His being here would be the conversation at tables around Newmalton by tomorrow afternoon. And he was talking to her: strange Aazar Salazar from Boyd St.

He caught his breath and stood up straight. He opened his left hand to reveal a small golden locket. Aazar recognized it and grabbed her throat, feeling for the locket where it should have been. He held it out to her.

"I found it outside the pool, where you walked by earlier. I tried to catch up with you then too, but you disappeared. You should join the track team.

I bet they could use you," he said, smiling again. "I see you wearing this all the time. I figured you'd want it back."

She stared at him for a moment and moved to grab the locket from his hand. Instead, he took a step toward her, and she took a step back. He gave her a gentle smile. He held the necklace up.

"May I?" he asked.

"What?"

Before she could protest, he stepped around her to put the necklace on her neck. Surprised by the gesture, she clumsily pulled her hair up, exposing her throat as Avery began closing the clasp. She felt his fingers brush the back of her neck as he fiddled with it. Each time his fingers touched her, sharp pangs of lust traveled from her spine down her body. After he was done, he grabbed her shoulders and turned her around to face him as she dropped her hair back down on her shoulders. He stood there for a second, looking at her as if taking in his handy work.

"Thank you," she whispered.

"It's nothing," he said, flashing another beautiful smile. "See you at school!"

Then he ran back in the other direction towards town without looking back. Aazar turned around and watched his back until he was no longer visible and watched a little while after that. Avery Kang came out here to give her necklace back. She brushed her fingers against it. The hairs on her neck were still standing on end as if he was still in front of her. He came out here, she thought, for her.

Chapter Three: Change in the Winds

Aazar hadn't been able to sleep that night. She couldn't get her mind off how he looked at her. Aazar tried to meditate as she did at the creek, but the stillness was interrupted by the feeling of Avery's gentle fingers grazing her neck. She knew he always made everyone feel like they were special, but she couldn't understand why he was bothering with her at all. Then she laughed at herself. He wasn't 'bothering' with her. He gave her her own locket back. It wasn't a sign of anything more than a good Samaritan. Hell, that explained why he had been looking at her in Church. But why didn't he wait until school the next day? She went back and forth for a while before convincing herself it was nothing, but it had taken all night.

She left for school a few minutes late to avoid the other kids in the neighborhood on their way to school. She didn't want to deal with the constant harassment they gave her. After the last kid had giggled down the street, she opened her door and looked down the crooked sidewalk. She tried not to think about Avery standing there hours earlier.

When she got to school, she headed toward the empty rooms where the theater program used to be. They had gotten rid of it when teenagers started making viral videos and lost interest in the slower roads to fame. Why study theatre when you could get rich and famous by making reaction videos? On the way down the hall, she saw a girl glance in her direction and smirk. Aazar ignored her and opened the door to the mini theater.

The room was larger than most classrooms, but not as big as an auditorium.

Chairs were stacked against the wall and on top of a desk covered in old playbills. Aazar sat with her legs dangling over the dusty stage and laid back to stare at the ceiling. The rooms air felt stale, and Aazar could hear muffled voices in the parking lot through the thin walls. She figured she had a few minutes before the first bell rang. She would head to class after the halls had emptied so she wouldn't have to deal with anyone. She wondered how many plays had been produced on this stage before it closed. How many kids had bowed and cried and bonded there? The door swung open almost immediately.

Aazar sat upright. Rebecca Bailey's red hair swung around her neck as she entered the room, and her brown eyes were filled with malice for Aazar. She was a furious girl who lived a few houses down from her. She was looking just as angry as ever as she looked at Aazar today.

"What are you doin' here?" she spat, looking around the room as though she didn't know this part of the school existed.

"Nothing, just sitting. Waiting for class to start," Aazar said. She pulled her backpack closer to her and Rebecca glared at the move.

"There ain't any classes in this area."

"There usually aren't any people here either, which is why I like it," Aazar said in a flat tone.

Rebecca put her hands on her hips. "You waitin' for Avery?"

"What?" Aazar asked, surprised. "Why?"

"You wanna play it like that?" The girl moved closer.

Aazar sighed. "I don't have time to do whatever you're trying to do here, so I'm just going to go." She stood up and grabbed her backpack.

Rebecca stepped in front of her, blocking her way to the door.

"Are you serious right now?" Aazar said, exasperated.

Rebecca was about to say something else, but the bell rang. She glared at her.

"This ain't over."

Rebecca turned and walked out of the room, slamming the door behind her.

"Perfect," Aazar muttered under her breath. She had only been seen with

Avery for a second, and it was already costing her reputation at school.

* * *

Before she knew it, the lunch bell rang. She loathed lunch. She had to go through the lunch line, and there was no way she could avoid people. She rushed to the cafeteria, hoping to get her food and return to the theatre before anyone could harass her.

She reached the front of the line before seeing Rebecca enter the cafeteria. Rebecca made a beeline toward her, getting more irritated with each step. Several girls walked up behind her, giggling at the upcoming drama. Rebecca was about ten feet away before stopping, forcing the other girls to bump into her back. Avery had walked into the room, making his way toward the popular table, looking in Aazar's direction with curiosity. Rebecca spat at her, narrowly missing Aazar's burrito. The other girls laughed as they followed Rebecca to the other side of the cafeteria.

She looked at Avery, who seemed to ignore the entire scene. Then his eyes landed on her. She had been staring again. Her face got hot, and she looked away as she headed out to the theater. He had never used to make eye contact before. It was like he sensed her now. She turned down the hallway. Of course, that was ridiculous, she thought. She was making things more intense than they were again. She seemed to be doing that a lot lately.

"So, what you been givin' him for him to come all the way out to our side of town?" a sinister voice said behind her. She felt her skin crawl at the sound of it.

She turned around to see Rebecca, who had a smirk on her face. She placed a hand on her hip, swishing her long skirt as she tapped her foot, waiting for the answer.

Aazar stared at her.

"Well? What you been givin' him?" Rebecca said.

"Nothing," Aazar said, finally finding her voice. She didn't want to tell Rebecca anything because Rebecca always lied. Even about the simplest of things.

Rebecca glanced at the necklace around Aazar's neck. She brought her glance back to Aazar's face with a glare.

"Why's he giving you gifts if you ain't givin' him nothing?" Rebecca spat.

Aazar fumed at the nosy neighbors spreading gossip around town about her. Someone must have seen him give her the necklace.

"He didn't give me anything," Aazar said, turning to leave, touching the necklace without thinking. "This was mine before. He was just giving it back to me."

Rebecca grabbed Aazar by the arm and pulled her forward so she could look at the necklace. "I don't think I've seen you wear this before."

Aazar struggled to pull her arm away. "IT'S MINE. Leave me alone!"

"Oh, come on, be honest about it. You're screwing him. The least you can do is share the wealth. Give it to me, and I won't tell anyone," Rebecca said as she held on.

"What are you talking about!" Aazar grunted as she struggled to get her arm free.

"Don't pretend you're innocent!" Rebecca growled. "You've always been strange, and no one could figure out why. You are always going out in the middle of the woods. It turns out you're just a little whore. It's disgusting."

Her entire body was pulsing with anger and rage as she tried to struggle free. Rebecca would tell everyone she was having sex with Avery because of a nice gesture She felt as if she was going to burst into flames. Then she felt herself grow hot. Immediately Rebecca fell back, yelping in painful surprise and Aazar felt coolness around her again, almost as fast as she had felt the heat. She stared at Rebecca in horror. Rebecca shrieked as she stared at her bright pink hands, seeing the severe burns to her fingers and palms. Aazar knelt to help Rebecca, but Rebecca jumped away. She stared at Aazar for a moment before sprinting toward the hallway, leaving Aazar alone in silence.

Aazar panicked. She grabbed her backpack and ran off campus toward home.

* * *

Aazar flung herself on her bed as her bedroom door slammed shut behind her. She didn't understand what had happened to Rebecca. She saw the events race through her head: her anger, Rebecca's shrieking, the hideous burns on Rebecca's hands.

Seeing that Aazar was in a mood, her mother said nothing as she ran past her to the stairs leading to her bedroom. She didn't even ask why Aazar was home early from school. Her mother had never been the nurturing kind anyway. She often watched Aazar from a distance as if she was contaminated. Since Aazar's father had treated Aazar like she could do no wrong, Aazar's mother drifted alone in the house, cleaning or cooking in silence, not a part of the family.

Aazar wished she had a comforting mother right now. She wished she could tell her what happened and how scared she was and ask what to do. Instead, Aazar sobbed without stopping into her pillow. Why had she gotten hot like that? Why had she gotten so hot that she had burned Rebecca but didn't burn herself? What was happening to her?

Maybe she made it happen. She started to think. She had been angry enough to kill Rebecca. Maybe her body knew that and wanted to take care of Rebecca on its own. Perhaps she was abnormal.

She sat for a moment and tried to do whatever she did again. She tried to get hot enough to burn. She felt ridiculous. She thought about Rebecca. She hated her but realized she didn't hate her as much as she used to. Now, she felt nothing but guilt.

A few hours passed. Finally, a door slammed shut downstairs. Aazar's heart leaped for a moment, realizing her father was home from the Arcade. She didn't move as she heard his footsteps thumping up the staircase. She heard a knock on her door. Without waiting for an answer, it opened slowly.

"Aazar," her father's voice came in through the crack, "are you decent?"

"Of course, I'm decent, Dad," Aazar said, allowing her father's voice to calm her nerves. "Come on in."

Her father came through the door, bending to get in. Seeing the sizable Mexican man walk through any door was like seeing a small giant enter a room. His size kept teenagers in line at the Arcade and kept them from breaking into his store when they were closed. Aazar believed people in town would bother her and her family more if her father weren't so large. He was like a large brown bear. And no one wanted to poke the bear.

"You weren't downstairs to greet me," he said. "Why would you miss an opportunity to jump all over your dad?"

Her momentary joy of speaking with her father came to an abrupt halt.

She looked back at her pillow, avoiding his eyes. She didn't know how to explain this to her father. She couldn't explain it to herself. What would he do if he found out what she had done? Rebecca would tell her parents, and they'd be beating down the door by the morning.

She sighed. "I accidentally hurt Rebecca today."

He smirked at the mention of Rebecca and said, "Accidentally on purpose?"

Aazar snorted, then she thought about the question. After a few seconds, she replied, "I don't know. But she got hurt, and now I don't know what to do?"

"Did you apologize?" her father offered.

She shook her head no. He didn't understand the gravity of what she had done, but she wasn't sure she wanted him to just yet. The truth of what happened would come out and everything would change. Maybe she could tell him in a way that wouldn't frighten him the way Rebecca had been.

"Well, the first step is to apologize. Ask for forgiveness. It's what God would want for you to do," her father said in a matter-of-fact tone.

Her father and mother had met in the Church long ago. Her father had been less active in recent years, but they still shared the faith for the most part. Sometimes, Aazar wondered if going to the Church was the only time, they spent with each other. She was pretty sure it was the only thing they had in common.

"Dad," Aazar asked, "do you think God blesses us in different ways?"

"Like how Brother Kang has a mansion, but I have a family I love?" her father asked, not understanding.

"No," she said. "I mean do you think he gives some people physical blessings? Like being able to throw a ball faster or being better at math?"

"Yes, of course," her father said. "Sometimes God gives some of us more strength than others to do his will."

Aazar perked up. "Really?"

"Sure." He smiled. "I think he made you smart and beautiful, so you can better do his will. People will listen and follow you when you know what you want."

"You think so, Daddy?" Aazar asked as she got up from the bed.

"Of course." He smiled again. "However, I believe God gave you quite the weakness in return."

Aazar's relief vanished as she thought about what happened to Rebecca, "What do you mean?"

"Stubbornness," he said. Aazar relaxed again and waited for him to go on. "I can see by the look on your mother's face when I came in that you came home early without an explanation again. How often do I have to ask you to mind your mother?"

Aazar gave him a grimace, "At least once more."

"Aazar." Her father said as he leaned against the door frame.

"What? I was stressed out. I told you I hurt someone."

"You could've told your mother that, Aazar. She loves you," her father said, crossing his arms.

"Are you sure about that?"

Her father walked to the bed and sat down, "Aazar, you're not being fair."

"SHE'S never fair!" Aazar protested as she punched her pillow.

"Even still," her father warned, "you should still talk to her."

A loud knocking noise came from downstairs. Aazar listened, wondering who it was and knowing precisely who. She stared at her father's confused face as he turned toward the door. Light footsteps were on the stairs coming towards the room. Her mother opened the door and peeked her head inside. She stared at Aazar in a way Aazar had never seen as she spoke to her father.

"We have visitors."

Mr. and Mrs. Bailey stood holding Rebecca by her shoulders. If Aazar's father was a giant, then Mr. and Mrs. Bailey were two elves next to a small girl. They had red hair just like Rebecca's and matching haircuts. Aazar often wondered if the Baileys were such horrid people that they ended up marrying their siblings. Her father lectured her for comments like that, but it was no secret that the whole town believed the same thing.

Rebecca shook in fright when she saw Aazar advancing down the staircase. She tucked her hands under her arms as she hugged herself. Mr. Bailey moved in front of his family and held a palm out, halting Aazar and her family in the spot.

"That's close enough, thank you very much," Mr. Bailey growled.

Aazar's father straightened his back, revealing his entire length and stared down at Mr. Bailey. The tiny man withered a little, but the malice never left his eyes.

"What is the meaning of this, Charles?" Aazar's father asked. "I don't appreciate you walking into my house commanding people's movements."

"Your daughter is a demon. That's the meaning of this!" Mr. Bailey said, pointing at Aazar. "She's a Variant!"

A thick silence filled the room. Aazar's face blanched. She couldn't be a 'Variant,' could she? Variants were mutant humans who had powers like telekinesis, control over water, and other unnatural things. They were known to kill without mercy. She didn't think she was one of those people.

Her father broke into a deep belly laugh while her mother stared at Aazar, skeptical.

"You think Aazar is a Variant?" Her father laughed again. "On what grounds do you have the right to accuse my child of something so heinous and ridiculous?"

Mr. Bailey grabbed Rebecca by the shoulder and thrust her forward. After another slight shove, her eyes looked at Aazar before dropping to the floor. She unwound her arms and revealed two heavily bandaged hands. Rebecca unwrapped one, showing the wounds to Aazar's parents. Aazar's parents took a step back as they gasped in shock. On her hand were second-degree burns. Puss and blood covered her meaty little red hands and fingers. Her father looked away, trying not to vomit, while her mother stared at the burns with wide eyes.

"Dear God in heaven, what happened?" Aazar's father asked, still looking away from Rebecca's outstretched hands.

"Your daughter…burned her!" Mr. Bailey yelled. "As if you didn't know! Where would she have gotten it if not from you?" He glanced at Aazar's mother. "Or maybe it's your suddenly mute wife."

"How dare you!" Aazar's father yelled back. "Aazar would never do anything to hurt a fly! You couldn't possibly believe such lies?"

"I'm not lying!" Rebecca boomed. "Your daughter did it after I asked to see what Avery gave her."

"You should've left me alone," Aazar growled. "You got what you deserved."

Rebecca opened her mouth to retort, and Aazar's father blinked in surprise, but Aazar's mother spoke all of a sudden.

"We'll handle this matter from here. Thank you, Mr. Bailey."

"The hell you will," he said, "I've already called the authorities. They're on their way to apprehend her!"

Aazar's mother slipped away into the home in deep thought. Her father stepped forward and put an arm on her shoulder with restraint. Aazar felt a rush of sadness. Her father was afraid of her. At least he stuck by her instead of hanging his head in shame like her mother.

"They're not taking my daughter, no matter what she is," he said with a violent tone. "I suggest you head out now."

"They'll be here any second, and I won't have a moment rest until that thing is put behind bars or burned."

"I said we would handle this," Aazar's mother said from the hallway. "The way it should've been handled a long time ago."

Aazar's mother was holding her father's hunting rifle. Aazar stared in shock as the end of the gun came up, pointing at her head. She froze in fear. Her mother was going to shoot her like a dog. She couldn't believe this was happening. The Baileys looked at her, unsure if they should feel pity or stand out of the way and let her mother shoot her down. Aazar's father moved in front of Aazar and the rifle.

"What do you think you're doing, Anaya?" he asked tentatively.

"I should've killed her when I saw it in her," Aazar's mother barked. "I didn't want to take her from you, Howard."

"Anaya, this is ridiculous. Put the gun down."

"You're the one being ridiculous, Howard," Anaya looked at Aazar, "she's a demon, and she's been possessed from the start. She's always been evil. Never listening to anyone. Always running off alone in the woods, consorting with Satan. I've suspected that she wasn't right for a while, but I never thought she would be a minion in a million years. Had I known, I would've done it when she was just a child."

"She's a child now, Anaya." Howard looked at her. "She's our child."

The Baileys stood in stunned silence, and Aazar's father hadn't moved. Aazar shook in violent fear. Had her mother always known something was different about her?

"You ignore everything except her. Don't you see, Howard?" Anaya looked to Aazar again. "It's a spell. She placed it on you when she was tiny. She's a strong Variant."

"That's just love for a child."

"How can you not see the truth, Howard? Think about it," Anaya said, holding the gun steady. "She's an abomination! What would God say?"

Silence filled the room again. Aazar felt she would die from the silence. Why wasn't he answering and standing up for her like he always had?

"He would call you a monster," her father said with shaky resolve.

"She's the monster!" Mr. Bailey spoke up, pointing a shaking finger at Aazar. "And she'll be apprehended. I worry for your whole family, Howard. It seems evil runs rampant in your home."

Howard leaped toward and punched Mr. Bailey square in the jaw. Mr. Bailey fell back and slammed into a bookcase behind him. Aazar was unprotected for that moment, and her mother did the unthinkable. She aimed and shot.

Aazar closed her eyes and waited to feel the pain. She opened them when she didn't feel the blow. She was hot all over, except this time, the heat was all around her. She realized it was a shield of fire. The bullet had melted before it could hit her. She looked at her mother to see her in a ball of flames, kicking and screaming.

Everyone in the room was stunned, even her father. She saw the fear in her father's eyes.

"OUT!" he screamed as he pulled curtains over her burning mother. "GET OUT, DEMON! OUT!"

Aazar stared at all of them. She had never felt so alone. She took a moment to stare at them. This was what abandonment felt like. She would never forget it. She decided at that moment that she wouldn't cry. She would never give them the satisfaction of seeing her cry. Aazar took no look back as she sprinted for the door. She no longer had any reason to stay.

Chapter Four: Rags to Riches

Her hair flung restlessly in front of her, competing with the wind and her will to move forward. She closed her eyes as she ran full speed ahead to a new life that she wasn't sure would last long. The houses on the edge of town had long faded from view as she chased the sunset and empty fields that stretched farther than she liked. She stopped running for a second, took a deep breath, and looked behind her. She blinked. Had she run that far that fast? The town looked about a mile away, even though she could've sworn she had only been running for a few minutes. Maybe she should've joined the track team, she thought with a twinge of sadness.

Aazar didn't feel as miserable as she thought she should feel, being alone and cast out of her family. Maybe she had always felt a little cast out, to begin with. She felt terrible that her father betrayed her with such quickness. How could he banish his daughter without explanation? Seeing her mother on fire was justification enough, it would seem.

Aazar pulled her small sweater around her shoulders as she walked toward the sinking horizon. As the sun set and the sky darkened, she noticed the chill settling around her. She wished she had time to get a bag ready. Her father instructed her to have a small bag ready in case of an emergency exit from the home. She'd thought he was silly, pretending to be tough, but she wished she had done it now. Tiny droplets of rain began to hit her face. The cold drops of water almost broke her resolve, but she thought of her mother as she shot the gun. Aazar hardened her heart and moved forward as the rain suddenly picked up speed. She was drenched in a matter of seconds.

After twenty minutes of heavy rain, Aazar realized she didn't like feeling her sandaled feet sinking into the mud. Her legs were getting tired, and she suddenly realized she had left without eating dinner. She wished the Baileys had at least let her have a meal before ruining her life forever. The rain stopped almost as fast as it began. She breathed a short sigh of relief before the silence settled in. The sound of the waking crickets made her feel more helpless and alone. And cold.

Mud was now caked up to her knees, and she was sopping wet. She stopped for a moment to ring the water from her mud-soiled dress. She wanted to stop and go to sleep, but Aazar knew it would be dangerous for her to sleep outside tonight. A car drove by all of a sudden, bringing a blast of wind with it. The force of it almost knocked her over. She moved closer to the trees and away from the pavement.

She couldn't think straight anymore. She was cold and starting to wonder where her next meal would come from. She hoped it wouldn't be from the garbage. Maybe she could beg for money and get a hamburger when she reached Broughton, six miles away. She was sure she had already walked three miles, but her legs were tired. She figured that in Broughton, she could stay at a local shelter for a while until she could figure out what to do.

Another car splashed by, flinging mud everywhere and covering Aazar in wet sludge from the road. She shook violently. She realized she wouldn't make it to Broughton in wet clothes if she tried walking. She decided to hope for good luck and hitchhike. Someone had to pick her up since she was just a petite girl. She wasn't intimidating in any way. Not in any way they would suspect, at least. She stood on the road's edge and thrust her thumb in the air as she had seen in movies.

After about an hour, the first two cars flew past her. She began standing on her tippy toes, stretching her body to be as tall as possible, but it seemed to make no difference. After another half an hour, she got tired. She took a moment to stretch and missed a car flying by. Determined, Aazar stuck her finger out and tippy-toed once more, wagging her arm back and forth. Finally, a small black limo slid to a halt, inches away from her legs.

"YOU ALMOST KILLED HER, YOU MORON! I'LL HAVE YOUR FUCKING BADGE IF SHE'S INJURED!" a muffled female's voice lectured in the back of the car.

The car door opened, and Aazar saw a pair of high-heeled feet slip onto the pavement. She knew the woman had stood up, but she was short and wasn't visible behind the car door. She came around it in a beautiful sparkling red gown and expensive fur around her neck. Aazar investigated her face and saw that, surprisingly, she wasn't much older than her. She was that beautiful age between teenager and adulthood. Her makeup was flawless, looked like it was drawn on, and took hours to complete. She looked like a model. The wind was blowing her blonde hair this way and that, which visibly distressed her. The woman wrapped the fur tighter across her shoulders and gazed at Aazar. It seemed that she was as far from the car as she would get.

Her voice changed into a sweet and soothing tone maintained even over the wind. "Hey," she called, "Hey, come here! Do you need a ride? Do you need a ride to your mom or something?"

Aazar was annoyed by the tone. She wasn't so young. "No," she said, feeling her face redden. She didn't want to tell this stranger her whole life story. It wasn't her business. She stood straighter and cleared her throat. "I need a ride to Broughton," Aazar stated.

"Is that where your parents are? Were you trying to run away?" she said in a sympathetic and knowing tone.

Aazar wanted the ride less and less as she spoke with this woman. She just stared at her.

"I remember trying to run away once," the girl commented. "You got much farther than I did, and in the rain too. I admire that." Her face got a little sad as she thought about it. Her smile came back within an instant, and she continued, "Well, come on then, we'll give you a ride wherever you need to go, okay?"

"Thank you," Aazar shouted over the wind and entered the car after the girl. The car pulled away from the side of the road and began rolling toward Broughton as Aazar sat on the warm heated seats and let her toes warm against the small heater on the car's floor. It smelled like a Western, with the air tinted with whiskey and leather. She noticed the back of the driver's head. He hadn't turned around even though the partisan was down partially.

They rode in silence for a few moments. Aazar was thankful to get out of the rain. She noticed the whiskey glass tucked behind a small counter with a mini fridge attached to it. Aazar still couldn't believe she was fleeing her hometown with a wealthy stranger. What would she accomplish on her own in a city she'd never been to and knew no one? The girl broke the silence all of a sudden with a loud gasp.

"I forgot to tell you my name!" she said as she smiled. "I'm Norma Belize. Oh, and I forgot to ask your name as well. What a horrible hostess I've been."

Aazar had realized this earlier, but she hadn't cared who Norma was. She'd just wanted out of the cold.

"I'm Aazar," she said.

Suddenly, she realized that she should have lied. She wasn't sure how long the authorities in Newmalton would look for her.

"What a unique name!" Norma said. "Aazar, I believe our meeting today was fate. Do you believe in fate?"

Aazar didn't answer. After this evening, she didn't know if she believed in anything anymore.

Norma hadn't noticed Aazar's lack of an answer and continued, "I believe in fate." She leaned in, nodding as though she had a secret. "Absolutely. I just got back from a charity benefit raising money for children in Yemen. I feel so compelled to help people now. After being there, seeing those poor children in need." She clutched her bleeding heart. "I couldn't just pass you by. I just want to help people, Aazar. I want to help you."

Norma's driver snorted in the front seat. He then cleared his throat and focused on the road. Norma shot him a glare before pressing a button to roll the partisan up.

"I haven't always been a good person," Norma admitted. "But I'm trying to be. Adam thinks I'm already a great person, but he's really the great one. Adam invited my family to the benefit, but he got me this limo and said I was the only one to use it. Of course, he couldn't come with me since he is running the benefit and couldn't leave early, but Adam would've if he could.

I know it."

The road winded, and they slid around on the leather seats of the limo. Aazar had never been in such a nice car. She tried to enjoy the ride as much as possible since she wasn't sure when she would be in a limo again.

"So, where are you heading? My parents are irritating too, but they give me everything, so I couldn't possibly leave."

Aazar thought about it for a moment. "I'm just going to the nearest restaurant in Broughton."

"You're not going home? Why?"

"I don't want to go home."

They rode in silence again.

Norma then exploded with joy, "OMG. YOU could live with US!

Aazar wasn't sure she heard correctly. "Wait…LIVE with you?"

Norma plowed ahead, "I'm sure my parents will allow it. They're almost never home anyway. You would love it. Everything except Pete, maybe."

"Pete?" Aazar asked.

"Pete's my brother. He's always around, but he's on the computer most of the time. It's easy to ignore him usually, so don't worry. We've got such a huge house! My father says our house is all new money, meaning he made it all himself. He's a self-made man, and he owns a big music company. He even signed B. Joskes. Do you know who he is?"

Aazar shook her head no.

"OH, he's so awesome!" Norma said excitedly. "I met him last year at the MusicBlast Festival. He hugged me and took a picture with me. It was amazing." Norma paused. "You're going to love it at my place! You must come. And you could stay for as long as you wanted! What do you think?"

"…No," Aazar said.

"Oh, come on! At least come for dinner. We've got loads of food. I know you're hungry."

Aazar wasn't sure how she felt about Norma, but she was hungry.

"You have to come," Norma insisted. "Come on."

"Okay," Aazar relented. "Just dinner."

"Great! Great! Great!" Norma said. She was almost jumping out of her seat. "Oh, I can't wait to tell Adam about this! He'll be so proud! Maybe he'll take me to the lake and make me his girlfriend after he hears! Oh, I'm so happy! Aren't you?"

Joy in the mists and because of my misery, Aazar thought to herself. She smiled with her mouth closed in a tight line and looked away from Norma as she stared out the window. At least she would get a free meal.

She watched as the city came into view. She'd never been there before. Her mother had sworn against it. Anaya often said cities were where good people lost their souls to flickering lights and other devilry, which she never discussed. Regardless, the lights twinkled beautifully against the horizon as they drove toward it. As they went down the hill, Aazar looked out at the tents lined up through alleyways and graffiti all over the walls. She could smell the piss in the air even though the windows were rolled up. She looked at Norma, who was staring at her phone in the nonchalant manner most people did.

Then the city all of a sudden went from a slum to the peak of perfection as they drove on. Tents and shabby homes gave way to fancy apartment complexes and restaurants. She looked out of the window in awe at the Hologram bear advertisement that danced back and forth in front of the bank it was promoting while they waited at a stop light. Norma was still deeply engrossed in her phone, never noticing the bouncing mascot. They finally arrived in a quiet, immaculate neighborhood where houses were three times bigger than most homes in her hometown.

The contrast shocked her for a moment.

She watched as a woman jogged by with her jovial holographic dog running in front of her. She thought about the poor starving animals in her neighborhood and became upset. Norma had perked up again and began pointing out celebrity homes. Her father was responsible for a lot of the neighborhood's wealth. Aazar had never seen such extravagance, and she wasn't sure she liked it.

They finally arrived at a large house that looked more like a mansion. The lawn was enormous and empty. It was the first time she'd seen a home without a garden in the front yard. It reminded her of 15th-century English lawns, and she wondered who maintained the grass for a moment. From what she heard in the car from Norma, her father came here as a music teacher and made millions after starting his music studio using his wife's money. He was almost never home because of it. Her mother was the daughter of the creator of a famous salsa company. She'd never had a job, and she sold the company when her father retired years ago. They all lived off the residuals of sales and stocks of SalsaCapt. Aazar found it disturbing how she hadn't heard a thing about Peter other than how annoying he was. It seems like Norma treated his existence like an old family dog everyone tries to forget is still alive.

The butler came around the limo and opened the door for the two girls. Aazar stared as she tried to keep her jaw from falling to the floor. She couldn't believe only four people lived there. She counted fourteen windows on the front of the house, evenly divided upstairs and downstairs. There was a balcony where you could sit and have tea or proclaim a grand announcement to the rest of the neighborhood. It was made of red and white brick, and all the windows were dark except one in the far-right bottom window. The enormous dark oak front door was anything but inviting. She felt that solicitors wouldn't dare knock on this grand door.

The limo drove back out of the driveway. Aazar and Norma stood there a moment as it left.

"That was fun, right!?" Norma said. "I just love limos. They're so luxurious. My mother says there'd be no war if everyone traveled in limos. Come on, let's go."

They crossed the porch and went into the house. A beautiful white and black marble covered the bottom floor. Aazar took her muddy sandals off with urgency. Her feet were so dirty that Aazar knew she would leave footprints down the hallway if she moved from the spot. The butler looked at her as though he was thinking the same thing.

"Allow me to show you to a bathroom, madam."

"Uh, sure, thanks," Aazar said.

"Oh, that's right! You're probably freezing!" Norma exclaimed. "Rodney, please, show Aazar to the guest room in the west hall, please?"

Rodney tried to hide his discontent as he led her up the white carpeted staircase leading to the bedrooms. As much as Aazar wanted to drag her fingers against the ornate metal railing lazily, she didn't because she didn't want to leave dirt on it. She hadn't seen any housekeepers but judging from the size of the house and how immaculate it was, she knew there had to be service people lurking about, possibly waiting on an order.

They reached the top and the wooden floors shined underneath her feet. They turned right. She tip-toed as they headed down a plain hallway filled with end tables and lamps.

Aazar looked behind her and glimpsed another hallway. She followed Rodney down the right hallway until she noticed an old family portrait and stopped. Norma's parents looked like Aazar had pictured them. The mother was tall and slender with large breasts that may or may not have been the pair she was born with and golden blonde hair. She gave a smile she'd given a million times. The father looked fit and content, his smile a bit more nervous. Norma was about ten and, excited to have an opportunity to look fabulous, gave a perfect smile. The boy in the picture had a smile that looked like it was plastered there in exhaustion. She peered at his little pale face and smiled. Clearly, they'd taken the photo many times. Rodney cleared his throat.

"This way, madam," Rodney said.

Rodney stood by an open door on the right. Opposite him was a bathroom. She could see the marble floor from where she was standing. Then she noticed another door painted bright orange. She assumed it was Norma's room. Aazar caught up to Rodney and looked into the room he gestured towards. She did her best not to gasp out loud and failed.

The room had a beautiful rug on the floor under a queen-size oak wood bed covered in what looked like millions of beige and dark-brown pillows. The comforter was a fluffy and soft golden color. The brown skirt at the bottom was resting centimeters off the floor. There were three tall white dressers near the windows. Everything seemed to match: the curtains with the bed, the bed with the dressers. There was a table covered in a white tablecloth and two matching reading chairs—yet another catalog room in the house of Norma.

"There is a robe and slippers in the bathroom. If you need anything, just call me," Rodney said with his hand on the doorknob.

"Thank you—" Aazar started, but Rodney shut the door quickly behind him.

She sighed. She felt she would always be considered a second-class citizen no matter where she went.

Aazar grabbed the towels and went to the bathroom. She blinked. It was covered from floor to wall with sparkling dark brown marble. There were two sinks, a large black mirror on one side, and a huge walk-in shower. The shower was big enough for at least four people and covered in glass, with no curtain. She turned around and closed the door behind her and locked it. No way was she getting walked in on in this room. She took off her clothes and caught her reflection for the first time. Her hair had been blown all over the place, and her body was covered in thick brown mud. She let her eyes rest on the locket Avery gave back to her. It had been a gift from her father. She resisted the urge to look inside at the pictures and took it off, laying it underneath her filthy clothes.

When she walked into the open shower, she felt like she was in a locker room instead of a private shower. After bathing, she dried herself off and looked in appreciation at the clean bathrobe hanging beside the toilet. She put it on and heard an urgent knock before she could dry her hair. She opened the bathroom door to see Norma bouncing up and down on her heels.

"Come on! I want to show you the rest of the house!" Norma was grinning.

Aazar didn't like the idea of walking around a strange house in just a bathrobe.

"But—"

"It will only take a minute! I just can't wait." She grabbed Aazar by the wrist and dragged her out of the room.

Norma gave her the whole tour. Room by room, besides the bedrooms upstairs. There was a front room with a dark fireplace and two comfortable lounge chairs in front of it. It was clear that no one had been there in years.

Aazar couldn't shake the feeling that she was in a magazine home. She was afraid to touch anything, let alone eat there. Norma had been particularly proud of the holography room being built in the backyard, even though it was still covered in tarps. They would have the first one on the block. Aazar couldn't believe her eyes. She didn't understand how she had so little, and they had so much. It was almost unreal. She was sure she could sell several things in this home and buy one of the biggest houses in her town.

There was a dining room with a massive chandelier hovering over a round table, an enormous kitchen with dark marble counters, and a computer room with a piano resting in the back, covered with a white sheet. Aazar went to take a peek when she realized the space wasn't empty.

A hunched figure was sitting in the dark with a luminescent screen outlining their thin silhouette. There were cups and chip bags all over the desk that had accumulated over a series of days. The fingers pecked furiously against the keyboard. Aazar knew that she had finally met her first Nomophobe.

Norma sighed. "And this is Peter."

Chapter Five: The Cage

Peter Belize didn't move at all. He continued to type with reckless abandon on the keyboard. Aazar looked at his screen. Words in bold letters stood out on the top of the page:

VARIANT CRIME IS ON THE RISE.

Aazar swallowed. He was reading about people like her. Or at least she thought she was one of them.

Peter continued to ignore their presence. Aazar then realized he was wearing noise-canceling headphones. Norma noticed, too, and huffed loudly.

"PETER!" She shouted as her hands tightened into a tiny, contained fist. He blinked, but now that he knew who was behind him, he continued to ignore her.

"PETER."

Peter pulled his headphones off and let them rest on his neck. He turned his chair toward his sister. He stared at her for a second.

"What?" He asked. He glanced around and saw Aazar standing a small distance behind Norma. He looked at her dressed in the robe with her hair wildly sitting over her shoulders. His face showed no emotion except a slight lift of his eyebrow. It was clear she didn't belong here. She shifted under his gaze. "Um…hi." He said after what felt like a decade.

"Hi," Aazar said. Aazar appraised him as well. Messy, short blonde hair that hadn't been washed in a few days. Dark brown eyes, an uninteresting nose, and a mouth that often smirked. He wore a gray hoodie that had once been black and faded blue jeans he'd owned for years. He also wore a pair of dirty sneakers with a non-descriptive label on the sides. She had to admit; she was a little surprised that this was the same little boy in the picture upstairs. Judging from the rest of the mansion, he didn't look like he belonged here either.

They stared at each other for a moment before he broke his gaze and wheeled on his sister.

"Well? What do you want?" he asked again.

"Peter, be civil for *once*," Norma said, clearing her throat for dramatic effect. "Peter, this is Aazar. She will be living here with us for a while. I expect you to treat her with more respect than the rest of us."

"What? Living here? Since when? Are you picking up strays now?" he asked incredulously.

Aazar glared. She hadn't agreed to live there, but she sure as hell wasn't a 'stray.'

"Peter!" Norma said through gritted teeth. "Just introduce yourself, please?"

"Why? Who is she? Who said she could live here? How do you even know her?" Peter asked.

"I don't need to know her to know that she needed a helping hand," Norma said, grabbing Aazar's hand for support. The move felt so awkward and forced that Aazar instinctively took her hand back.

Norma looked at her hurt for a moment, then whirled back to Peter. "She was on the side of the road wearing this cheap little dress in the rain and didn't have anywhere to go! What was I supposed to do?"

Aazar didn't appreciate them talking about her like she wasn't there.

"What the fuck, Norma? Just give her a twenty or something. Not the keys to our fucking house!"

"Why do you always have to be so disgusting, Peter? Can't you just open your heart?"

"What? Are you high right now? Did they lace those fucking crackers they serve at those events with molly this time?"

"Peter, just DO IT!" Norma yelled.

"Fine, fine." He turned to Aazar and got up from his chair. He was a little taller than she'd thought. He stood straight, tucked one hand behind his back, and took Aazar's hand with the other. "Hello, My Lady Aazar, I am Lord Peter Belize of the Upper East Side Belizes. Since we just met, would you like my car?"

Aazar bit her lip.

Norma was furious. "Peter, you're a fucking asshole sometimes!"

"Perhaps I can interest you in a yacht or a small vineyard?"

"Oh, fuck off!"

"Ahhh, and her true nature is shown," Peter said. "Such a foul mouth. Show our guest some respect."

Aazar forced her face to relax so she wouldn't burst into laughter. Norma glared at him. If looks could kill, he'd be dead. If emotions could kill…she thought of Rebecca, the girl she burned. Norma took a deep breath and let it go. She slit her eyes at Peter.

"Just grow up," Norma spat.

Peter sat down and then laughed at her. "Like you? Walking around like you're the heir to the throne? You, with your fake manners, your fake causes, and your fake hair. You're a little girl playing dress-up in her mommy's jewelry with her daddy's wallet. And I need to grow up?" He turned back to his computer.

Aazar couldn't see how he was much different. He sat in the same house in front of the newest computer she'd ever seen in person. Who paid for all of that?

Norma was fuming. "You always take your problems out on me, Peter, but it's not my fault you don't have any friends."

"I know," he said, looking back to his computer screen, "it's my fault. I do it on purpose. Everyone around sucks. I don't want friends here."

"You never GO anywhere. How would you know how anyone is?" Norma spat.

"Hey, I go to a lot of places, okay, just not your bullshit places. The world's a lot bigger than Mill Avenue, you know. Plus, I meet people online from all over the world."

"You've always been jealous of me," Norma spat. "You're just mad because you don't have charisma. I can talk to all kinds of people face to face, and YOU have to hide behind a computer screen."

Peter continued to ignore her as his fingers pecked the keyboard.

Norma continued, needing no audience, "You know I try to be good to people. I try to help everyone. And all you do is hate me because I like to enjoy myself."

"You're trying to help yourself," Peter said, turning away from the computer again. "I bet that asshole Adam was there, wasn't he? I bet you saw this chick on the side of the road and creamed at the idea of being able to show her off, right?"

Peter stood up and mocked Norma, sticking his butt out and pushing back his hair. "*Oh*, Adam, I helped this poor innocent soul on the side of the road,"

He took a few seconds to fix his hair and dress. "I love helping people. I'd just *love* to be a part of your next benefit. How about we discuss it over dinner."

He kissed the air with a dramatic, sloppy kiss meant for Adam.

Aazar bit her lip. She didn't like being the scapegoat in this narrative, but his impression of Norma was spot on. Norma's face went scarlet. "Come on, Aazar, let's go get ready for dinner."

They returned to the double staircase and walked up the one to the right. Norma didn't say anything as they walked down the hallway. Aazar knew she was still mad about how things worked out with Peter. Aazar felt sorry for her. Norma had been gracious enough to open her home to her, regardless of what she intended. She knew a twenty wouldn't have been enough to help her that night.

When they reached the guest room, Norma turned to her.

"If you need anything, our maid lives down the hall, past my room, so you can ask her directly. I assume you can find your way back to the dining room for dinner. Mom and Dad will love to meet you, I'm sure."

"About that." Aazar said, "I'm only here for dinner, remember? Just stopping for food."

"Oh, of course." Norma waved the question away. "Just for dinner.

Whatever you say. Dinner is in about a half-hour. See you soon!"

Norma walked out the door without another word, closing it behind her as she left. Aazar stood staring about the beautiful room in silence. Could she stay here? She hadn't given staying here a real moment of thought when Norma first mentioned it, but now that she was here, looking at the soft bed, the new clean towels lying on the table, and the beautiful view from the window, she was starting to have second thoughts.

All of a sudden, she realized that she didn't have anything to wear to dinner. Aazar refused to have dinner with these people in a bathrobe. She left in search of Norma's room.

She looked at the orange door. She had her name engraved inside of it. "Norma Jane" in fancy calligraphy. She knocked, and the noise was too soft to be heard. She heard light rock music and some shuffling.

"Yes?" Norma said from behind the door.

"Um, do you have something I can wear? My clothes were—"

"Yes, Oh my gosh!" Norma exclaimed. "Hold on, for just a second."

She heard more shuffling behind the door and a few swears muttered under the music. She listened to a few drawers opening. Finally, Norma came to the door and opened it about three inches. Aazar could smell the sweet apple-scented shampoos and lotions from where she stood. Aazar caught a glimpse of a light orange wall, but Norma blocked the rest of the room with her body. She wore a bathrobe, too.

"I don't know your size, but I have a sweatshirt and sweatpants for you. I got the biggest shirt I could find for pajamas." Norma hesitated, "We can go shopping for clothes tomorrow…if you know, you wanted to…maybe stay another day?"

Aazar took the clothes and sighed. She could use another pair of clothes. She didn't know what she was going to do tomorrow. It made her stomach hurt just thinking about it.

"I'll see you at dinner," Aazar said simply and walked back to her room.

When she got there, she closed the door and put the clothes on the bed. The blinds were wide open. She walked toward the window to close the blinds but looked out for a moment instead. It was a beautiful city, much bigger than her hometown. She saw a young couple walk hand in hand down from the street below. She wondered what it must have been like being raised in a huge house like this. She didn't understand why someone would want to leave.

All of a sudden, she saw a movement from beneath her. She tightened her robe and watched a figure slip out the downstairs window. She saw the figure's feet hit the ground and turn around. Peter stood up and looked at the full moon. His hoodie slid back a little bit to reveal his face. A slight smile flickered over his face for a moment in the moonlight. Then he pulled his hoodie up and began jogging down the long driveway. She watched him until he could no longer be seen.

* * *

"Oh, of course, you're staying," Gloria Belize announced in a sugary sweet voice over the dinner table. She grinned as she cut her carrots up into small pieces on her plate. "It would be our pleasure. Stay here for a few days until we can find a more permanent place for you. No one should be forced to live on the street as long as an empty bed is around."

"That's what I thought too, Mom," Norma said, bouncing in her chair.

Aazar wanted to protest but was cut off by Mr. Belize, the thin, dark-haired man with horned-rim glasses who had been leery of her the second she walked into his immaculate living room that evening. He wasn't the kind of man who liked things out of place, and it was clear that he was mad about Aazar's presence and Peter's clear absence at the table.

"But what of her parents? There are bound to be people looking for her," John said, cutting up his smoked ham with more aggression than he needed. "Surely, this is against too many laws for even you two to ignore."

"Oh, John, please." Gloria pouted as she moved the tiny carrot pieces around her plate.

Gloria and John looked like the perfect couple. They both kept in shape, had money beyond what they knew what to do with, and were very high standing in the community. However, it was clear that the love had faded years ago, and now they were left with an innovative partnership for appearances. Gloria dressed like she was still sixteen, even though she was in her early forties. Her long and curvy body wore the look well, however. With her stunning green eyes and long blonde hair, she looked like she had walked out of a fairy tale and was committed to keeping it looking that way. Even though Gloria looked like a siren, it did nothing to keep Mr. Belize from his line of questioning.

"How do you think it will look if her parents come around snooping for her? We'll go down for kidnapping. Maybe we should be calling the cops—"

"My parents are dead," Aazar said without thinking. She realized how outlandish it sounded as soon as she'd uttered it. "That's…that's why I left. My parents died…in a car accident. I'm almost eighteen and didn't want to go to a foster home, so I just got out of there…"

It was shaky, but it would have to do.

Gloria and Norma looked as if they were going to burst into tears. John lost some of his resolve but was still on his guard.

"I just need a meal anyway, and I'll be on my way to the nearest shelter." Aazar offered.

John nodded and pointed his fork at her in triumph. "Well, that solves…"

"Shelters are *horrible*, Daddy!" Norma said, her big green eyes wide in fear. "They do things to those girls you couldn't imagine. They don't care for any of them there. I saw it on the History Channel, I know."

"But…"

"Surely a couple of weeks won't hurt, John," Gloria said in her sugary voice. She still hadn't taken a bite of the carrots she forced back and forth on her plate with her fork. " The kids are out of school for fall break, and they can watch her around the house. Plus, she's almost an adult anyway. We can't just leave her anywhere. The poor girl is so frail they'd eat her alive at the wrong one."

"I don't think we should…"

"Only for a few weeks, Daddy," Norma begged. "PLEASE!?"

Aazar assumed that because she was found on the side of the road like a dog, they thought she was one.

"I don't need to stay here. It's fine. I'll eat and leave." Aazar chimed in.

Aazar wasn't sure she wanted to stay with them, but she had nowhere to go. And after hearing how the shelters treat people, she didn't want to go there anymore. Maybe this wouldn't be such a terrible place to stay after all. She could crash for a few weeks and then move on after she had collected a few things to help her on her way. All of a sudden, she hoped John wouldn't send her away. He narrowed his eyes for a moment, then rolled them.

"No, that's not necessary," John said before looking at his wife, whose eyes widened dramatically in a plea. He released a large sigh. "Oh, fine. She can stay."

The two other women jumped in their chairs as they whispered plans to each other.

"Only for two weeks," John told her, ignoring the other girls. "Starting today."

Aazar had the feeling that Mr. Belize knew she was lying, but he couldn't prove it yet. She hoped no one was looking for her. She knew that John would be the first person to give her up. She could tell she was a thorn in his side that he wanted to be removed.

There was a loud crash on the opposite side of the house. Everyone froze and stared at each other. John gathered his resolve, stood, and headed into the living room. He grabbed a rifle that was resting on the mantle. The women all stood and followed him into the hallway. They all tip-toed down the hall to a door with an old sticker smashed across it reading, "GET THE FUCK BACK."

"Peter, are you okay in there?" John said through the door.

"Fine," Peter said, muffled through the door. There was the sound of glass being stepped on.

John rested the rifle down by his side and rubbed his temples. He sighed.

"Peter, open this door."

"Why?"

"Peter, open the damn door," John bellowed.

The door swung open, and Peter stood with a smirk as he saw everyone crowded around his father, holding the rifle.

"Did all of you come to save me or watch me be killed?" Nodding toward the rifle. Peter looked at Aazar. "You never can tell with this bunch."

"What in God's name happened in here?" John said as he stared behind Peter.

The cool breeze was flowing through a now-broken window. There was glass all over the floor of the bedroom. You almost couldn't tell since the floor was littered with loose papers, clothes, and God-knew-what-else.

"Peter, have you lost your mind? What were you doing?" Gloria asked, frightened.

"I went out the window earlier, but I forgot to prop it open, so it locked behind me. I broke it to get in. It's fine." Peter shrugged.

"*It's fine!?*" John yelled. "What the hell is wrong with the front door?"

"I didn't want you to know I was gone. I failed." Peter said as he shrugged.

"Where would *you* be going?" Norma asked with a snide smirk resting on her face.

Peter met Norma with a smirk of his own. "Out, Norma. You always say I should."

"You are grounded," Gloria said behind Mr. Belize. "And this comes out of your allowance."

"I was already grounded," Peter said, annoyed. "Or do you not remember? Slow down on the Xanax, Mom."

"Don't speak to your mother that way!" John said, irritated. He shoved past his son and entered the cluttered room. He snatched a blue laptop up and tucked it under his arm.

"Hey, what gives—"

"No computer for three weeks," John said.

"What? Oh, come on!"

"You just broke a *window*. You also left the house while you were already grounded. I should beat you. My father would have. He would've beat me like a dog. I think the least you can do is use the house computer in the hall for homework. No allowance, no leaving the house, which includes the front lawn," John growled. He shoved his way out of the room and stormed down the hall.

Norma and Gloria followed him in a huff. Aazar stood in the doorway of Peter's room, looking at him.

"Well," he said, "can I help you?"

"Why are you like this to them?" Aazar asked. "They're a little weird, but I don't see anything wrong with them. Why do you treat them this way?"

Peter looked at her, confused. "What do you mean, nothing's wrong with them? They're assholes."

"How are they assholes?" Aazar asked.

"You mean you can't tell?" Peter said, shocked. "They're all in denial of what's happening. They're walking around like princes and princesses when the whole world is on the brink of war. They ask for more drinks as the Titanic sinks."

"I don't understand," Aazar said.

Peter leaned forward and lowered his voice. She wondered why he bothered. It was clear he didn't care what his family thought.

"These people with powers. They're coming from everywhere. They all just showed up one day. Like weeds."

Aazar felt her face grow warm in embarrassment.

He said, "They're all born with it. Like, they evolved or something, I don't know. But they're here now and want to be included in the world as they are instead of being test rats in a lab. We should all be on board with integration. But most of us aren't. They're stuck in the past and ignoring the problem. The Variants will not keep waiting for the laws to change much longer. They're going to start a war." Peter said. "And they're going to win."

Aazar was rooted to the spot. She couldn't breathe as she thought about war. She didn't want to be a part of it. Not to mention that being a lab rat had never even occurred to her. She couldn't tell anyone what she could do and couldn't let it happen again if she could help it. She was faced with a whole new element of fear.

"And my family? Look at them! They ignore everything. Walking around pompously with their charity functions, Christmas parties, and awards shows. Their indifference is fueling the Variant community with hate. If we don't make negotiations soon, they'll attack us in full force. We'll be defenseless. I mean, do you know what they can do?"

Aazar shook her head.

"All kinds of things!" Peter gestured with his arms. "They're going to take over the world. They're going to change everything, whether we like it or not. We have to jump on board with them or fight back."

Aazar found her voice, "What are you going to do?"

Peter smiled and pulled her into his room. He closed the door behind them. Aazar felt his hand on her arm as he pulled her close and whispered in her ear.

"I've got some friends," Peter said softly.

Chapter Six: Larceny

"Friends?" Aazar whispered. He was still holding her arm. He looked as if he had climbed out from under a pile of dirty laundry, yet somehow, he managed to smell like deodorant, grass, and shampoo. She felt herself swallow. She suddenly hoped her breath didn't smell.

He let go of her arm as he leaned back and nodded with a huge grin. He looked attractive when he smiled. Aazar had to keep herself from shaking her head to clear the thought. She still wasn't sure if he was an enemy or a friend.

"Evolved humans," Peter said, getting excited. "Real Variants. I met them in a chat room a couple of weeks ago on 7chan. You know, for hackers and stuff? We all started chatting about what's happening and everything, and then I got an invite to a meet-up tonight at the Café Moana."

Aazar was astonished. At least he wasn't against evolved people. That was a relief. She still thought it was dangerous for him to be with these people calling themselves Variants. She had powers and wasn't bad, but not all of them were like that. She had seen the news.

"You met them once," Aazar said. "That doesn't make them friends."

"You don't know them," Peter said, his grin faltering a little. She decided to change strategies. She wanted to keep him talking.

"Are you going to see them again?"

Peter's grin melted from his face. He put on a hard stare.

"I'm supposed to meet with them online tomorrow to find out the new meeting date. But I can't since my dad took my computer, and the home computer isn't encrypted."

"Can't you go to the library?" Aazar asked.

"And access a secure site with an open IP address? At a public place? Are you kidding? We'd be found out in ten minutes. I must have my computer or another secure network," Peter grumbled.

"Can't you call?" Aazar asked.

"What century are you from? We don't exchange phone numbers. It's too dangerous." Peter said, "We only talk online from secure networks. Now I can't talk to anyone."

"You can talk to me," Aazar said without much strength in the comment.

"Yeah," Peter smiled a little, "you're not that bad." Then he looked away, distracted.

"Don't you have any friends around here at all? Don't you know where anyone lives?" Aazar asked again, anxious.

"No," Peter said. "If talking on the phone is dangerous, meeting up at their houses isn't going to work out either. I don't know anyone around here. They're all just like my parents in this neighborhood."

They were silent for a moment. Aazar needed to know more about these people. Maybe they could help her if they were decent. She knew she couldn't stay here long without more questions about her parents and past.

"I can help you get your computer if you want," Aazar said.

Peter looked at her and smiled. "I thought you were Norma's friend. Norma wouldn't want her friend helping me get my computer. Norma thinks I deserve it."

"I'm not anyone's friend," Aazar said. "And I don't care what Norma thinks about this."

"So, what do you care about?" Peter asked. "Because I don't see why you'd want to help me."

"Because I'm a good person, and you need help."

"Bullshit," Peter said. "Try again."

Aazar paused. She decided to be as truthful as she could. "Because I want to meet Variants too. In the end, I want to be on the right side of things."

Peter's grin came back. "Another revolutionary. Nice." He grabbed her by her arm gently and opened the door. He pushed her, "I'll meet you in the hallway by the upstairs office at eleven."

"There's an upstairs office?" she asked.

"It's across from my parent's room."

"And you know that your computer's there?"

Peter glanced around, then whispered, "Of course it is. It's never in the same place but always there when confiscated."

"This happens a lot?"

"I was going to get it myself anyway," Peter said.

"Then why did you make the task seem impossible a few minutes ago?"

Peter smiled. "I just wanted to complain. I never thought you'd offer to help me. Most people wouldn't. Stealing from your hosts the first night you're in their home. That's just bad-ass."

Peter closed the door, leaving Aazar standing alone in the hallway. Aazar stared at his door.

"Still here?" Norma said, coming down the hallway. She had changed into her nightgown with orange ruffles everywhere. Her hair was now up in curlers, and her makeup was off. She looked much plainer without her hair extensions and her face painted on. Aazar could see why Peter had called her fake, but she didn't understand why Norma did it. She looked nice without all the makeup.

"I know exactly how you feel," Norma said, reaching her. She stood looking at the door as well. "Sometimes, when I walk by Peter's door, I just stand there mad, too. He's so disrespectful and mean. I imagine him in there, plotting against us on that computer. I bet he steals people's credit cards or something. He's just so vile."

Aazar didn't understand why he would do that since they were already rich, but she said nothing.

"Come on!" Norma said, grinning. "I have so many things I want to show you! I just got this brilliant Italian dress on Mill Ave last weekend. It's so wonderful! I hope to wear it the next time Adam picks me up for the opera!"

Aazar followed Norma down the hall. She realized Norma looked just like Peter when she smiled. She glanced back at the door. The "GET THE

FUCK BACK" Sticker was still visible down the hall.

* * *

Aazar stared out of the two-story window of her room at the busy city, waiting to help Peter. She saw buses, heard nosy cars, and watched planes leaving trails of smoke; all of them destroying the air quality. She hated the smell of cars. She always had. It was something about the gasoline. When it was burned, it reminded her of death. She'd watched as they built the new roads in Newmalton a few years back. She remembered how excited the town was for paved roads and streets. There was no more dirt on Sunday shoes, rocks, or potholes when they drove or rode their bikes. But Aazar had noticed how much she missed looking at the grass growing on the side of the roads. She also noticed how the boys were left with harsher cuts when they fell on the pavement and how hot the street became after installing the concrete.

Looking at the city below, she wondered if Newmalton would look like this city someday. A sizable gray metropolis with pavement and cement and few trees. It was like a giant gray blanket suffocating nature.

She finally looked away from the window and checked her watch. She was happy that she'd worn it on the day she left. There were no clocks in this house since most people relied on their cell phones to tell them the time. It was near enough to eleven. She walked away from the window and headed toward her door. She gave herself a quick check in the mirror in the bathroom and noticed her clothes were missing. Her locket sat resting on the counter. She couldn't believe her life had gone so haywire over a small piece of metal. She left it on the counter and left the room, tip-toeing down the hall toward the extra room.

Peter was standing against a wall near a door that was cracked open. The faint light washed over his shoes as he waved her over urgently. Aazar slid next to him and knelt. She still couldn't believe how clean he smelled. He looked like he hadn't showered in decades. She had to keep herself from sniffing him.

Peter leaned down as he whispered, "My dad's still up, so we have a change in plans."

"I thought you did this all the time," Aazar whispered.

"I do," Peter said, exasperated. "Seems like the old man finally caught on. I figure he'll go to sleep in his chair, but we'd have to wait longer for that, so I've got a new idea."

"What was the original idea?"

Peter sighed, "I was going to go in there and search while you kept guard, but now you'll have to look for it while I keep my dad occupied. Look in boxes or under some furniture first before going to the drawers. Half of those are locked and make a ton of noise when opened. He's pretty lazy, so it shouldn't be hard to find."

Aazar felt a rush of panic cool her skin. "But what if I can't find it?"

"Then you don't find it."

"How will you know when I've given up?"

"You aren't in charge of that," Peter said. "I am. I'll keep talking until I think you've had enough time to look. You're done looking when I'm done talking; you got it?"

"But what if your dad gets up and leaves before you're finished talking? He'll see me, and we could both be in trouble."

"I'll just say you were stealing," Peter said, throwing her an evil grin. Noticing Aazar's angry face, he continued, "I'll take the fall, okay? I'll tell him I told you that if you didn't help me, we wouldn't let you stay here."

"But that makes me look like a coward and an idiot," Aazar stated.

"You want to do this or not?" Peter said, irritated with all the questions.

"Okay," Aazar said, her fears not swayed at all. She knew if she got caught, there would be nothing she could do to stop Peter's father from blaming her. She sighed. "After you."

Peter gave her a mischievous grin before walking into the dim room.

Aazar peaked her head around the corner. To her surprise, this wasn't one room but two. There was a television with a couch on the left and an elliptical machine by a large window. To the right was a cracked door through which she could see a desktop computer. Peter's father was sitting on the couch with his back facing the door and his legs crossed. Peter walked in front of the television, ensuring his father's gaze stayed away from the door.

"Thought you could take your computer like you usually do, Peter?" Aazar heard Peter's father comment to Peter's smirking face, who glanced at Aazar, letting her know to go.

Aazar crept into the first room. Her heart was pounding out of her chest. If his father looked over his shoulder, they'd be done for.

"I was hoping you were awake, Dad—"

"I don't believe you are here to apologize for a second, so you can just come off it right now."

She slipped into the computer room and started breathing again. She hadn't realized she had been holding her breath. The computer room was nothing more than a desk and a computer with a bookshelf on one wall and a filing cabinet on the other. She went to a small chair beside the bookcase and looked under it.

"No, I wanted to ask you something," Peter said sheepishly.

After the computer was not under the chair, Aazar stood on it to feel the top of the bookshelf. There was no luck there either.

"Well, go on. Some of us sleep at night, Peter."

Aazar tiptoed to the small desk. She felt like she was making a ton of noise, but Peter hadn't made any notion that she was. She tried not to breathe again.

"I was just wondering…How do you feel about this girl Norma's brought home like a lost puppy?"

Aazar froze mid-step.

"Oh, Peter, it's just one of her projects. You know that."

"Well, yeah, but I mean, do you think she's safe? Do you think she's trustworthy?"

Aazar glared in Peter's direction and continued to check the desk. She looked under a file.

"Peter, she seems like a decent person. Is there something else you need?"

Peter shuffled a little. "Yeah…How would you ask a girl out? I mean so that she'll say yes and all."

Aazar placed the file back on the desk and darted toward the drawers as her face grew crimson from embarrassment.

Peter's father sounded embarrassed, too. "Oh, well…yes…well…First, you have to be polite to her. No rude business like what you do with all of us…"

Peter's father droned on about relationships and women, while Peter would throw in a "really?" or "this is great stuff, Dad" while pretending to listen. Aazar opened and closed each drawer, careful not to make any noise. When she reached the last drawer, she opened it and felt a smooth metallic material under her hands. She relaxed in relief and lifted the laptop from its drawer.

As she stood up, she kicked the chair behind her by mistake. It made a loud squeak. Aazar closed her eyes and felt herself grow hot. When she opened her eyes, her mouth dropped in awe. She was on fire from head to toe. Fear was the only thing that kept her from screaming. She noticed the laptop in her hands wasn't burning. It didn't make any sense. The computer seemed to be protected by the fire instead of destroyed. She couldn't understand why any of this was happening. She twirled around, looking toward the door, waiting for Peter or his father to burst in to see her covered in flames.

"What was that?" Peter's father said.

"You were telling me you and Mom were friends for three years before dating her—"

"No, that noise," Peter's father said.

Aazar closed her eyes and forced herself to breathe.

"I didn't hear anything, Dad," Peter said.

She looked at her arms as they flickered with fire and realized for the first time how quiet fire was. She breathed in and out slowly, trying to cool herself down. She felt the heat leave her body, and the fire went back into her pores almost as soon as it had started.

"Oh…Never mind then, where was I? Oh yes! I courted your mother for an entire three years before…"

Aazar looked at the laptop and turned it over. No burns, no twisted metal, no nothing. She tiptoed back out of the room and back into the hallway.

She took another big breath and peered back into the room.

"Anyway, that was when things got a little bit more intimate. Your mother and I were always—"

"Dad, try not to be gross." Peter saw Aazar's head, and she gave him a thumbs up.

"Well, Dad, off to bed now. Thanks for the advice. Later," Peter said to end the conversation and hurried out the door. As he reached Aazar, he pushed her by the waist, leading her away from the study. When they got down the stairs, Peter let out a sigh of relief.

"Man, what a rush!" he said, grinning from ear to ear. "I thought for sure we were dead when you—What did you do in there?"

Become a character out of a comic book, Aazar thought.

"I kicked the chair."

Peter shook his head in disbelief. "I can't believe I sold him. Too easy. Where were you when I was ten? I could've used someone like you."

Aazar was trying to keep her mind off what had just happened. She was starting to think she could become a human torch the next time she stubbed her toe. What if it happened at dinner? At a park? In a mall?

"When are you going to contact them?" Aazar said. She needed to meet people who could help her control her power.

Peter's demeanor changed as his smile was replaced with a straight line, "As soon as I get the email about tomorrow's chat. They're pretty cool. I'll probably have to do some initiation stuff again, though."

"When will you meet up? Soon?" Aazar asked.

"I'll let you know."

They had reached Peter's room. Aazar was surprised when he didn't invite her in.

"I'll see you."

"Wait," Aazar said. Peter stared at her with raised eyebrows as she shuffled under his gaze. "What was that all about me being trustworthy?"

"I figured if you would feel guilty and tell my dad what happened, you'd do it then. If not, you were worth keeping in the loop."

"What about the whole dating thing." Aazar stared at her shoes.

"Something to freak my dad out. Don't worry about it." Peter said.

Before Aazar could look up to judge his eyes, he closed his door in her face.

Chapter Seven: Café Moana

"DAMMIT, PETER, I DON'T KNOW HOW YOU DID IT, BUT YOU WILL HAND OVER THAT COMPUTER RIGHT NOW!" Aazar sat straight up in bed with her heart racing. It was morning, and Peter's father had noticed the confiscated laptop was no longer in his 'secure' hiding place.

Aazar made her way down the stairs in the over-sized gray T-shirt Norma had given her the night before. Aazar hated the color gray more than she hated going up in flames at random, but she didn't feel right sleeping naked in a strange bed in an unknown home with the most eccentric people she had ever met. This morning's outburst was no exception. Norma and her mother stood outside Peter's door with hands on their hips and scowls on their faces while his father pounded the door making his fist turn red. The shade of his face was comical, but Aazar didn't think it would be wise to laugh. She watched them in the hall.

"PETER, OPEN THIS DAMN DOOR!"

"Sweetheart, he's not going to listen," Mrs. Belize said. "You're just wasting your time."

"You baby him!" Mr. Belize growled. "Do you think he'd disrespect me this way if you didn't?"

"You're constantly coming at him like a deranged animal! That's why he ignores you."

"And you hide like a damn mouse," Mr. Belize said, rounding on Norma's mother.

Norma held a hand to his chest. "Dad, this isn't about Mom, don't let Peter manipulate you into fighting each other."

Her father sighed and turned to the door. "Peter, goddammit…you open this damn door, or I'll kick it open!"

Aazar bit her tongue. This man would never kick down a door—especially not one in his exuberant house. Aazar slipped past them unnoticed and headed for the front door. She passed a maid or two, but they paid her no mind. She walked into the backyard and straight to Peter's room window.

The window was still broken, and Peter was nowhere to be found. She could still hear John's idle threats outside of the bedroom door. Aazar was furious he'd left without her. She was sure he was going to meet up with those guys. Then she noticed the laptop still sitting on his desk. Careful not to cut herself on the glass or moon the entire neighborhood, she climbed into the disastrous room.

"Peter, for God's sake, can you be a member of this family for once!" Mr. Belize bellowed.

She tip-toed around the glass on the floor, darted to the laptop, and opened it. She was happy it was still on, but she was almost disappointed. Aazar hated computers. She had never had one in her house, and she almost never needed to use them unless at school, so navigating them wasn't easy. Her typing skills were non-existent. She noticed a password login area, but she had no idea what his password would be.

Fuck off. Aazar typed one letter at a time.

Access denied.

"I'm giving you to the count of three!"

"John, you can't start giving him ultimatums like that. He'll never respect you."

"He doesn't respect me *now*, Gloria."

Fuck Dad, Aazar typed.

Access denied. She sighed, exasperated.

"One!"

"And exactly what do you plan to do, John? You know you don't intend to kick the door down. What will happen when your bluff has been called?"

"It's not a bluff! I'll kick it down!"

Aazar heard Mrs. Belize's muffled laughter.

"See! You don't respect me, either!"

Fuck you, Dad, Aazar typed.

She blinked in shock when the screen lit up to a desktop with an anarchy sign dripping blood as the background. For someone so security-conscious, Peter's password was pretty easy.

"I respect you, Daddy," Aazar heard Norma offer her father from the other side of the door.

"That's it, Peter, you want to play games? You want to pretend you're a man? Fine, you can stay there. No meals! Do you hear me? NO. MEALS."

"John—" Aazar heard the party making their way back down the hall.

"Don't you dare, Gloria…"

Aazar noticed that the last browser window hadn't been closed. She clicked it and saw a DM conversation between someone called PBhatesitall and Energy56. The conversation wasn't lengthy, but she noticed the meet-up time and realized why the computer was still on. He had just left for the Café about five minutes earlier and was running late.

Aazar closed the computer and looked down at herself. She needed pants. She found a wrinkled pair of Peter's pants on the floor that looked clean, shoved herself into them while rolling up the top so they wouldn't fall, and headed for the window.

She paused at the window frame. She needed money. Aazar dug around Peter's desk and found a few dollars and some change. Hopefully, that would be enough for the bus.

* * *

Navigating through town wasn't as difficult as she thought it would be. Most people were so absorbed in their problems that no one thought about a young girl in over-sized clothing at the bus stop. As luck would have it, the bus that showed up ten minutes late went straight to the street she needed to go to, so she was glad she only had to catch one. The city was vast, and if she got lost, she knew she wouldn't be able to find her way back to the Belizes. Aazar knew she would be about half an hour late to the meeting, no matter how many stops the bus blew past. She wasn't sure how Peter would have made it on time to the meet-up if he'd woken her. He might have missed it altogether if he had. She hoped someone would be there when she arrived.

What would they be like, she wondered. She looked around the bus and saw people dosing in seats while others stood holding the railing while looking at their phones. She knew the Variants would just look like everyone else, but would she be able to tell them from out of nowhere? Would they be able to sense her or something like that? She felt herself getting warm and tried to get her nervousness under control. It seemed like any emotion would trigger her…affliction. Aazar's eyes darted back and forth around the bus as one of her fingers flickered with a spark. She needed to get this under control. She took a deep breath and felt the heat leaving her again. Then Aazar tried to focus on keeping her serenity until she reached her destination.

The Café Moana looked like something out of a 1930s movie. The exterior paint, once white, was gray after a century of water damage. Nothing could be seen through the filthy windows, and the dead palm tree stationed outside had tall weeds growing around its base. The large sign that bared its name didn't have the last "A," making it Café Moan instead of Café Moana. Aazar bet the boys got a kick out of that.

She felt she might have judged the windows too soon because she had only been standing there for a few seconds before Peter came barreling out the squeaky doors straight for her. He wore the same pants and hoodie he'd worn the previous day.

"What the hell are you doing here?" Peter asked, panicked. "How'd you even find me?" He took in her appearance for a moment. "Are those my *jeans*!?"

"Well, your laptop was still on, so I—"

"You broke into my room, had the balls to touch my computer AND steal my clothes!? Are you crazy!?"

Suddenly remembering the kind of person Peter seemed to be, it was clear this had been a poor way to get on his good side.

"Well, you were gone!" Aazar said, and then she remembered she was mad. "You were gone without me! You said you would take me to the next meet-up if I helped you, and then you slip into the city without so much as a note!"

"I just got the meet time an hour ago. You saw how long it took to get here. I had to leave right then!"

Aazar felt relief to know she'd been correct.

"But by all means, break into my room, steal my pants, go through my compu—how'd you get the password?"

"'Fuck You, Dad'? Anyone with you for ten minutes would figure that one out. Why is it so easy?"

"Because no one ever had the balls to break into my room and go through my damn computer!" Peter grumbled again. "Plus, I never remember my passwords when they're complicated." He sighed as he looked at her, exasperated.

"You look fucking ridiculous."

The door of the café creaked open before she could answer. A tall Black teen with dark brown hair and dark blue eyes stepped out of the building, keeping the diner door from closing with his foot. His huge muscles bulged and flexed under his white T-shirt as he forced the weathered door open and glanced around the street. The teen had a handsome face, but he looked tired. More tired than someone his age should look. Aazar instinctively pulled up her pants, caring about her appearance for the first time.

"Are you guys coming in or not? We don't have time for things like this, Peter."

Peter gave Aazar one last scowl before turning to the guy. "Sure, KJ, we'll be there in a second."

"Now, Please," said KJ, not moving an inch. "Bring the girl."

Peter sighed, grabbed Aazar by her arm, and pulled her along with him. Annoyed, she snatched her arm away from his grasp. Aazar was getting sick of him dragging her around everywhere. Aazar could've sworn she saw a flicker of a smile from KJ as he stood back to let them through.

The Café looked much better inside. Instead of the 1930s, it looked more like a 1960s diner. It was still old but spotless and well-kept. It looked like the place people might have had secret meetings during the civil rights movement. She figured it was fitting since they were having their own secret meeting.

Peter and KJ led her to a booth in the back of the café with five people crowded around a laptop and dozens of empty coffee cups. Clearly, Peter had been invited at the tail end of the meeting. They all stared at Aazar with tentative eyes.

"This is Aazar," Peter said when they had stopped in front of the booth. "She's…uh…interested in the revolution."

At this, Aazar looked at her shoes. She didn't know if she was interested in the revolution yet. She just wanted to know how to stop catching fire whenever she felt anything. She wasn't sure if she was willing to fight alongside these people. She felt on the spot and had no idea what to say. And they felt the same way because their tentative looks became more questioning. KJ shook her hand.

"Hi, Aazar." He smiled in a soft tone. "Happy to have you."

After he made this greeting, everyone else grumbled a half-sincere greeting of their own and went back to staring at the one laptop between them all.

"You shouldn't be bringing people to these meetings, Peter. This is a severe breach of our agreement," a light-skinned Black teen with dark brown hair and hazel eyes commented in an annoyed voice as he shoved his glasses up on his nose. He was a petite, frail teen whose long fingers pecked away at a laptop in front of him. He was in the middle of the group, hunched in front of the computer, and didn't even glance up at Aazar.

Peter swallowed. Aazar didn't think she would ever see anyone Peter would be nervous around. Then again, she was shy around them too.

"It's fine, Todd," KJ said. "Peter knows our meetings are secret. I'm sure he wouldn't have told her about it if he didn't think she was trustworthy."

"Most people aren't trustworthy, KJ," Todd remarked. "You, of all people, should know that by now."

The whole group went silent as tension rang throughout the table. Then

Todd deigned to look at Aazar for the first time. She didn't know much about their cause, but she did know it wasn't the best idea to barge into a secret meeting. Aazar just needed to find others like her. She didn't care about the repercussions at the time.

She looked at the boy. Something about him felt familiar. All of a sudden, she realized there was something familiar about all these people. Todd must have felt the same because he looked back to his computer and moved to the left, letting the group know they could make room for Peter and Aazar to sit. The group shifted, and they sat at the edge. KJ grabbed a chair and was on the aisle.

"So, the building we're talking about is pretty small considering the number of chemicals they've got down there, but the security is tight. We're going to need a good front man to walk us in there," said Todd.

Aazar couldn't see anything on the computer, but she knew he must be looking at blueprints or something of that nature. A small Indian teen girl with long black hair looked over Todd's shoulder. She had a perfect body. She looked like she could be in 'male videos,' as her mother always called them. The black-haired girl licked her lips in a seductive way.

"You should let me do it," she said. "I can handle a security guard or two."

Aazar didn't doubt her for a second. She probably had power over all the men in the room. Aazar then wondered what these teens' abilities were. Did anyone catch on fire as she did? What else could they do? She was bursting with questions but had no idea how to address any of them without sounding rude.

She wasn't interested in the mission, but she didn't want to be excluded either, so she kept her mouth shut as the others debated strategies to get in. KJ sat saying nothing at the end of the table, taking everything in. He nodded quite a few times but didn't say anything when he seemed to disagree. He watched to see how the group would handle the problem without him. He wasn't saying anything, making her want to know his opinion even more.

"KJ…What do you think," Todd said as though he'd read Aazar's mind.

KJ shifted in his seat. He cleared his throat.

"Although I think everyone is skilled enough to get it done, I think we should send in Peter."

There were more than a few eye rolls from the group at the thought of bringing Peter into the fold after the stunt he'd pulled this afternoon with the unwanted visitor.

KJ continued, "Peter has the best hacking abilities out of everyone we know." The group nodded in agreement. "If you can get Peter to disable the building in some way…make it unusable and force them to close for a day, you could destroy the supply without the risk of harming anyone."

Todd took his eyes off the computer for the first time so he could roll his eyes.

"Oh, you and your body count. Don't you know this is a war? They'll never listen unless we take something important to them. Their numbers are the reason we must behave this way. Destroy a few, and you'll free up space for people like us," Todd stated.

"Todd," KJ replied, "I don't want to destroy anyone. I want to keep them from destroying us. If we can do that without killing anyone, isn't it worth a shot?"

"I can do it, you know," Peter spoke up. "It would be easy. I could do something simple like make the heater stay at a hundred-ten degrees. They'd have to close due to excessive heat. Including security. We'd only have to worry about five guys instead of twenty while they try and figure out what's wrong."

"Revolution by air conditioning failure," Todd said sarcastically. "With all the things we can do, we hit the air vents. Original." He slapped the table. "We need to make an impression. We're stronger than them. We need to let them know you can't just do whatever you want to us. We are people too."

"What you all can do?" Aazar was surprised that the question came from her. However, her curiosity got the best of her in the last few minutes.

Todd and the others stared at her for a moment; then, a few smiles swept the group. There were also a few nervous glances around the café. KJ was one of the latter.

Todd spoke for everyone through his slight smile. "That's a conversation for another time. I think we've talked enough for now, anyway.

How about we meet up on another day?" he continued, addressing the rest of the group. "Okay, everyone, pay attention to your emails and DM's at about one this morning."

"These times get later and later, Todd," the black-haired girl said.

"It's because times are getting tougher, Britney. We have to go underground a little more every day," Todd said.

Everyone rose to leave. Peter was talking to a red-headed boy who looked like he had played many sports in high school. Aazar stepped away from the group and looked around the café. There were only a few other patrons, and they all looked like they'd had a long night in the bar. No one here would be interested in any conversations that didn't involve them.

"It's stuffy in here," KJ said behind her. "Want to step out? Everyone's going in that direction anyway. We might as well be the trendsetters. You know, have an opportunity to be the 'cool kids.'"

Aazar smiled and walked outside with KJ in front. They leaned against the wall of the Café and enjoyed the weather while watching a family walk across the street holding hands. They were smiling at each other.

"Todd can kind of read minds," KJ started, his eyes never leaving the family. "It's not as strong as he'd want it to be. Todd can get a few sentences from one person a day. He's always sitting at home trying to make it stronger. Three weeks ago, he could only hear a few words, so whatever he's doing, it's working."

Aazar was afraid that if she spoke, he would stop talking.

"Britney has a pheromone she gives off. It's a seductive thing. She can make anyone lust for her. It was bad for her when she was younger, and she couldn't control it. Then there's Brian, the redhead. He's got super strength. You should get out of the way if he goes to slap you on the back. He broke one of our friend's collarbone last weekend on accident by punching him in the chest as a joke." He stared at the family holding hands.

"What can you do?" Aazar asked.

KJ smirked. "Mine is a little scarier. I think you can understand."

Aazar blinked. "What?"

KJ looked away from the family and looked at her. She felt shivers go up her spine when she looked at him. She didn't know why he'd been able to elicit that kind of response from her. She noticed the contrast of his brown skin against his blue eyes as he looked at her.

"Your power is kind of the same, right? It made you cause pain to someone; I know that much." He looked away. "I know mine did."

"How did you know I had one," she whispered to him.

"We all knew when you came in," KJ said, surprised. "You didn't think we would've allowed you to sit with us if we hadn't."

"But how?"

"We can sense each other," KJ said. "You know you felt it when you saw us didn't you?"

She thought about the familiar feeling when she looked at Todd in the café.

"Oh," Aazar said stupidly. "Yeah. I did."

KJ shrugged. "There you go."

"Peter and his family don't know."

"Of course, he doesn't. He wouldn't have yelled at you or grabbed you the way he did, had he'd known," KJ stated. "Why would his family matter?"

"Well, I'm staying with him," Aazar said.

"Wait…You're staying with Peter?" KJ said in shock.

"Yeah, I—"

The door swung open. Todd chased Britney out of the Cafe. She giggled as she darted and dodged out of his reach. They were flirting. Aazar wondered if he was interested in her or if Britney was using her power. She wished she'd had a simple ability like Todd or Britney. They didn't have to worry about destroying things.

"How about I give you my email, and you can send me questions whenever you have any?" KJ said.

"I'm horrible at computers, and I mean bad."

Britney squealed in delight as Todd chased her back and forth across the street. He was laughing like a maniac. Aazar didn't know how anyone could run and laugh at the same time. It seemed like too much pressure on the lungs.

"You can't be that bad if you hacked into Peter's computer."

"I didn't really hack—"

"Come on, we have to head back," Peter said, walking out of the diner. "My dad's figured that I'm gone by now."

"Oh," Aazar said, upset for some reason. "Well, fine, let's go." She turned to KJ. "It was nice meeting you."

"Likewise," KJ said, staring at the family again as they turned the corner. "Have a nice evening, you two."

Chapter Eight: The Penny Drops

"I like KJ, but he always walks around like someone died," Peter said as the bus swayed back and forth. The lighting was so bright inside the vehicle that they couldn't see from the reflective glass windows.

Aazar shrugged. She felt like KJ was very realistic. Peter seemed to love the smell of adventure instead of realizing the trouble that came with it. She thought about KJ's sad blue eyes.

"What can KJ do?" Aazar asked. "He was going to tell me earlier, but we got interrupted."

"Oh, he can control electricity," Peter said. "It's really something to watch him do it. I hope you get to be so lucky to see it."

Aazar nodded. So, he'd hurt someone by electrocuting them, Aazar thought. KJ must feel so guilty. She tried to push her own guilt away about burning Rebecca and her mom. Peter interrupted her dark thoughts.

"You don't follow me anymore, you got it? You come when I say you should come. It can be dangerous," Peter said.

"KJ told me to come whenever I wanted. I'm a part of the group now, I suppose." Aazar thought about how they had allowed her to sit down. She'd never been so readily accepted by a group before. She wondered how they would've reacted if she hadn't been a 'Variant.' Considering what they could all do, she didn't want to know. Brian could break her like a toothpick. The bus slowed as it dropped off a tired-looking man. She wondered how far he had to go.

"Just like that?" Peter said, astonished. "I had to go through three levels of tests before even getting an email, and you get invited by stumbling in on a meeting? Must be nice being a pretty girl."

Her looks weren't what got her into the group, she thought, angry for a moment. But then, Aazar blushed. No one had called her pretty before. No one that mattered anyway.

As they bounced through Broughton's slums, the bus let people on and off as they went. Most of the patrons were smiling or frowning at their phones the entire ride, but Peter stared gloomily out of the window. Aazar noticed that he didn't seem to have a cell phone for the first time.

"Why don't you have a phone?" Aazar asked.

Peter shoved a bored hand into his pocket and produced a brand-new phone with a neat blue and white cover. She looked at it in shock. She'd never known anyone to have a cell and *not* be on it.

"It's a tracker for the government," he said, looking at the contraption with distaste. "Every website you browse is monitored, every social media post is saved, and every picture is tagged with facial recognition. I try to avoid using it as much as possible. That's why I don't Uber or do rideshares."

"And your computer at home has all of that security stuff, right?" Aazar asked.

Peter looked at her like she was from another planet. "Encryptions, VPNs, Secure Servers…yes. It's the only way to be on the internet."

"So, you do social media on your computer?" Aazar asked as the bus hit a large bump. None of the passengers looked up.

Peter snorted, "No. I don't do socials at all. I hang in chatrooms and forums. No pictures, no status updates, or 'hearts'. I deal in questions and answers."

"Oh," Aazar said, "I don't do any of that stuff."

Peter smiled, "I gathered that much."

They were quiet for a moment before Peter spoke again.

"You're probably better off without it." He said, "It's nice talking to someone who doesn't take a picture every time they change locations."

They sat in silence the rest of the way home. When they reached their stop, they headed through the winding neighborhood back to the house. It was getting dark, and they had been out all day. She couldn't believe how long they'd been at the meeting.

"Peter," Aazar asked as they walked in the fall evening. "Why don't you have your license? I mean, couldn't you just drive to meetings?"

Peter shoved his hands in his pockets and kicked the pavement. "I'm not allowed to have the car."

"Why's that?" Aazar pressed.

He sucked his teeth in annoyance. "Because my parents are assholes."

"Do they allow Norma to use the car?"

"Norma has her own car, but that's because she's a suck-up," Peter growled. "And I'm not a suck-up."

"You didn't do anything to make them not trust you?" Aazar said.

"I sneak out of the house all the time, including today," Peter said, walking faster. "Why would they trust me?"

He was a few feet ahead of her now. The woods lining the road seemed darker and more sinister the farther away Peter got. She jogged up to him.

"Did you do something specific to piss them off, Peter?"

Peter ignored her, but he didn't speed up again. She decided to let it go and they walked the rest of the way in silence. Aazar saw a dirt path winding into a small forest behind the affluent community and wondered what was down there. She made a mental note to check it out one day. The road gave way to the Belize's immaculate neighborhood and when they reached the house, Peter spoke again.

"Go in through the front door. I'll sneak back in through my window," Peter said. "I'd like it if they didn't know we were together. I can't have Norma having you followed."

"Do you think she'd do that?"

"She's had me followed before."

"What?" Aazar asked, shocked. "Why?"

"Go inside, Aazar," Peter said and sprinted toward his bedroom in the back.

Aazar walked to the front door and opened it. She looked around the quiet, dark foyer. The smell of fresh popcorn filled the room, which surprised her. Then she heard a noise in the front room. She walked into it and saw Norma sitting in a large armchair with her feet propped up and her hands behind her head. She had toe-openers on her feet since she had finished painting her toenails and her hair was full of curlers. Norma had a green paste on her face as she watched TV, her face glowing with light. She looked up and grinned.

"There you are!? Where have you been? I thought you left! I've been looking for you all day!" Norma said, picking up a bowl of popcorn and offering it to Aazar.

"I went exploring the city. It's…massive," Aazar said as she grabbed a few pieces of popcorn then plopped them in her mouth. She had to lie better than that.

"Oh, I know! It's huge!" Norma said. "I wish you would've told me." She glanced at Aazar's clothes and tried not to grimace. "I would've *loved* to take you shopping."

Aazar squirmed, despite herself. "I just caught the bus and rode around—"

"THE BUS!?" Norma looked as though someone had shot her. "Oh, we can do so much better than that! You must have gotten a terrible impression. The city is charming after you get past some of the…rougher areas. You can only see the good places if you own a Maserati if you know what I mean."

Aazar thought about the neighborhood where the diner was found. She bet these were the 'rough areas' Norma was talking about.

"Anyway, come on! Sit down! America's Best Singer is on! I'm hoping Krista wins, don't you?" Norma said, looking back at the television.

"I don't follow it, actually," Aazar said.

"REALLY?" Norma said, with genuine shock. "OH, you should! It's such an inspiring show. It reminds us that dreams really do come true!"

Aazar found it interesting that a girl living in a mansion didn't realize she was already living many people's dream life.

"I'll check it out later. Let me go to my room and get changed."

"Sure, sure," Norma said, already engrossed with the show again.

Aazar charged up the stairs and heard noises from the study. She glanced in and saw Norma's father watching TV. He was also watching America's

Best Singer. She wondered why they weren't watching it together.

As soon as she reached her room, she went straight for the shower. For some reason, she felt sweaty. Probably because she'd been so nervous meeting the other Variants.

She stepped out of the shower and noticed her dress had been washed and was hanging in the closet. Aazar looked at the side table near the bed and saw her locket sitting by the phone charger that she had no use for. The house cleaner must have wanted to make sure she didn't lose it. Aazar stared at it for a moment before opening the side table drawer, dropping the locket in, and slamming it shut. She didn't want to think about that right then. Aazar grabbed her clothes and headed downstairs to grab a bite to eat.

When she went there, she saw Norma's mother gazing at a small television with America's Best Singer on. She stood leaning against the kitchen counter, with a glass of wine and a phone in front of her.

"Hello, ma'am," Aazar said like her mother had always taught her.

The woman looked up from the TV. She smiled at Aazar.

"Hello, how are you fitting in around here?" she said. "I'm sure you've met all Norma's friends by now."

"Not yet."

"You'll love them!" Gloria said, grabbing her glass of wine a little too fast, allowing a few drops to spill on the counter. "They're outstanding. So ambitious and stylish. They'll all go far, I tell you."

Aazar smiled as she thought they would all do well since their parents would have the money to pay for it. She walked to the refrigerator and grabbed two sodas and headed to Peter's room instead of joining Norma. She wasn't very interested in watching a bunch of people singing old pop songs and being judged by everyone.

She knocked on his door.

There was no answer.

She knocked again. And still got no answer.

"Peter, I know you're there."

Silence.

"I got you a soda."

Peter opened the door a crack. He peeked through and saw the soda. He put a hand out to grab it, but Aazar stepped back.

"Let me in."

With a loud sigh, Peter held the door open. He closed the door and snatched the soda from her hands as soon as she was inside. He cracked open the lid and sat at his computer. She noticed he was watching America's Best Singer.

She laughed. "You watch this show too?" she asked, sitting down on his bed.

"Yeah," he said, taking a sip of the soda. "Only to make fun of the masses. They put up a bunch of people willing to do anything for money. These people dance and sing just to make a dollar. They're singing strippers. Strippers to aspire to. Strippers to keep our eyes busy, with their glitter and perfect smiles and flowing hair…"

He pondered for a moment as he watched a woman shaking her hips in a circular motion while she belted out a note. "Actually, it would be more accurate to call them Sirens. We're all captivated by them. We can't take our eyes off them. And all the while, we're on the brink of an evolutionary war between Variants and us." He looked at Aazar.

Aazar nodded in silence. They watched a few more sirens sing and dance before Peter broke the silence.

"I'm not going to lie, though. The chicks on here are hot," Peter said as he watched a blonde sway back and forth in a short skirt. Aazar witnessed a hungry look on his face that made her cheeks warm. She swallowed.

"I hear Krista is the one to beat," Aazar offered.

Peter snorted. "Krista is a tone-deaf shrew."

She smiled and said, "You know, your whole family watches this show."

"Psh," Peter said, looking at her. "I'm not surprised."

"Why don't you all just watch it together?"

"Why would we?" Peter said. "Mom likes watching it with low volume, so she can get her stock options while she watches. Dad likes it loud so he can feel like he's there. Norma wants to talk on the phone with her girlfriends at the same time, and I like talking about how it's making society dumber and dumber by the second, and they all think it 'brings down the mood.'"

Aazar frowned. Aazar and her family didn't have a TV, but they always spent the evenings together.

"That sounds sad."

"What's sad is watching everyone fight all night," Peter said, staring at the blonde again. "It's better this way."

"So, how long have you been communicating with the Variants?" Aazar said, changing the subject.

"For a little while, maybe about a month," he said. The blonde had stopped dancing and was waiting to be judged.

"How long have they been meeting, though?" Aazar pressed. "Like, how long has everything been happening?"

"You mean how long there have been Variants? How long have they been planning a war?" Peter looked at her like she was insane. "Have you been living under a rock?"

"Basically," Aazar said, looking at her sneakers.

Peter turned his chair to face her. He calmed his expression. "People believe Variants have always been around. Back in the Middle Ages, they were called witches and wizards, but actually, these were evolved human beings."

Aazar sat up straighter.

"They kept themselves hidden for a long time, just trying to make it by without being slaughtered. After the LGBT rights movement and the liberation of the Indigenous People, Variants came up as a small group to fight for rights. They had grown too, so many that the government couldn't arrest them for experimentation without showing its true power. For the last thirty years, the Variants have wanted more rights. They've petitioned and have had several issues on the ballot for a vote. But the world is still suppressing them. They have found a leader who isn't against using violence to get his wants. He is building an army to take over the country. Probably the world. They're everywhere, you know."

Aazar sat in stunned silence. All of this had been happening the entire time she had been alive. She looked back at Peter.

"And that's what this rebel group we met with does? They answer to this leader?" Aazar said.

Peter put his feet up on his desk. "Well, yeah. The guy is supposed to be young, so he's ambitious. He joined a few years ago, and he's moving up through the ranks fast."

"Aren't you afraid of what will happen if they win? What if they wipe out all humans or something?"

"They're human too, Aazar. Besides, they don't want to wipe us out. They want equality."

"They call themselves 'Variants.' That doesn't sound like they believe they're still human. It sounds like they think they're something more than that," Aazar said, worried.

"People who join them won't get hurt. They just want us all to work together for a positive change."

She thought about KJ. She knew he didn't want to hurt anyone. And he seemed to be important to the group.

She sighed. "I just don't think violence is the only way."

Peter smiled. "Well, we're open to suggestions."

Aazar smirked.

"Look," he said, "I don't want you thinking I'm down for annihilating my species or anything like that. But I believe Variants deserve rights. Rights can be shared. I don't know why we always feel we should keep them from other people."

She thought about that for a moment.

"You should go out with my sister tomorrow."

"What?" Aazar said. She didn't know why she felt so insulted.

"You need to have girl time with her, or she'll turn on you and convince the family you've been here too long."

"That's not true," Aazar said defensively. "No one's that cruel."

"She only picked you up because her heart was bleeding about puppies or whatever she was trying to save the other night with her ass-hat boyfriend."

Aazar sucked her teeth, annoyed. "She's a little annoying but give her a break. She's trying."

"She's faking, you mean," Peter said, turning back toward the television. "Faking."

Aazar sat down on a nearby box and opened her drink. She didn't know how she felt about everything going on, but she knew it would be hard to hang out with Norma after everything Peter had just told her.

Chapter Nine: Just Us Girls

As she hurried toward her room after going to the mall the next day, she pulled the hairpins from her hair. She'd had a headache all day from her hair being pulled so tight. She couldn't wait to wash her face. The amount of makeup she had on was making her face itch. She didn't understand how Norma always walked around with hairpins, makeup, and lipstick on without touching her hair or face. Or how she managed not to smear her makeup throughout the day. Plus, Aazar kept getting flicks of mascara in her eye, burning and blinding her every few seconds.

When Aazar found Norma that morning to hang out as Peter had suggested, Norma declared that she had to let her do her hair and makeup before going to the mall to buy her some clothes. Aazar did admit she looked pretty nice with pouty lips and longer eyelashes, but her face felt heavy and unnatural. When Norma started putting pins in her hair, she had to keep herself from crying.

"Aazar, don't be a baby. You're a woman. This is what women do." Norma said matter-of-factually as she twisted a strain of Aazar's hair.

"Why?" Aazar spat.

"If you don't do your makeup and hair, you won't get married, get a good job, or become a model or anything for that matter!"

"You believe that?" Aazar asked.

"Of course," Norma said, annoyed. "My mom told me so. Girls must be pretty, dress nice, and wear makeup; otherwise, they don't do anything but bitch and complain. When's the last time you saw a woman who didn't wear makeup do anything important?"

"Whoopi Goldberg?" Aazar offered.

Norma rolled her eyes and continued pulling her hair.

"I bet Whoopi would've made even more money if she had bothered to do something with her face. I mean, a little plastic surgery never hurt anyone."

"I'm pretty sure plastic surgery hurts everyone if you think about the recovery time and the medical bills—"

Norma yanked another strand. "Oh fine, fine, fine. It hurts, but only for the first few weeks…as long as there are no complications… Afterward, it's worth the pain."

"Have you ever had any work done?" Aazar asked, turning her head to look at Norma's nose.

"Hush up and turn around."

After about an hour of plucking, waxing, shaving, and lotion, Norma decided Aazar was presentable.

Aazar and Norma headed down the stairs and into the kitchen. Gloria was at the bar with her back facing them. She jumped when she heard them come in and dropped the phone in her hands. She threw a quick smile on her face as it clattered onto the counter.

"What are you up to this afternoon, ladies?" Her smile looked much too painted on.

"Aazar doesn't have any clothes, Mom," Norma reminded her mother. "We need to buy her a whole new wardrobe."

Gloria looked like she might cry out of pride for her daughter. Just then, John came into the kitchen holding a small notepad, reading something disturbing. He muttered the words as though he was trying to memorize them.

"Hello, ladies," he said, distracted. He glanced up for a moment at the phone on the counter near Gloria.

"There it is! I've been looking for it all morning. I had to use my notepad." John chortled.

Gloria sat as still as a statue. John didn't notice as he pecked her on the cheek, grabbed his phone, and took an apple off the counter while walking out. They heard the front door close behind him.

Gloria cleared her throat. "Have a good time, ladies." She got up from the chair and headed out of the door.

Norma didn't seem to notice anything and grabbed her keys. Aazar wondered if she hadn't seen it or if this kind of awkwardness happened so much that it no longer deserved a reaction.

"You have to check out my car." Norma smiled as she opened the front door. "I know the limo was cool and all, but my car is cooler. It's so beautiful. Come on."

She couldn't believe anyone would pay for their entire car to be painted bright orange, but she hadn't met Norma yet. It had bright orange custom leather, rims, and even wheels. She didn't understand how Norma didn't throw up whenever she saw it. Aazar felt she had a hard time holding down her nausea.

"Do you like Orange?" Aazar offered.

Norma burst into laughter. "How could you tell?" Her smile was a mile long. "Come on, we're going to meet up with Adam."

"I thought we were going to the mall to get clothes." Aazar didn't want to go meet some guy that Peter had referred to as an 'ass hat' even though Peter seemed to be pretty harsh with his judgment of everyone.

"We'll meet him there," Norma said as she opened her door and sat down. Aazar opened the passenger door and noted the orange radio.

They jumped into the car and headed toward the mall. Besides being a reckless and self-centered driver, Norma believed she missed her calling as Britney Spears as she sang her heart out in her car. She didn't seem to notice that if Aazar sat any closer to the door, she'd fall out of the vehicle. Norma just kept singing pop song after pop song with full hand gestures and choreographed arm moments. Although most of Aazar was terrified, she also wondered what it was like to be so free.

When they finally got to the mall, Norma pulled her keys from the car, ending the longest episode of *American Idol: Car Edition.* As Aazar reached for the door, Norma grabbed her other wrist. Everyone in this family had boundary issues.

"I like Adam, you know?"

"I know," Aazar said, reaching for the door again. Norma's hand remained on her wrist.

"What if he doesn't like me back, though?" Norma said, pouting. "I mean, what if he thinks I'm shallow and self-centered."

You are, Aazar thought. "I'm sure he likes you. Guys hang around when they like you, right?"

"Well, yeah…"

"Then there you go."

Norma smiled. "Yeah, you're right. I'm just worried about nothing, that's all."

They sat in the car, and the doors remained locked. Aazar realized she wouldn't be allowed to leave this car until Norma was no longer worried.

"I promise you he thinks you're great. I mean, you picked me up and went to his gala thing."

Norma still didn't look convinced.

"Plus," Aazar said, digging, "you're stunning. I mean, he'd have to be crazy not to look at you and know you're great, right?"

Norma relaxed. "You know what, you're right. I look great, do great things, went to that gala, and my car is amazing. Why wouldn't he like me?" They sat silently for a moment. "Okay, let's go."

Aazar was starting to understand why Peter hated these people. Being pretty was essential for Norma. All the good qualities about her didn't matter to her at all, which was sad.

They walked in and out of stores. Aazar changed into blouses, skirts, and jeans hand-picked by Norma. Aazar didn't care for any of it, but she knew dealing with Norma, and her obsession with fashion and makeup was part of keeping a roof over her head. Aazar smiled when she was supposed to smile and laughed when appropriate. She started to have a good time. She was the perfect companion, even picking out a few items here and there to try on, even though they were all turned down by Norma and her fashion eye.

When they headed to the food court, Norma's phone started ringing. She pulled it from her purse and glanced at it.

"Oh my god, it's Adam!" Norma said, jumping out of her skin. She stared at the screen, reading the text message he'd sent. Her face lit up in excitement and joy.

She hugged the phone to her chest as she announced, "He'll meet us here in ten minutes! Oh-my-God!"

Norma sent Aazar to grab some food for them, too afraid to leave the spot and be missed by Adam while they were in line. Aazar watched her from her place in the Mexican food line. She wondered what it must be like to have a boy want to meet you somewhere. When she was in Newmalton, no one had ever wanted to sit with her. Maybe if she had stayed, Avery would have sat with her.

She brought the food to the table, but Norma was distracted and hadn't looked from the large hallway since the text message came in. She gave a halfhearted attempt to eat some chips and salsa. Right before Norma had decided to start her taco, she dropped it and stood up. She began waving frantically toward the crowd.

Aazar saw a swift wave from a guy with blue eyes and a short beard that looked like it had been touched up by a professional every day since he started growing it. His hair was dark brown and was almost a military cut. He was a huge guy, and his muscles could be seen under his black shirt. He threw them a gorgeous smile. He looked like a junior weightlifter.

Aazar almost laughed at the idea of small Norma holding hands with the Hulk. At least he wasn't green. He looked annoyed to be there, but Aazar felt he looked like that all the time. Norma was grinning so hard that Aazar was sure you could see all her teeth. He made his way over to them, eyeing Aazar as he approached. He fixed his face with a smile as he looked at Norma.

"Sup."

"Hey," Norma said, beaming, "how'd practice go?"

"Cool," he said as he eyed Aazar again. "This her?"

"Yes, Aazar," Norma said, gesturing. "This is Adam. Adam's the Quarterback of our school's football team. He's totally into saving the rainforest and protecting animals, right Adam?"

"Yeah," he said. "So, you're staying with Norma, right?"

"Oh…yeah," Norma said. "She was lost and doesn't have family, so I told her she could stay with us for however long she needed to."

Adam smirked for a moment at Aazar, then changed the smirk into a smile at Norma. "You're better than me. You really are."

"Oh, you would've done the same thing," Norma said, blushing. "You're amazing, Adam."

Somehow, Aazar didn't believe Adam would've done the same thing. She was sure Adam would've hit her with the limo to ease her suffering before offering her a helping hand. But Adam liked Norma calling him amazing.

"So, there's another gala in a few weeks for world hunger," Adam said matter-of-factly. "Maybe you should bring your friend."

"Oh yeah, she would totally want to go, right, Aazar?" Norma plead with her eyes.

"Sure," Aazar said, unsure what to say and hoping she'd be gone by then.

"Awesome," Adam said to Norma, trying to pretend Aazar didn't exist. "How's your family?"

"You're so great to ask," Norma said. "They're good."

"Company still in good standing and all of that?"

"Adam's totally interested in business," Norma said to Aazar as if she cared. "The company is stellar."

"Great, great," Adam said, looking at Aazar in the eye for the first time. "I hope you fit in well with Norma's family. They're great people."

Aazar just smiled.

"Oh, she totally gets along with everyone," Norma added. "Even with Peter, and almost no one can stand to deal with him."

Adam's fake smile disappeared. "Peter is a waste. I wouldn't spend any time with that kid if I were you. No good could come from it."

"I think Peter is pretty cool, actually," Aazar said, unsure why she was so mad.

"Yeah, he totally is," Norma said, giving Aazar a panicked look. "When he's not being a jerk, he's a totally cool person."

"No." Adam said. "Peter is worthless. All he does is whine. He's always in his room. I wish he never left it."

"Adam," Norma said, "that's mean."

Adam seemed to remember his place. "You're right, Norma. I'm sorry. See, you're a better person than I am. Always so thoughtful of people's feelings. Even people like Peter."

Norma smiled and giggled. "Oh, come on."

Aazar wanted to puke. She didn't think anyone could be more superficial than Norma, but this Adam guy had proved her wrong. No wonder Peter didn't like him. There didn't seem to be much to like at all. He seemed dull and quite angry for some reason that no one probably knew.

They walked around the mall a bit. Norma and Adam chatted about meaningless topic after meaningless topic. Aazar began to wonder if they would even notice if she disappeared. She doubted it. Norma did try to include Aazar in the conversation a few times, but soon she realized Aazar did not know pop culture references and celebrities and gave up. The more Aazar didn't seem to know, the more annoyed Adam got at her being there. It was clear she wouldn't fit in with this crowd. Aazar wondered what KJ and the other Variants were doing. Maybe she should attempt to email KJ when she gets home.

After what seemed like hours, Adam had to prepare for a party Norma wasn't invited to. Instead of feeling small because of this fact, Norma seemed to be even more enamored. Exclusion meant Adam was even more popular than Norma could imagine. The couple said their goodbyes and Norma and Aazar headed to the parking lot.

"Oh-my-god, that went almost perfectly!" Norma said with excitement as they got into the car. "He totally liked me. I mean, he TOTALLY liked me, right?"

"Oh yeah," Aazar said in a sarcastic tone. "Totally."

Norma laughed. "Okay, I know. I get ditsy when he's around, but he's so awesome, funny, smart, and cute. I, like, totally lose myself, you know?"

Aazar felt she could understand. That's how she had felt when Avery was around. She tried to brush the thought of Avery from her mind. He didn't matter anymore.

"Why does he hate Peter so much?" Aazar asked.

Norma's smile faded and was replaced by a frown Aazar hadn't been sure she was capable of until today. Her eyes sank to the floor.

"It's kind of a long story."

"What happened?" Aazar said, even more interested.

Norma became silent for a moment. She took a deep breath. "Last year, Peter and Adam were in a car accident together."

"What?" Aazar said. "They were together in a car accident?"

"No, like Adam hit Peter. Or Peter hit Adam. I don't know. They both say it was the other guy's fault."

"Well, what do you think happened?" Aazar pressed.

"I don't know," Norma said again. She sighed and started again, "So, Adam was coming home from a party one night. He was with all his friends, and they got into a car accident with Peter. Peter was sober, but the cops found paraphernalia in the back of his car, so he was stuck doing community service for six months."

Norma shifted in her seat as she made a turn. "Adam says that Peter came out of nowhere and should've taken all the blame, but he didn't, so Adam had to do community service too. Peter says he never had any paraphernalia and that it was planted on him by Adam after he didn't take a bribe."

Then Norma's voice began to speed up in Adam's defense, "But Peter always says outrageous stuff like that. He's always talking about conspiracies. It's hard to decipher the truth from him."

Aazar thought about this for a moment. It had to be why Peter was not allowed to have the car. "Do you think Peter's lying?"

"Well, one of them is lying," Norma said sadly. "I convinced my parents to hire a private eye to follow Peter for a while to see if he actually did have paraphernalia or if he was doing drugs, but after he found out about the private eye, he threw a fit, so I don't really know. But Peter lies all the time. It's not shocking if he made up something like that."

This was the reason Peter hated his whole family. It seemed that they all sided with someone else and deserted Peter for being strange. Then again, Peter did seem to be quite the conspiracy theorist. It couldn't be surprising that people wouldn't believe him. If she hadn't been a Variant herself, she probably would've thought he was just an over-exaggerator a few weeks ago. It seemed like Aazar, and Peter had more in common than she'd known.

They drove up to the house and into the garage. Aazar was relieved to leave the car.

"Well, that was totally awesome!" Norma said bright and cheerful again. "We should go again!"

"Sure," Aazar said with as much enthusiasm as she could.

* * *

When Aazar got to her room and kicked her shoes off, she thought about Peter again. She wondered why he hadn't just run away. Then she realized she wouldn't have run away if Aazar didn't hurt anyone or felt that she had to. At least his family somewhat accepted him. She had been run out of town. It had almost been a witch hunt. She shook her head at the thought.

Then she heard a knock on her door. She rolled from the bed and opened it. Peter stood there with his computer open in his arms. As he balanced and looked at the screen, he spoke to her.

"So, Todd emailed me last night, and told me they're meeting up again tomorrow afternoon at four at the Café. No one has your email, so—" He looked at her. Then he busted out laughing.

"Look at your face! What happened to you?" He jeered.

Aazar realized she still had the makeup on her cheeks. She must have looked like a prostitute.

"Oh, shut up."

"Norma *clearly* got her hands on you." He laughed again, ignoring Aazar's glare. "Oh, come on, don't look like that. You look nice."

Aazar ignored the compliment as she took the edge of her sleeve and wiped her face.

Peter grinned at her discomfort. "No, really, you look nice. Just lay off the lipstick…and eye goop…and are those fake eyelashes?"

"Leave me alone."

Peter bit his lip to control the grin and then cleared his throat. "Okay,

okay. Here I have something for you."

He walked toward the dresser and put his computer on it so he could grab a small piece of plastic out of his pocket. He handed it to her. She looked at it as she turned it back and forth in her hands.

"A debit card?" she asked.

"For the next time you go to the mall with my sister," Peter said. "Maybe you'll come out looking like yourself instead of a Norma clone." He laughed again.

Thinking about Norma's clone, Aazar was suddenly reminded about Mrs. Belize and the cell phone that afternoon.

"This might sound weird, but your mom was digging around on your father's phone when we came downstairs today."

Peter shrugged, picked up his computer and sat on Aazar's bed. "That doesn't sound weird since he's cheating on her."

Aazar blinked. "Really?"

"Well, to be fair, she started cheating first," Peter said as he began to type on the computer. "The funny part is she's insecure about *him* plowing someone else."

"That's so sad," Aazar said. "Why don't they just get divorced?"

"What would that accomplish?" Peter said. "Neither one of them want to split the money down the middle, so they'll probably just stick it out."

"Do they even love each other?" Aazar asked.

Peter shrugged, bored with the conversation. It seemed that neither one of their children cared about the state of their parent's marriage. Aazar found that sad somehow.

Peter changed the subject. "Anyway, we're to meet at Café Moana tomorrow at four. I figure we can catch the bus together?"

"Norma told me about what happened with you and Adam."

Peter's face contorted into a grimace. "The fictional version, no doubt."

Aazar was quiet.

"That tool was drunk off his ass when he hit me. He had friends at the police department, so they covered up the fact he was drunk, but when I wouldn't take responsibility after he bribed me, they planted paraphernalia in my trunk."

Aazar was still quiet.

"Look, I don't care if you believe me or not. That's what happened. That guy was pissed that he couldn't buy me off and decided to ruin my life. He always gets what he wants. I guess I should've known my fucking place," Peter snarled. "Now my parents don't trust me, not that they did in the first place…but now they *really* don't trust me, and I have that falsified shit on my record for ten years."

"I believe you," Aazar said. "Adam seemed like a tool anyway."

Peter smiled. "Well, at least someone believes me. The Variants do, but they've got their own problems. They don't have time to worry about mine, you know?"

"Yeah," Aazar said, pondering. "I do."

"Anyway. Tomorrow at four."

"Aren't you still grounded?"

"Probably. Doesn't matter. Four. Okay?"

"Okay. See you." Aazar said.

Peter turned to leave but then hesitated. He looked over his shoulder.

"You know, my sister does know about colors and makeup and shit. If you're into that stuff, she's given you a good outline of what looks good. Just…use less…"

Aazar blushed. "Thanks."

Peter nodded and walked down the hallway.

Chapter Ten: Living Sack of Potatoes

Aazar woke up the next morning still thinking about how nice Peter had been to her. She was starting to think he was a good person, regardless of what Norma and the rest of his family said.

She stretched in her new pajamas. Although the shopping trip had been anxiety-inducing, she did manage to get a few decent clothes from the journey. Norma wasn't as bad as Peter thought. Maybe they should spend more time together; then, they could see their similarities instead of their differences. Somehow, she didn't see that happening soon, not with Norma dating Adam.

Her door flew open with no warning. Norma was standing there, dressed and ready for some sort of physical activity, judging from the pink and orange active wear she sported that morning. Norma was grinning like Peter, so Aazar knew she would be asking her to do something she probably wouldn't enjoy.

"Hey, there, sleepyhead!" Norma said, jogging in place as her blonde ponytail bounced behind her. "Let's hit the gym!"

She held a bundle of cloth in her hand. Aazar could tell it was sports attire.

"No."

"Are you always such a stick in the mud?" Norma said, slowing her jog to a half-hearted march in place.

"No, I just don't go to the gym."

"That's because you haven't gone to the gym with ME!" Norma exclaimed. "Here!" She threw the clothes on the corner of the bed. "Get dressed, and let's go!"

Aazar sat up and looked at the clothes in confusion. "I don't remember buying any active wear when we went to the mall."

"That's because I bought them while you were changing out of that red dress I wanted you to get."

"The one that was too short?"

Norma smirked. "Noooo, the one *you* thought was too short. It was a perfect cut. I wear dresses like that all the time."

"Maybe I don't want to be like you," Aazar said, lying back in bed and throwing the covers over her head.

Norma leaped onto the bed and snatched the covers from Aazar's face.

"You've been hanging out with Peter too much." Norma pouted. "You don't mean that."

Aazar pulled the covers back up over her head.

"You HAAAVVVE to go with me, Aazar!" Norma pleaded.

Aazar stayed quiet.

"This isn't fair!" Norma growled. "I didn't tell Dad that you and Peter snuck out, but I get no credit for that!"

Aazar took the cover from her head. "You know about that?"

"Oh, come on, you were gone for hours, and you don't know anyone. Obviously, you went out with Peter," she muttered. "You were even wearing his jeans."

Aazar stayed silent. Norma wasn't as dense as Peter thought she was. Aazar wondered how often Norma hadn't snitched on Peter and let him sneak out.

"Why didn't you tell anyone?" Aazar asked.

"Peter is a dick, but he's still my brother." Norma shrugged. "Plus, he seems to get grounded more since the car accident. Mom and Dad won't let him sneeze without punishing him for it."

Aazar nodded.

"But I *will* tell them if you don't go to the gym with me." Norma said with an evil grin.

Aazar sat up straight. "What the hell, Norma?"

"What?" Norma shrugged. "I need a gym partner, and none of my friends are available!"

Aazar sighed. The truth at last.

"What did you and Peter get into anyway? Did he take you on a date? Show you his favorite cyber bar?"

Aazar rolled her eyes. "All right, all right, I'll go as long as I don't have to go through the Third Degree."

Norma sprung from the bed in glee.

"Yes!" She fist-pumped the air. "Be downstairs in twenty minutes!" She skipped from the room.

Aazar sat up with a frown and started to get ready.

* * *

The gym Norma wanted to go to seemed more like an office building outside than a place for physical fitness. It was in the middle of the city (the nice part) and had four stories. Aazar looked around at all of the foreign trees planted around the building. She wondered for a moment why they didn't use trees native to the area. They weren't considered pretty enough to remain in the city. The thought saddened Aazar. They entered a bland lobby with a few chairs and a homophone charging station when they walked through the doors. Norma had the receptionist scan her gym card and stroll past the double doors next to the desk.

Aazar was shocked to see how much workout equipment seemed crammed into this room. She couldn't believe there were so many kinds of machines and weights. She looked at the people working out; they were all the gym type, with perfect bodies and skin. There were lots of guys drinking water from water bottles, sweat-drenched towels thrown haphazardly on ellipticals, and women taking selfies of themselves on workout equipment. She knew this would be Peter's nightmare.

Norma and Aazar headed upstairs to the pool. Norma took out a bathing suit and went to the dressing room to put it on. She tried to convince Aazar to go swimming, but Aazar reminded her that Norma neglected to buy a bathing suit without her permission. Norma was annoyed with herself until

Aazar said she didn't mind watching Norma swim.

Aazar looked into the water. No one was in the pool now. She wondered if she could get it hot enough to make the pool boil or even make it burst into steam if she used her powers. She almost wanted to try, but after hearing about Variants getting put into laboratories, she didn't want to get caught. She took off her shoes and put her feet into the cool water. She watched her toes get covered in tiny bubbles and wiggled her feet around. The last time she had seen a pool was when she had been watching Avery as a lifeguard. Avery and Newmalton felt like a lifetime ago. It had only been a few days, but it felt like an eternity.

Norma came out in a bright purple bikini with a matching swimming cap and jumped in the water. She began swimming laps back and forth across the pool with grace and skill. Aazar watched her in amazement. Norma was an outstanding swimmer. Her arms stretched into perfect half-circles as they spread the water, and her legs were as straight as boards behind her. Norma was graceful, and her face had a look of determination that Aazar hadn't witnessed before. Norma swam to the side pool side Aazar was sitting and popped up from under the water. You could see how young she was without all the makeup and hair. She grinned like a child.

"I can't believe I forgot to get you a suit," Norma said, wiping the last of the water from her eyes. "I swim about twenty laps before heading out, but since you can't get in, I'll just get out now." She pulled herself up and sat next to Aazar. Water spilled from the pool over the tile in front of her. Aazar moved away to keep from getting wet.

"Do you like swimming?" Norma asked breathlessly.

"I know how to swim…" Aazar said.

"Well, next time we come, I'm teaching you. You'll love it!" Norma wiped the water from her face.

"Are you on the swim team at your school?" Aazar asked.

Norma laughed. "What? And have people see me without my makeup, looking like a drowned rat? No, thank you." The laugh felt forced.

"But wouldn't it make you popular?" Aazar said, thinking that would be a plus.

"Well, maybe, but what if I suck and end up in last place? Or what if Adam feels like less of a guy because I became a jock?" Norma shook her head. "Plus, I want to be popular for my looks and style, not because I can move fast in a pool."

Aazar didn't know what to say to that. It seemed sad not to do something you liked because of other people. Norma didn't seem to have any self-confidence outside of fashion. It didn't look like thinking that way was helping Norma, but she knew better than to contradict Norma's logic.

"Plus, I already AM popular," Norma said before standing up and grabbing the towel resting on the bench next to a water fountain.

Aazar waited for Norma to change, and they went to the next level at the gym. It was full of treadmills and a few rooms with glass walls. She saw cycling stands in one glass room and yoga mats in another as Norma headed straight for a treadmill facing a television with a fashion show in front of it. Aazar grabbed the one next to her. She looked at the controls, unsure where to start.

"Here, just start with beginner so that you won't over-exert yourself," Norma said, leaning over and pressing a few buttons on the control panel.

The treadmill turned on, and Aazar stepped onto the moving belt like a baby giraffe. It surprised her that it wasn't going too fast. She started to get into the groove of things, running rhythmically on the machine. Aazar wasn't irritated about having to come anymore. This was fun. Plus, she liked "Gym Norma." She seemed more natural and a little nicer here. Maybe it was because you had to focus on what you were doing and not how you looked at doing it.

"So, what DO you and Peter do together?" Norma said, still watching the screen. Someone had just walked out on stage wearing a dress that looked like a piano.

"What?" Aazar said, being taken off guard.

"Oh, don't be all coy," Norma said, smiling at Aazar. "Do you have a crush on him?'

"What is this? The fourth grade?"

Norma still smiled. "Sounds like you do."

"I don't," Aazar said, unsure if it was a lie.

"Bogus."

"I don't!" Aazar repeated with more force.

Norma was silent for a moment.

"It just seems like you do, though."

"He's teaching me about computers!" Aazar lied.

Norma laughed. "Is he teaching you about the computer that is your heart?"

"That doesn't even make any sense!" Aazar spat back.

"Love never makes sense…" Norma pretended to look out into the distance.

"Oh, shut up."

Norma laughed. "But, seriously, if you like Peter, it's fine. After you get him into something that hasn't been sitting on his floor for six months, he's not a bad-looking guy."

Aazar was silent.

"Maybe get him a decent haircut and some new shoes…" Norma said, looking back at the screen.

Aazar spoke up, "I think his haircut is fine."

"AH HA, so you DO like him!" Norma grinned like the devil.

"I just said his haircut was fine!"

"Yeah," Norma said, licking her lips. "It's FIIINNEE."

"He's your brother," Aazar laughed, looking at Norma.

Norma giggled. "I'm just messing with you."

Aazar smiled and shook her head.

"You could do worse, you know."

Suddenly, two men wearing all-black clothes with bulletproof vests and guns holstered came into the room. They began walking around asking for IDs.

"What's going on over there," Aazar whispered to Norma.

"I don't know," she said. "This has never happened before. What if they're looking for a criminal or a Variant?"

"A Variant?"

"Yeah, I heard they are everywhere, now," Norma whispered. "You never know who you can trust. They're monsters."

The two men reached a dark-haired man with a tank top and black shirt. Aazar's heart began to drum against her chest. She didn't have any ID. Would they take her too? She began to feel warm and tried to breathe. The men began speaking to the gentlemen in quiet but aggressive tones. Norma leaned toward Aazar to spill some gossip.

"Last weekend, Tiffany said they were out to dinner with her family, and guys just like that came up to them and took her aunt. She said none of them knew she was a Variant. Could you imagine how betrayed Tiffany's family must feel? I can't believe she'd lie like that."

The dark-haired man bent down to the bag sitting next to the machine he was working out on. He must have been looking for his wallet. Then, without warning, he took the bag and slammed it into one of the armed guard's faces. As soon as the bag left his hand, he sprinted out of the room while both guards followed him, screaming for him to stop.

Aazar looked on, paralyzed with fear. Norma looked excited.

"Oh my god, did you just see that!" Norma said. "I can't believe I didn't have my camera out. That was so crazy! Come on, let's see if they caught him."

Norma began digging through her bag for her phone as Aazar jumped off the treadmill and sprinted toward the door, leaving a shocked Norma behind. She had to know if they caught him. She had to see what had happened.

She was about to run straight past the receptionist but stopped dead in her tracks when she saw the black-haired man having a bag thrown over his head with his hands zip-tied behind his back. He resisted, attempting to kick one of the officers, who grabbed his feet with no struggle and dragged him to the back of a black van like a sack of potatoes. They slammed the van doors and jumped into the front seats. Norma came up behind her breathlessly with her phone out. The van drove down the block. Aazar ran out the glass doors with Norma close behind her. Aazar noticed the block was full of people with their phones out, trying to capture a few seconds of the kidnapping.

"Damn, I missed it," Norma said, dropping her phone back into her bag. Aazar stared at the back of the van, drifting farther and farther away.

***

"They did it right in front of us," Aazar explained.

Peter nodded. "Yeah, I've been hearing about kidnappings like that. No one knows exactly what happens to those people. Nothing good, though."

They were sitting in Peter's room. Aazar had dismissed herself from Norma's presence as soon as she got home from the gym. She knew going straight to Peter's room would make Norma think she had a crush on him even more, but she didn't care. She needed to talk to someone who understood.

"Norma was excited," Aazar fumed. "Like she was a part of a once-in-a-lifetime reality show event. I couldn't believe it."

"I can," Peter said. "Other people's lives aren't that important or interesting to her."

"What if that happens to someone we know?" Aazar said, almost unable to keep herself from talking about her skin in the game.

"I..." Peter faltered. "I don't know."

They sat in silence for a moment.

"It's probably online by now. Do you want to see if we can find it before it gets taken down?"

"Why would I want to do that?" Aazar said, annoyed.

"I mean," Peter offered, "I know people are lame for wanting to film it, but these things need to be documented. Someone must know this is going on. If I can save the file before the government takes it down, maybe I can share it with some people, get the word out."

"I guess that's true," Aazar said.

Peter put his hand on her knee. "Look, I know it feels impossible. Watching that probably made you feel helpless, but we can't give up. Sharing the video, keeping it on the internet, keeps the conversation going."

"Maybe someone will recognize him. Maybe they can get the word out to his family." *If he had a family*, Aazar thought.

"Exactly. Let me see…" Peter rolled his chair around and began typing on his computer.

Aazar looked out his window in silence, thinking about herself running away from men with black bags and a dark van.

Chapter Eleven: Free Food

Aazar woke to a gentle tapping on her bedroom door. She felt like someone was constantly waking her since she moved to the Belizes. It wasn't too different from home. Back then, she used to wake up to Mariachi music her father played before doing chores around the house. He said it reminded him of his mother. Aazar's mother, on the other hand, couldn't stand the noise and complained every day. She was surprised that she had missed it.

The tapping came again, so she rubbed her eyes and blinked as they adjusted to the light drifting in from the window. She grabbed a robe resting on a dresser by the bathroom and flung it around her. Aazar opened the door and saw Peter leaning against the wall.

"So, I'm gonna head out," he said.

"Out?" Aazar yawned. "Where are you going?"

"It's Monday," he said as he shoved his hands into his jeans. "I'm going to school."

"Oh, right." Aazar had forgotten about the entire concept of school. "Why weren't you in school last week?"

"Fall break."

Aazar remembered her fall break started this week. At least she wouldn't miss anything important since she wouldn't be there. She almost laughed.

Peter stood from the wall and rubbed his hands over his face and hair. She noticed bags under his eyes and wondered if he'd slept that evening. She knew Peter spent a lot of time on the computer when she wasn't around. He saw her looking at him and cleared his throat.

"Anyway, I just thought I'd give you a heads up since Norma already left. She's got cheerleading practice in the morning and likes watching her meathead boyfriend run drills."

"What am I supposed to do?" Aazar asked.

"Whatever you want, I guess. See you later."

Peter walked down the hallway and the stairs without looking back.

Aazar closed the door and sighed. She wasn't sure what she'd do that day. She didn't know anyone in the area, and she didn't know where anything was. Standing around in her pajamas wouldn't help, so she picked a floral blouse that Norma said looked beautiful and a pair of jeans Aazar slipped under the stack of approved clothes bought at the mall trip.

She headed downstairs. She slowed down when she heard muttering in the kitchen. She looked around the corner.

Mrs. Belize leaned toward a man standing in the kitchen. She shifted, and Aazar realized it was Rodney, the butler. Aazar leaned back so she couldn't be seen. Rodney muttered something in a silky tone, and Mrs. Belize laughed and rested her hand on the man's arm. He moved closer to her.

"You know you shouldn't have done that. I was sure he'd pick up on it," Mrs. Belize said.

"He wouldn't have noticed the detail I put into the meal," Rodney said. "I'm pretty sure he just inhaled it without looking at it at all."

Mrs. Belize laughed. "You're right, but still. It was risky...I loved it."

Rodney whispered something into her ear that made Mrs. Belize bite her lip. Then he leaned back. "I've gotta go. I'll see you later?"

"Of course," Mrs. Belize said in a sultry voice.

Aazar tip-toed halfway back up the stairs to avoid Rodney walking out of the front door. He hadn't seen her. Aazar then made her way into the kitchen.

Mrs. Belize stood straight when she saw her and plastered a large smile. "Aazar! Oh dear, I forgot you were here!"

"Good morning, Mrs. Belize."

"Oh, just call me Gloria." She said with a voice a little too high.

Aazar smiled. She knew she would never call that woman by her first name.

"So, what are you planning to do today?" Mrs. Belize asked.

Aazar put her hands in her pockets. "I wasn't sure. I should probably start looking for a place to stay."

"Oh, you don't have to do that right now," Mrs. Belize said. "I know John made it seem like it was immediate, but we have all the room in the world. You can stay as long as you want."

"I won't, but thank you," Aazar said.

A small older woman with peppered gray hair walked in wearing a dress covered in a worn but clean apron. The woman smiled politely at Aazar as she went to the kitchen pantry and grabbed a broom hanging behind the door.

"Have you met any of the staff?" Mrs. Belize asked. "This is Melissa. She's our live-in housekeeper."

"That's right!" Aazar said, surprised. "Norma mentioned having a maid down the hall, but I've never seen you."

"That just means I'm doing my job properly." Melissa smiled.

"Melissa lives in a room down the hall from you. She's a very quiet tenant."

"No kidding," Aazar said. She hadn't heard anyone in the hallway, but she also hadn't gone past her room.

"How about you go with Melissa to the store!" Mrs. Belize offered. "You could see a little bit of the city, maybe get a few things for yourself. What do you say, Melissa?"

"I could always use a helping hand if you're willing."

Aazar thought Mrs. Belize was a little rude for offering Melissa's help as her tour guide, but considering how big the house was, she didn't think Melissa was kidding when she said she needed help.

"Sure, that sounds good." Aazar smiled.

"I'll be leaving in about fifteen minutes," Melissa said. She threw another smile and disappeared around the corner.

* * *

Melissa had a small sun-faded blue car with a small dent on the front bumper. Aazar looked out of the window at the city. Norma was right. There were a lot of very nice areas in the city.

"It's wonderful," Aazar commented.

"It is," Melissa said. "I could never live here without the Belizes' help. It's too expensive."

"Would you want to live here?"

"Well, who wouldn't?" Melissa laughed as she gestured at the passing mansions. "Of course, I would be just happy with any home. I've been saving up, but it seems like something always gets in the way."

"What do you mean?"

"Last month, I saved four hundred dollars, but then I had to go to the emergency room and spend it there. Three months ago, I had saved eight hundred dollars, but my car needed a new part. Every time I get ahead, something knocks me back."

And here Aazar was, living rent-free in the Belizes home with shopping benefits. Norma didn't need to pick up a stranger if she wanted to help someone. She could have just walked down the hall.

"I'm not going to give up, though," Melissa said. "Living with the Belizes just makes me realize that the American dream is real and attainable."

"How do you figure?" Aazar said.

"Well, if it were impossible to get the American dream, then that would stand to reason that no one would have it. The Belize family has it, meaning it's 'getable."

"But didn't they inherit most of their money?"

"Sure," Melissa said. "But someone had to make it. People just don't want to work for anything anymore. Gloria's father attained the American dream and gave it to his kids. What's wrong with wanting your kids to profit from what you've created?"

"Do you have any kids?" Aazar asked.

"Oh no," Melissa said. "I could never afford them."

It seemed silly to worry about giving wealth to children she didn't even have and couldn't afford. The America Melissa was talking about hadn't existed in over a decade. Aazar had a feeling Peter would have a few good points about that, but Aazar didn't argue. It was rude to tell people about themselves. At least that's what her mother had always told her.

"Here we are."

They reached a crowded supermarket with people spilling from every entrance and exit. She saw long lines that stretched around the building. Aazar's mother told her that supermarkets used to be full of food when she was young and that other countries around the world were jealous of how many choices we had, but after the Climate Crisis, most stores only carried the essentials.

After waiting in line for fifteen minutes, they headed inside. A small older woman at the front was checking for membership cards. Melissa flashed hers and began walking into the store. They had every staple one would need: beans, rice, flour, and sugar. Everything had a limit to how much was purchasable.

They slowly weaved back and forth down the aisles, with Melissa grabbing items from the invisible list in her mind. There were women in hair nets handing out food samples to the passersby. Aazar looked away. She knew she wouldn't buy anything and didn't want to be a mooch since she already felt like one.

"Aazar?"

Aazar looked at KJ, grabbing a sample of sausage from a hairnet woman. He thanked the woman and walked up to her.

"Do you want some?" he asked.

"No, thank you."

"What are you doing here?" KJ asked, looking at Melissa, trying to decide between different potato sizes.

"Oh, I'm just shopping with Peter's housekeeper."

"Why aren't you in school?"

"Why aren't YOU in school?" Aazar asked.

"I graduated last year." KJ smiled.

"Oh," Aazar said. "No college?"

KJ stopped smiling. "I can't focus on college right now…"

"Right," Aazar said. He had a revolution to carry out. She felt a shiver go down her spine.

"Hello," Melissa said, turning toward them both. She had a very stressed-looking smile on her face looking at KJ.

"KJ, this is Melissa. She's the housekeeper from Peter's house."

KJ offered a hand. "Hi, I'm a friend of Peters."

Melissa visibly relaxed. "Oh, you know Peter? That's a little surprising. I didn't think he had many friends."

"Well, I'm one." KJ smiled. He looked at Aazar. "What are you doing after this?"

"Me?" Aazar said. "Um, nothing, I guess."

"Melissa," KJ looked back at Melissa, "do you mind if I steal Aazar from you for the rest of the day?"

"Oh." Melissa blushed. "I don't mind."

"I guess I don't mind either," Aazar said, annoyed that he'd asked someone else about what SHE would want to do.

KJ's smile melted away.

"I'm sorry, I didn't mean to be…I just thought…"

Aazar softened at once. "No, no, it's fine." It was too much like her mother to get upset at an invite she would enjoy. "I mean, I wasn't doing anything anyway, so yeah. We can hang out, I guess."

"Cool," KJ said.

Melissa looked back and forth at them excitedly. "It's not a problem. I'll tell the Belizes you caught a ride from a friend." She began walking back down the aisle. "I'll see you at home."

Aazar waved at her. She looked at KJ.

"Do you have any more shopping to do?"

"Oh, no, I'm not shopping. I was just here for the samples."

Aazar laughed. "That's a little dishonest, right?"

KJ looked at her with his eyebrows furrowed. "It's free food."

"Never mind," Aazar said. "What do you want to do?"

* * *

KJ took Aazar to a small store about three miles away from the Supermarket where they had just been. The faded sign above the building said "BPS." It was part of a dying strip mall and was one of the only open stores, while the others had windows boarded up as they collected dust and became lined with trash.

The man sitting behind the counter seemed like he hadn't slept for centuries. His eyes were bloodshot and hardened. He looked at KJ and threw a clipboard at him without saying hello.

"Ten just this fucking morning, can you believe it?" the older man said, grabbing a vaporizer and taking a huge drag. He blew the vapor from his lips in a massive cloud and continued, "It's like the grid has been running for one hundred years without maintenance."

"But isn't that exactly what—" KJ started.

"OF COURSE, IT IS. DON'T GET ME STARTED," the man bellowed from his small swivel seat. He slammed his fist on his desk, which was covered with papers, fast food wrappers, and one lamp that seemed to be on its last light bulb. He took another vape drag.

"Well, what the hell are you still standing there for!? Get going!" the man growled at KJ. As soon as he finished his sentence, the phone rang.

"Oh, for the ever-loving fuc—" He picked up the phone. "Broughton Power Systems, how can I help you…" He waved them away and turned back to the call.

KJ and Aazar walked back out of the store.

He handed her the clipboard. Aazar looked at the list of ten locations on a sheet of paper. They looked like requests for an electrician.

"Sorry about Tom, He's got a lot on his plate. The electrical grid has been faulty for the last few years. The city should've implemented power rationing years ago, but they haven't since rich people don't like to conserve. Power outages are becoming more frequent, and he has to answer all of the complaints."

"You work there?" Aazar asked.

"Not exactly," KJ said, looking at the clipboard. "What I do isn't really certifiable, so I can't work there in a technical sense, so he pays me under the table to help out once in a while for issues that are severe or hopeless."

He studied the paper. "We'll go to this one first," he said, pointing at a location on the clipboard.

KJ and Aazar walked toward a bus stop at the edge of the street. The bus pulled up just as they got there and climbed on. Aazar noticed the permanent marker drawings under the bus windows. The windows were clean enough to look through but not enough to touch. KJ sat next to her and looked out of the front window.

Aazar looked at the list. "Are we going to all of these places?"

"Not all of them, only the first one. It will take a while to get there." KJ looked at her. "Probably most of the day."

"What?"

"You said you didn't have anything planned," KJ said, looking worried.

"Well, no, but…" Aazar couldn't think up a good excuse. "Well, okay, I guess it's fine."

KJ leaned back and smiled.

They drove away from the beautiful buildings and manicured lawns toward a darker part of town. Aazar watched as the fancy restaurants and extensive shopping areas gave way to dirty gas stations and dilapidated houses. The sun began to set, and the bus became cold. It stopped at each stop along the way, letting off people as they went. A small boy and his family got onto the bus. KJ looked at them for a moment, then looked away.

Aazar looked at the boy. "How did you know you had powers?" she asked.

KJ was so quiet for a moment that Aazar didn't think he would answer.

"It was a few years ago," KJ started. "We were at the city pool…"

He looked into the distance in the silence. Aazar held her breath, waiting for him to continue.

"Me and Todd had finally convinced our parents to let us go after Todd had gotten in trouble for manipulating our parents into buying him a new car and a laptop for his birthday by telling one the other was covering it."

"Todd's your brother?" Aazar asked, surprised.

KJ nodded. "My younger brother." He paused for a moment. "He always seemed smarter than me. We thought he'd be grounded all summer, but

Todd has a real way with words, and he managed to talk his way out of it before school started."

He looked down at his shoes, smiling. "It was a big deal because Cindy Lopkin had started wearing bikinis, and she was a little…top-heavy, and everyone was talking about it."

"Gross," Aazar said.

"I know, I know," KJ said. "I thought it was immature, but Todd wanted to get a shot at talking to her before she got popular when we went back to school. Anyway, we got to the pool, and about five guys surrounded her. But like I said, Todd has a way with words, and he doesn't like to lose, so needless to say, the other guys didn't stand a chance."

He smirked. "Unfortunately, Cindy had already got a boyfriend this summer. He just wasn't at the pool…or so we all thought."

"Uh oh," Aazar said.

"He came out of nowhere and started shoving Todd around. Cindy got pissed off and broke up with the guy on the spot. She said she hated violence and aggressive guys. That didn't land well with him."

He looked up to the ceiling. "So, this guy starts beating up Todd. And I mean nasty stuff. Punching him in the nose, kicking him in the chest. Cindy was screaming, and I couldn't just let him beat the crap out of my little brother, you know."

KJ looked down at his feet again. "So, I shoved him. And he shoved me into the pool."

Aazar frowned.

"I wasn't a good swimmer, so I panicked. I started flailing around and couldn't tell which way was up. I felt myself getting hotter and hotter, which freaked me out even more. I finally reached the surface, coughing and choking. I shoved my way around people in the pool, even though it seemed like no one would get out of the way. I got to the edge and pulled myself out."

KJ got silent for a moment. His eyes glazed over.

"When I looked around, I realized everyone was staring at me. No one was trying to help me or make sure I was okay. They were just staring horror and shock. I remember being a little offended by it even. Then I looked at the pool."

His eyes welled.

"Everyone was dead."

Aazar blinked. "Dead!? Dead how?"

"When I fell into the water and panicked, my body released electricity. It was like throwing a live telephone pole in there. I electrocuted everyone."

"…Oh God," Aazar said, covering her mouth.

"There…" KJ looked down. "There were kids…families…"

"Oh wow," Aazar said. "I'm…I'm so sorry."

"No one knew what happened," KJ plowed on, determined to finish the story. "They ruled it as a mass heart attack, which didn't make any sense, but no one could think of a better explanation. I went for weeks thinking I was a walking plague until I saw sparks shoot from my fingers when turning on a TV remote. Todd was the one who figured it out. He added it up."

Aazar sat in silence.

KJ looked away from her. "I…I just try not to panic anymore. I try not to feel any emotions too severely…"

"Isn't that hard?" Aazar said.

KJ gave her a half smile as he tapped her leg. "Sometimes, but I've got a mentor. He's been helping. I'm sure he'll help you too if you want."

"I…" Aazar thought out loud, "I think I might like that."

"This is us," KJ said, changing the conversation.

They exited the bus on a dark street whose streetlamps were long out of commission. KJ placed his hand on the electrical substation a few feet away. She saw his hands glow light blue. Aazar watched in awe as each streetlamp lit one by one. She watched as rats scurried away into new dark corners created by the shadows. Aazar looked around. She thought the street was being renovated because of all the tarps and sheets she saw. But with the lights on, she realized that there were tents and shelters placed up the street for the homeless. Cars were left on any empty curb regardless of the "NO PARKING" signs.

They walked to another BPS store since it wasn't that far from the substation. This time, a woman was asleep on a pile of papers at the front desk. She had a phone dangling out of one hand and a pen resting in the other. There was a lamp at the back of the room that she'd turned in a way that kept the light from hitting her while she napped. She jumped awake as the door closed behind them.

"Hello, welcome to Broughton Power Systems."

"Hey, I'm KJ. I'm here from the main branch."

The woman looked surprised. "What?"

"I'm from the main branch."

"They said they couldn't send anyone."

"Well, someone sent me."

"I…" the woman started. She then shrugged. "I guess if you think you can help. Come on back. The power grid is here."

They went through a small door in the back of the office. The office had been very misleading because of a large power grid connected to the small building. It was very dark except for a few ceiling lights that blinked dimly throughout the building.

"The main power substation is through there," the woman said. "Go one aisle down and make a left. It's huge. You can't miss it."

"Okay," KJ said.

"They say it can't be fixed," the woman offered. "We haven't had power in this area of town for almost three months. I don't know what you think you can do." She sucked her teeth with frustration.

"I'll give it a shot."

She shrugged and went back through the door.

"She didn't even check if you had an I.D. or anything."

"I don't think anyone cares at this point," KJ stated. "I've been doing this for a while. People don't care who you are if you can bring them power."

They went down the aisle and saw the vast substation. KJ took a deep breath.

"Okay," he said to himself.

He placed his hands on the substation and closed his eyes. In the dark, Aazar could see his hands turn blue again. Then she gasped as she saw the blue turn to white lightning glowing from his arms like vines. He grunted, and the sparks went from his hands straight into the substation. The entire building lit up at once. Aazar looked at the ceiling and realized that the room had been filled with light bulbs, but none had power. Her jaw hit the ground.

Before they reached the office, the woman burst through the door with a giant grin on her face.

"WHAT DID YOU DO!?" she exclaimed. "The WHOLE area is lit up like a damn Christmas tree! The whole area. I couldn't believe it when the air conditioning kicked on."

"I'm an excellent electrician."

"Well, bless you!" the woman said. "Do you two want some coffee? Some tea."

"We're fine, thanks," KJ said. "We've got to go. There are more places to help."

They walked out of the office to muffled cheering inside homes. Lights lit every building that had been dark before. Even the homeless looked out from their tents at the glistening lights above them.

"This is amazing, KJ," Aazar said.

"Yeah," KJ said, "it's the least I can do…considering…" He stared sadly into the distance again.

Aazar realized she had never met someone so selfless in her life. He looked tired after lighting up the grid, and she knew what he did drained him, yet he would do it another ten times that day to help people. She decided right then that having powers didn't make someone evil or vicious. Sometimes it made people kind.

"I think I can go to one more stop," Aazar said.

"Really," KJ said, surprised.

"Yeah." Aazar looked at him. "It's nice to see powers used to help people."

He smiled a little as they walked toward the bus stop and looked at the clipboard for another location.

Chapter Twelve: The Nomophobe

Aazar and KJ fixed three more substations before dropping her off at the Belizes. As she walked down the lawn's pathway, she hummed to herself in a pleasant tone. It felt good to help people today. She even started thinking about ways she could help people with her own powers. KJ had shown Aazar a new side of his personality. He'd been kind to everyone they'd come in contact with, and she even caught him giving some cash to a homeless man while he thought she wasn't looking. She hoped she could spend more time with KJ soon.

Aazar reached the deck and tried to open the door to the house, but it was closed. She raised an awkward fist to knock on the door. Aazar could almost hear her mother mocking her for being so meek. Aazar wondered if she'd ever be rid of her. Rodney opened the door, and after realizing who it was, his face settled into an irritated smirk.

"Hello, ma'am," he said, his voice filled with sarcasm. "It's great to see you've made it back."

"...Thanks," Aazar said awkwardly, waiting for him to move out of the way.

Rodney continued to block the entrance when a noise behind him caught their attention.

"WHAT THE FUCK!" Peter cried from inside the house.

Rodney turned and walked inside, leaving the door wide open for Aazar. She closed it as she walked into the foyer.

"He can't do that!" There was a loud crash in Peter's room.

Aazar and Rodney rushed down the hall. Gloria stood against the open door with her arms crossed. When Aazar looked inside, she saw a wild Peter flinging a book to the floor.

"Peter..." Gloria started on the brink of impatience.

"No!" Peter yelled back.

"Your father thought it was bes—"

"That motherfucker doesn't know anything!" Peter raged. "He can't just lock my shit away!"

"Your father saw a documentary on Nomophobes and—"

"This is fucking ridiculous!" Peter bellowed as he picked up a mug and threw it against the wall, shattering it into ceramic pieces on the floor. It was the first time that Peter had ever reminded Aazar of his father.

Aazar and Rodney jumped, but Gloria didn't even flinch. It seemed she wasn't surprised by this kind of violent behavior. It was clear Mr. Belize ensured Peter wouldn't get his laptop this time.

"Look at yourself," Gloria said, irritated. "You've lost your mind."

"You can't do this to me!" Peter roared as tears welled in his eyes.

Aazar was stunned. So, this was Peter without his computer. His wild expression and his jittery movements seemed foreign. He always seemed so in control of himself. *You never know a Nomophobe until they don't have their gadgets*, her mother sang in her head.

"It's only until your father gets back in town, which is in a couple of days," Gloria commented.

"A couple of *days*!" he screamed. "Do you have any idea how much goes on in a day online!?"

Gloria sighed. "Honey, you still have your cellphone for—"

"Get the fuck out!" he yelled.

"Peter..." Gloria started.

"GET OUT!" He picked up an empty bowl and hurled it toward Gloria, who jumped this time. The bowl bounced off the wall and landed softly into a pile of laundry.

Gloria glared at Peter for a moment before releasing an exasperated grunt and turning to leave. Rodney followed Gloria, rubbing her back for a second as they walked down the hallway. Aazar stood outside the door looking at a breathless Peter, whose eyes darted every which way. She wasn't sure if she wanted to go in.

"Hey…" Aazar began.

"He just *took* it!" Peter said, sounding frantic. "He took my laptop and locked it in the fucking computer room upstairs!"

Peter walked up to her and grabbed her shoulders as he stared into her eyes. "What am I supposed to do for two days!?"

He didn't wait for Aazar to answer and kept going, "I have algorithms to create. People I need to contact from a secure location. I can't do this."

He let her go and walked back into his room. Aazar followed him with a grain of caution she'd never needed before.

"It's only for a couple of days," Aazar said. "We could take some time off, maybe do something fu—"

"Don't be ridiculous," Peter said, pacing again. "I need to get my computer. How do I get my computer." He began muttering to himself.

"You can just use the house computer, right?" Aazar said.

"Are you fucking joking?" He spat at her. "No. I can't use the fucking house computer."

Aazar stared at him in shock. She understood why people were afraid of Nomophobia. Peter had lost all sense of himself over a block of metal and plastic. It was like she didn't know him at all. Aazar knew that Peter needed professional help, but Gloria didn't seem to care. Aazar sat on Peter's bed as he looked under it for a computer he already knew wasn't there.

"You know what, fuck this!" he said all of a sudden. "I'll just buy a new one."

"That's ridiculous, Peter," she said. "If you just wai—"

"I'm not fucking waiting." Peter bolted out of the room and into the hallway, leaving Aazar standing in his room alone.

This was stupid, she thought. Peter had lost his mind, and she wouldn't sit around listening to it. Aazar sucked her teeth in irritation and headed up the stairs toward her room, only to be greeted by Peter's back as he leaned into Norma's open door. Aazar heard Norma's muffled voice from the hall. She walked toward them against her better judgment.

"...me alone. Just get out," Norma said from her bed as she ignored Peter's frantic gestures. She wore a fluffy orange robe and a face mask as she watched a video on her phone.

"It would only be for, like, a half hour," Peter reasoned.

"NO!" Norma said. "Dad's going to flip when he finds out you bought a new one. I'm not going to be complicit. No way. You can't borrow my car."

"How would he find out?" Peter said. "He's not going to go through your gas receipts."

"Mom will tell him."

"I'll sneak out," Peter pressed. "She won't know a thing."

"Just get out!" Norma yelled.

Peter stepped into the room. Aazar looked on from the hallway. She saw Peter move near Norma's vanity.

"Look," Peter started again, "I'm going crazy, okay? I can't just sit here while—"

"Why can't you just sit, Peter?" Norma asked, never looking up from her phone. "I mean, this shouldn't be an issue if you don't have a problem."

Peter leaned against the vanity with his hands behind him. Aazar watched as Peter's fingers found a pair of orange car keys sitting there.

"It's not an issue." Peter pretended to cough to cover the sound of him shoving the keys into his pockets and continued. "It's a preference."

"Well, I prefer not to help you," Norma said, looking up finally. "You're on your own."

Norma saw Aazar standing in the hallway.

"Are you spying on us!" Norma said with an evil grin. "Or are you just spying on Peter?"

Peter pivoted in her direction, his eyes wide with fear and his face flushed red.

"I was just going back to my room," Aazar said, staring at Peter.

It was quiet for a moment before Norma sucked her teeth in disapproval. "Well, whatever, you guys can both leave. Adam is supposed to video chat with me in like five minutes, and if I miss it because I was talking to you, I will freak out."

"Fine, fine." Peter threw his hands up in surrender. "I'm out of here."

Peter gave Aazar a nervous glance before walking back down the stairs. Aazar followed him, unsure why.

"You can't just steal your sister's car, Peter," Aazar spat out. "What are you doing?"

Peter turned around, surprised. "I don't know—"

"Don't lie to me!" Aazar said louder than she wanted to. She began to warm and tried to breathe. Not now, she thought. Not now.

Peter stared at her, shocked that she'd yelled.

"I…" Peter said. "Look, I can just get a new computer and stash it when my dad gets home. I need access to my files. It will only take a few minutes to get to the store, download my cloud, and get back before my mom notices I'm—"

"Do you hear yourself?" Aazar said. She felt her fingertips begin to warm.

"What are you talking about?" Peter asked with impatience. "This can be done if I leave right now—"

"You shouldn't go," Aazar said. "You need to—"

"And how the fuck do YOU know what I need?" Peter snapped. "You've been here for a total of, like, four minutes; you don't know me at all."

Aazar's whole hand was warm now. She hid it behind her back and took a breath. No. She wasn't going to lose control. Aazar looked at Peter as he scratched the back of his hand vigorously, and realized she felt sorry for him. He was a mess. She sighed as her pity for him washed away her anger.

"You're right," Aazar said. "I don't know you. I'm going to my room."

She turned to leave.

Peter's voice softened. "Wait…come with me."

"What!?" Aazar's forehead ruffled with confusion as she turned around. "You've got to be out of your mind if you think I'm going anywhere with you after all of this."

"Please," Peter pleaded. "I'm sorry. I don't want you mad at me."

"Too late."

"How about I get you something from the mall while we're there," Peter said.

Aazar looked at him like he'd swallowed a hammer. *"You're* going to a mall?"

Peter scratched his arm with vigorous force. "They have the best Kiwi store in Broughton. I have to go there if I want something decent. Can we go?"

"Kiwi?"

"Yeah, Kiwi Computers," Peter said, exasperated. "Largest computer distributor in the world. Can. We. Go?"

Aazar stared at him for a moment. He bounced a little bit on the staircase, waiting for her reply. As much as she didn't want to go with him, she also didn't think it would be good for him to be alone now.

"Okay, fine," Aazar said. "But I want something nice."

"Sure, anything you want." He grinned, looking like himself, for a few seconds before dashing down the rest of the stairs and out of the front door. Aazar rushed to catch up with him.

* * *

The ride to the mall was quiet. Aazar stared out of the window while Peter cussed and swore at every vehicle on the road. Maybe it hadn't been the best plan to follow him while he was in a fit of rage. Aazar felt like she was always following someone else into trouble. Peter seemed to forget that she existed, muttering with fury as he looked out the window. She didn't like him like this, Aazar decided.

The mall was more crowded than the last time and going with Peter was a jarring experience. Being with Norma meant stopping at kiosks, trying on makeup, and giggling over sodas at the food court. Peter, on the other hand, had thrown the hood of his sweater over his head, shoved his hands into his pockets, and walked briskly through the crowd like a fish through water or ghost through walls. Aazar had to jog to keep up with him. People looked startled when the hooded blur came rushing by and even more surprised when Aazar came after it, apologizing for Peter's rudeness.

When they got to the Kiwi store, Peter rushed straight to the sales counter without looking around. He began barking orders at the poor representative. The person smiled as though they weren't being yelled at by a man who'd lost all control. Aazar gazed at the high ceilings and the fact that there were no doors in this store, only large glass walls that shifted for closing and opening. The room looked sterile, like they should've been performing surgeries, not selling overpriced computers. People crowded around different displays, pushing buttons and checking out new features. She only saw a few people who'd bothered to take a seat and those who had looked lost to the world. Aazar felt people wouldn't look up if she broke out in a flash mob dance. Despite herself, Aazar looked over someone's shoulder to see a bouncing green blob smiling back at her as it danced to the next level. She smiled at it.

"Aazar!" Peter yelled from across the room.

Aazar looked up, and Peter waved her over. She noticed that he had relaxed. His hand rested on a new laptop as he smiled. There was no doubt that Peter was a Nomophobe.

"Look," Peter said as she stood next to him. "It's like my old one, but it has more memory and a better graphics card."

"Six-times faster," said the employee behind the counter.

"Oh," Aazar said. "So, it's good then?"

Peter and the employee looked at her like she'd just asked if rabbits have ears.

"Yeah," Peter said, "it's good."

"Okay, let's get out of here," Aazar said, looking around at the people. She wondered if they'd all go into a fit of rage if their phones were taken away. Would they start throwing things and screaming at each other?

"Do you want a phone?" Peter offered. "I did say I'd buy you something nice."

"What?" Aazar said.

"I know you don't like this kind of stuff," he responded. "But it comes in handy. What if you get lost or—"

Just then, a man walked up to the counter. His clothes were disheveled, and his hair was dirty. His eyes were as wide as Peter's had been before he'd purchased his computer.

"Hey, brother," the man spoke. "I don't have enough for a phone, but if you could just hook me up with a battery—"

"I'm sorry," the employee interrupted with a scripted answer. "It's against our policy to sell anything other than phones and computers at this location. If you need other components, you'll need to go to our department store in New Haven."

"But my battery's dead now, man!" the guy begged. "If you could just give me a battery, I could—"

"Sir," the employee said, "I'm going to have to ask you to leave."

"Oh, come on, man!" the man pleaded. "I can't get kicked out again."

The employee pressed his hand to his ear and whispered a code into a hidden microphone. A large security guard came from a back room.

"Please!" the man begged as the security guard grabbed him by his arms. "Just a battery! I JUST NEED A BATTERY!"

Peter and Aazar watched as the security guard dragged the man away. Peter looked back at Aazar.

"So, do you want a phone or…" He trailed off.

"I don't want one," Aazar said.

She knew she'd hurt Peter's feelings, but it was true. After what she'd seen today, she decided she would try to stay away from them for as long as possible.

* * *

Aazar ate her ice cream as Peter pecked away at his new computer. He complained about its new settings and features to her, but Aazar ignored him. He didn't seem to care. She never realized how much her Regressor upbringing would stick with her. Aazar hated electronics now.

Peter smiled all of a sudden and closed his laptop.

"Finished the set up," he gloated.

"Good for you," Aazar smirked and took a lick of ice cream.

"What flavor did you get?" Peter said, seeming to waking up from his mad episode.

"Like you care," Aazar said, staring off into the distance.

Peter swallowed. "Look, I know I lost control today…"

"Yeah, no kidding," Aazar spat. She was surprised at how angry she was. Aazar didn't want to admit it might be because she had feelings for him and worried about his health. It was strange to be confronted with the fact that she cared for him and disliked something huge about him at the same time.

Peter ran a nervous hand through his hair. "You're not going to make this easy, are you?"

Aazar sucked her teeth in disapproval.

"I just need my files. I can't do anything for the resistance if I don't have a secure line. It's understandable."

"You think throwing things and freaking out is understandable? For any reason?"

"If you understand it is." Peter grinned.

Aazar rolled her eyes, and his grin disappeared. She didn't want him to be funny right now. He seemed back to normal, but Aazar would never be able to erase the image of his massive temper tantrum earlier.

Peter reached over the table and touched her hand. Her eyes darted to his.

"Okay, I'm a little weird about my tech. But I promise I'll work on it," Peter said. "I don't want to lose you as a friend. You're the only one I have."

Aazar's face softened as she moved her hand over his.

"You're not going to lose me," Aazar said, realizing she meant the words. "I'm not going to abandon you, but you need to get this under control."

"I will," Peter said.

"I think you should ditch the computer for a couple of days."

Peter removed his hand from hers.

"I don't think I need to do all of THAT," he said. "I'll just use the computer a little less, you know. Everything in moderation."

"Have you ever been without a computer?" Aazar asked.

Peter's eyebrows furrowed. "I don't see what that has to do with anything. Most people get their first piece of tech before they turn five. It's not like I'm any different from anyone else."

"But you have a problem—"

"I just need to have a little restraint," Peter cut her off.

She wanted to continue, but she realized it didn't matter. Peter didn't believe he had a problem, so nothing would change. She looked at her ice cream and began licking it once more.

Chapter Thirteen: Unplanned

"You're ignoring reality!" Todd said as he stood up from the table and glared at KJ. He'd almost knocked his computer over.

It had been three weeks since Aazar and KJ went to fix the power grid and Peter's meltdown. Peter hadn't done much in the way of working on his Nomophobia, but he seemed as though he was back to normal. It bothered Aazar that Peter had a rage monster hidden beneath an exterior of cell phones and computers, but she hadn't brought it up again. She didn't want to upset him.

Todd and KJ bumped heads the closer they got to the mission. They'd been going back and forth for about an hour at the Cafe. Todd now wanted to explode the chemical factory, regardless of who was inside, and KJ took a stand against it.

"You create your own reality, Todd," KJ said calmly. "You want to believe violence is the only way to change anything. Therefore, you only pay attention to the things that validate that belief."

"Don't psychoanalyze me," Todd growled. "I believe in violence because it works. Regardless of how I feel about it. And most people agree with me!"

"How would you know?" Brian spoke up. "When's the last time you spoke to someone who wasn't on our side? I mean, they can't all possibly want this."

Todd ignored him. "The Normies will never recognize us as people! We scare them, we're more powerful, and they know it. As long as we keep pushing around paper hoping they'll feel pity for us, we'll never be treated as equals."

"Killing them won't make them any less afraid of us," said KJ. "And it doesn't sound like you want to be treated as equal. You want to be treated like gods."

The table got silent. Britney agreed with Todd, but with Brian and KJ disagreeing, it was clear she wouldn't say anything. Peter looked uncomfortable with the entire conversation while Aazar sat eating her bagel, not participating in the discussion. She wasn't sure how she felt about violence to achieve means. She didn't want to believe it was the best option, but if she had been violent in her hometown before she had powers, maybe things would've turned out differently.

"Do you remember what they DO at this medical facility, KJ? Do you remember the mission at all?"

They had clear leads that surfaced, stating this medical facility produced an ability-inhibiting drug used to subdue Variants who 'lost control' of their powers. After injection, many Variants lost their powers, became paralyzed or died. The mission was to dispose of the chemical by any means necessary and free the Variants imprisoned for experiments. It was up to Todd as squad leader, to devise a plan. Everyone believed his next promotion was linked to how he handled this situation, and he wanted to do it with a bang.

"I understand the circumstances," KJ said. "But that doesn't give us just reason to kill innocent people."

"Those people aren't innocent!" Todd yelled. He sighed as he rubbed his temples and continued, "How about we let Peter do his tech thing, and then we blow the place up. No one will get hurt, but we'll send a clear message."

"Todd, there are numerous shops and stores around the building. The shrapnel could hurt anyone who was in or around those places. It's just too dangerous."

"That's a risk I'm willing to take," Todd replied.

"Well, it's not a risk I'm willing to take, so how are you going to make an impression unless I do it?" KJ said with an edge in his voice.

Todd was silent again.

"You wouldn't have to do it yourself, right?" Aazar asked. "Couldn't we just use explosives or something?"

"You agree we should explode the building?" Peter said, speaking for the first time in what felt like a decade.

"Well, not exactly," Aazar said. "I just don't understand why KJ would have to do it."

Todd smirked, still glaring at KJ. "KJ's ability to control electricity could explode the place from the outside. It would look like lightning struck on a night it wasn't raining and would be seen by the whole city." Todd's eyes glazed over as he gestured. "I want KJ to stand on the roof of a nearby skyscraper and strike it. A huge lightning bolt would come down straight onto the medical building. There would be no doubt about how it happened. Only one of us could do it that way. I want to email some choice journalists and vloggers to witness so the real story would spread."

The table was silent again.

"That's," Aazar said, "that sounds…terrifying."

"That's the point," Todd said. "The Normies would know that they can't ignore us. They would know we were capable of more than they could imagine."

"They would start a war," KJ said. "Find someone else to do it. I won't be the key factor in why things escalate beyond our control."

KJ stood and walked toward the door.

"This war is coming, KJ," Todd called after him before sitting back down. "Whether you like it or not."

KJ opened the door and walked out. He leaned against one of the Café windows and stared across the street. Todd looked at his outline and sucked his teeth in frustration. He sighed.

"Okay," Todd said. "Peter, you'll do your thing. We'll have Brian handle the remaining guards, and after that, we'll create the explosion."

"But KJ just said he wouldn't do it, Todd," Brian said.

"We can find someone else who has electro kinesis," Todd said. "Plus, I'm sure I can talk him into it. Just in case, though, Britney, I want you to scout for talent."

Britney frowned. "But I thought you said I didn't have to do that anymore after what happened last time."

"We need a guy who you can control," Todd said simply. "Do your part. I can send Brian with you if you're scared."

Britney smirked. "I'll be fine, whatever. Don't go wasting Brian's time."

"It wouldn't be a waste of time," Brian said. "I'll go."

"Great," Todd said. "Well, I think we'll end this meeting right here. Check your emails at three in the morning."

Aazar stood and headed straight for the door. KJ looked pained as he stared at nothing across the street. Aazar leaned next to him, trying not to mind the dirty windows.

"He's looking for another guy with your power," Aazar said.

"I know." KJ frowned. "He'll probably find one."

"He said he thinks he can talk you into it."

"He says a lot of things," KJ said, staring off.

"How can he ask you to do this after what…happened that summer?" Aazar said.

"He knows that he's the reason I'm probably not dead. Instead of fearing me when he figured out my ability, he was scared FOR me. Todd realized that if they found out how I was responsible, they'd kill me. So, he convinced me to run away."

Aazar was surprised. "I'm a little surprised he took care of you like that."

KJ nodded. "After that, we joined the resistance. They've been taking care of our room and cover identities. But now, things have been becoming more violent. I believe our leader gave Todd this mission for the sole purpose of causing violence."

"But why Todd? You're older and have known about your powers for longer. Why aren't you in charge?"

"I didn't want to be. Plus, Todd is always looking for a chance to lead," KJ said. "He's always taken charge, even when we were little. I let him because it's easier than fighting, but now I think that might have been a mistake…"

Britney came bursting through the doors, being chased by Todd. Todd gave them both a look before turning back to Britney. Peter and Brian were right behind them, talking in low whispers.

"I don't want to hurt people," KJ said. "I came to the resistance to learn how to control my power, not to start a war. I can thank them for helping me with that, but now I feel like they want to use me to destroy others, and that's not what I want."

"Maybe you should leave?" Aazar said. "You've learned enough. I'm sure you could make it on your own now."

Todd tickled Britney for a moment before she took off again into the street.

"I even have a better mentor," he said. "But don't want to leave Todd. He's a mess, but he's still my brother."

"Well, maybe you ca—"

Aazar's sentence was stopped by the high-pitched scream of Britney being struck by an oncoming car.

The car sped around the corner and disappeared, never putting on its brakes. Britney lay crumpled in the road with Todd frantically holding her head, screaming her name over and over again.

The bar patrons come out of their stupors long enough to file out to the street and see what the fuss was about. Aazar stared at the scene in frozen horror as blood began to pool under Britney's head. She had never seen that much blood before. KJ ran into the street and helped Todd drag Britney from the middle of the road. The people from their group came running, all covering Britney, trying to stop the bleeding with frantic hands covering wounds on her head and stomach. Britney whimpered. Peter stood next to Aazar in shock.

"She's not as bad as she looks," KJ said, assessing Britney's wounds. "That head wound is bleeding a lot. We have to get her out of here, now."

"We need to take her to the hospital," Aazar said.

"She can't go to a hospital! We'll never see her again!" Todd wailed.

"If she survives, they'd know she was a Variant because of her blood test," Peter explained.

"What do you mean?" Aazar asked.

"After Variants activate their powers, they no longer have a normal ABO blood type," Todd said. "We have what they call C blood, something brand new and very obvious when you run a test."

"So, they'll kill her?" Aazar asked, terrified.

"No, not right away," KJ said, not looking away from Britney. "They'll experiment on her until she dies. It could be days or years, depending on how well she'll handle the treatment."

Aazar stared without saying anything, taking it all in. This was her government. It just seemed ludicrous.

"Well, where are you going to take her?" Aazar asked.

The group looked around at each other with nervous faces.

"You mean you don't know?" Aazar asked. "What about her family?"

"She doesn't have any," Todd said.

The group got silent again. The only noise was Britney's soft moaning.

"What about your place?" Brian suggested to Todd.

"We don't have room at our place," KJ said. "If we brought a bleeding girl home, our roommates would send her straight to the hospital, and we'd all be in danger of our covers being blown. They follow hospital leads to other people like us."

"Can you take her to headquarters?" Peter said.

Todd hesitated. "Since she wasn't injured on a mission, they wouldn't help anyway. We need to get a reliable doctor and a place to let her heal."

"Okay..." Aazar said, thinking. "You can keep her at our place."

Peter looked at her as though she'd eaten a squirrel. "You've been staying with us for what, a month? And now you want to bring a bleeding, dying Variant to my house?"

"Yes."

Peter looked at her while he crossed his arms and sucked his teeth in frustration.

"Your family wouldn't notice anyway," Aazar said, looking at him, 'Come on, Peter, you said they're so stuck up their asses, they never look at what's happening around them. You have an extra room by mine. No one ever goes by it except for the maid. If we put her in that one and stay quiet during the day, the only person who might find out is Melissa, and we can pay her off, right?"

"We?" Peter said. "What money are you adding to this? And you met

Melissa. She's a drone."

"We don't have time for this, you guys," KJ pressed as Britney whimpered.

"Look," Aazar said. "This is the most rebel thing you could ever do to give the finger to your dad."

"I'll get grounded!" Peter tried.

"You're already grounded," Aazar said. She realized she had hit a nerve when he bit his lip. She understood. It's harder to help when your neck is on the line, even when you want to do the right thing.

Peter thought about it for a moment. The group stared at him. Aazar knew that if Peter didn't help right now, the group would turn on him. He smiled. "Well…it would drive my dad crazy if he ever found out. Let's do it."

Todd stood up. "Get her to the car, Brian, and protect her head. We need to get her there now."

Brian sprang into action at once, moving Britney with care, who was unconscious. He rushed to a brown Sedan parked behind the café. The group followed as patrons and workers of the café stared. She didn't understand why no one had called the cops. Then she realized this wasn't the kind of neighborhood that called the police about anything.

"She needs attention," Todd said, retaking control of the situation. "We'll send someone by to check on her from the resistance as soon as we can. KJ and I will go to our city headquarters on foot to see if we can bribe a doctor into coming while Brian takes my car to your place. See you soon."

With that, Todd threw the keys at Peter, who struggled to catch them. Then Todd and KJ sprinted in a northerly direction down the street.

Peter opened the car door, and Brian placed Britney in the back seat. Aazar ran to the back and opened the back door to sit with her. Peter gave Brian the car keys.

"This better work," Brian said, jumping into the driver's seat.

"It'll work," Peter said with confidence. He climbed into the passenger seat. "Aazar has cased my house and she's right. My family will be too busy pretending to save the world to notice someone else is under their roof. I'm pretty sure they think Aazar, and I are still there right now."

Aazar sat in the back with Britney's head in her lap. Aazar was happy

Britney had passed out because she looked terrible. She found an old T-shirt stuffed under the car seat and used it to press against Britney's head to stop the bleeding. Aazar tried to find a way to keep Britney's blood from soaking through the back seat of the car, but there was nothing to stop it, and the seat was a lost cause anyway.

They drove in silence. The trip felt much longer even though they were in a car this time. Usually, it was the opposite when you came back from somewhere, but death lingered in the air this time. It was like they were all holding their breath.

When they reached the house, Peter directed Brian to drive into the backyard at a slow speed so it wouldn't destroy the grass. Aazar tied the shirt around Britney's head. They all carried an unconscious Britney into the house, upstairs, and straight to the back guest room. Aazar was surprised at how easy the task was. Britney wasn't bleeding much anymore, meaning they managed to get her into the room without spilling blood on the marble floors. They ran into no one on their way to the room, making her even more confident about her idea.

Brian sat her onto the bed when they got her to the room.

Aazar looked out into the hallway. She couldn't hear anyone in the maid's quarters or the small office down the hall. The whole house seemed quiet and strange. Brian found a chair, sat close to Britney, and held a pillow in his lap.

"What's with the pillow?" Aazar asked.

"If she makes noise," Brian swallowed, "I have to drown out the sound."

Aazar stared at him in horror.

"I won't kill her. It's not like that," Brian said, waving away all suspicions. "She might not be able to hold a pillow to her mouth to scream if she wakes up in pain. She'll need someone to do it for her if it comes to that."

Peter and Aazar still looked at him.

"She knows how important it is not to be found," Brian said in a soft tone. "She'd want this."

Aazar pulled a seat next to Britney's other side. "I'll stay here just to make sure that's okay with you."

Brian almost smiled. "Fine. Do what you want."

"Sorry, but you need to make an appearance," Peter said. "I'll stay right now. If my sister doesn't see you at least once a day, she won't feel fulfilled as your guardian. Just walk around looking sad and poor, then you can disappear again for another three or four hours."

"But what about you?" Aazar said. "I'm sure they'll be looking for you too."

Peter laughed. "Are you kidding? I stay in my room for days sometimes. I come out when I want. They all know that regardless of how much they think they can change it."

"Fine," Aazar said. "I'll look for your sister." She looked at Britney's unconscious pale body. "I'll be back."

"I'd be surprised if you didn't," Peter said.

Aazar turned and walked out of the room, closing the door behind her.

Chapter Fourteen: Drafted

Aazar wondered how Norma would react to a Variant bleeding all over her family's beautiful sheets. After going to her room to change her clothes and wash her hands, Aazar knocked on Norma's door. When the door opened, she was greeted by the smell of expensive perfume and flowers.

"Hey! I was just about to go to your room. Come on!" Norma said, grabbing a purse from the dresser behind her. She wore a bright blue blouse, a jean jacket over her shoulders, black pumps, a short white skirt, and dark blue makeup around her eyes. It was clear that Norma was ready to show off. She hadn't even noticed Aazar was gone today. If Peter was the old dog, Aazar had become the young family dog. She was only remembered when she walked into a room. No one cared about what Aazar was doing with the rest of her day.

Norma started digging in her bag for her car keys as she headed down the hall.

"We are going to the mall to see if we can find you something for the gala." As she walked down the staircase, she said, "Adam said he might stop by too, isn't that great?"

"Oh," Aazar said, stopping in her tracks and feeling more like a dog by the second. "I kind of had something else to do."

"What was that?" Norma asked.

Aazar started thinking up a lie. "Well, Peter—"

"Oh, please," Norma said, dismissing the idea altogether. "Anything you were doing with Peter can wait. You need more clothes. I'm not letting you

leave my care without at least ten new outfits to start your new life with."
Before Aazar could comment that she wasn't under her 'care,' Norma was
already at the door. Aazar sighed and walked out with her. While Britney
was there, one less person in the house was for the best.

They sped off to the mall. Norma was still dancing and singing, not
noticing a more distant Aazar sitting with her. Aazar wished she was normal.
She was having way more problems being a Variant. She wondered if it was
a good time to tell Peter her secret. But after the laptop tantrum, who could
know when Peter would just snap? She wasn't sure how long she could keep
it from him since her fingers seemed to light on fire the second, she felt an
emotion.

* * *

While Norma was changing into a green dress with a short neckline at the
mall, Aazar held Norma's purse looking at the store clock every few seconds.
She wanted to get back home. When Norma's phone began to buzz, the girl
shoved a blonde head and a bare arm through the dressing room curtain,
signaling Aazar to give it to her. She had a ringtone by an artist Aazar didn't
recognize. Norma looked at the screen, and her face fell.

She sighed. "It's Peter," she answered. "Hello, brother."

Norma grew silent as she listened to Peter on the phone. Aazar looked
around the store, feigning disinterest.

"What!? But I'm meeting Adam!" Then she added snidely, "Why don't you
pick her up if you need to have your date so bad."

Cheap shot, Aazar thought.

Norma's anger melted from her face and was replaced with sadness. "Oh.
Well, she didn't tell me that."

There was no way Peter just told Norma the truth, Aazar thought.

"Okay, okay. Here she is." Norma sighed as she handed Aazar the phone.

"You could've told me, you know," Norma said, sounding hurt. "I would've
helped you look for some of your relatives too."

"Oh, well I—"

133

"I get it, though. Peter's the computer whiz. If anyone can help you find someone, he can," Norma said, reflecting. "I guess Peter's got more of a heart than I thought."

Aazar thought Peter's heart was much bigger than Norma could comprehend. He was helping a bleeding girl while Norma was shopping for another outfit. Aazar put the phone to her ear and walked a few feet away so she could speak in private.

"Hello?"

"Aazar? What happened? Where are you?"

"I'm with your sister at the mall. She wouldn't let me leave."

"Figures."

"How's Britney?" Aazar asked in a whisper.

"I snuck the doctor inside about fifteen minutes ago, and he's still here. He said she wasn't that bad off, with no internal damage that he could see. It's just cuts and bruises. Luckily, the car wasn't going that fast. He's doing the stitches right now."

"Okay, well, I'll be back soon."

"K."

Norma tried not to look disappointed as they headed toward the parking lot. When they were halfway to their car, Adam's bright red convertible drove up next to them. He threw them his brilliant smile, and Aazar's stomach turned.

"Leaving so soon, ladies?"

Norma lit up. She ran a quick hand through her hair. Aazar realized she did the same thing before seeing Peter every day.

"OH, Adam! I'm so sorry! But I have to go!" Norma said.

Adam's smile faded. He was so furious that Aazar felt like she could feel the heat of anger from him.

"I just got here, and you're going to ditch me?"

"It's not like that," Norma said quickly. "Aazar just needs to get back for personal family reasons."

Aazar had a sneaky suspicion that Norma would tell Adam all about her problems as soon as she was gone and only pretend to respect her privacy.

Not that it was the real problem, anyway.

Adam sighed and smirked. "Fine." With that, he sped out of the parking lot with his tires squealing down the street.

Aazar looked at Norma. Norma smiled. "He's just a little temperamental sometimes, that's all. He's a beautiful person, I swear. He came down here, and we're leaving, you know? It would make anyone mad."

Not that mad, Aazar thought.

* * *

Aazar ran up the stairs two at a time. Instead of going into her room, she moved toward the back hall and headed straight to Britney's room. She looked behind her, then opened the door.

A man in black cargo pants, sneakers, and a red T-shirt hunched over Britney's unconscious body. When he turned to her, he smiled. He was the oldest member of the resistance she'd ever seen. He looked to be in his mid-thirties. He was a dark man with light brown eyes and an aggressively average face.

"You must be Aazar," he said, holding a blood-covered hand. Aazar stared at him. He looked at his hand.

"Right," he said as he wiped his hands on his pants. He stuck his hand out again. Aazar looked to Peter, who looked at her in a way that said she should shake this man's hand, covered in blood or not. Aazar felt that strange feeling of familiarness again. She shook his hand.

"I'm happy to know we have such strong people joining the resistance," he commented.

"I'm not sure if I'm joining the resistance yet," Aazar said.

He smiled again and gestured to Britney. "You are already a part of it if you haven't noticed yet."

"How is she?" Aazar asked. She turned to Peter. "Is something wrong?"

"No, she's fine," the doctor said.

Peter smiled. "Yeah, I just called so you'd come back. I know you didn't want to be shopping with my idiot sister. It looks like some of her rubbed off on you again." Gesturing to her new manicure.

Aazar shrugged. "You told me to hang out with her, and I did. This is what she likes. It's not so horrible, you know."

"No, it's horrible," Peter said.

The doctor cleared his throat. "Britney will need a lot of rest and painkillers. I'll send as many as possible with Todd when he comes by later. I'm not sure when she'll wake up. Hopefully, sooner rather than later. Sooner would mean that there is no internal bleeding or brain swelling." The man stood. "Anyway, I have to go. Make sure to change her bandages and get her something to eat when she wakes up. It was nice to meet you both."

"What's your name?" Aazar asked.

"Oh, that's right, I'm sorry," the doctor said. "I'm Ivan. I hope to speak with you more later."

"Let me walk you out," Peter said, standing up. "Can't have my sister stumbling onto you when you get lost in this place."

As Peter and Ivan left the room, Aazar grabbed Peter's chair and sat next to Britney. She looked at Brian, sleeping with the pillow tucked under his head. She looked at Britney, whose long black hair stuck to her forehead. Aazar hesitated a moment, then moved the hair from her face. Britney didn't move. Aazar couldn't understand how anyone would drive away from an accident like that. Her father taught her to be kind to people you've wronged and try to make it up to them if possible. She couldn't believe parents out there taught their children to hit someone and run away. The whole world was changing right in front of her.

Britney coughed, sending Aazar and Brian jumping out of their skin. Brian sat up straight, holding the pillow between his hands, ready to silence her if needed. Britney sighed and lay down, not moving again. Brian looked at Aazar.

"When did you get back?" Brian asked.

"A few minutes ago," Aazar replied. "How long have you been sleeping?"

"Only a few minutes," Brian said. "So, what can you do?"

"Oh," Aazar said, uncomfortable with the whole thing. "I can kind of…set myself on fire, I guess."

"Pyrokinesis?" Brian thought about that for a moment. "Cool!"

"What can you do?" Aazar asked, deciding not to let Brian know she had been talking about him behind his back.

"Super strong," he said. "I could throw this bed across a football field if I wanted to."

"That must be fun," Aazar said, unsure what to say. She wanted Peter to come back. She felt uncomfortable talking about her power because she didn't know much about it.

"It can be," he said, looking out of the window.

"Do you, uh, help people move a lot?" Aazar asked awkwardly.

Brian laughed. "Well, it's easy when I do. It's only good for when someone's under something no one can pick up or if I'm in a fight." His smile faded. "Sometimes it's not so good in a fight, either."

Aazar looked at her shoes. She knew he must have hurt someone. She wasn't sure how great it was to have these powers if all they did was injure people. It seemed more like a disease than a power—something you should be pitied for having.

Peter walked in a few moments later. He leaned against the wall nearest to Aazar.

"So," Peter said, "now what?"

"We wait, I suppose," Aazar said.

"No, you'll wait," Peter said, standing. "I've been here all day. If you've got nothing else you need, and she's got nothing else, I will head back to my room. I haven't been away from a computer for this long in years."

"Really, man?" Brian said, concerned. "That's pretty sad."

"No one asked you," Peter spat. He looked at Aazar. "Come by later?"

"Oh, y-yeah, sure, c-cool," Aazar stuttered.

Peter nodded and headed toward the door.

Brian and Aazar stared at each other for a moment.

"You know you don't have to stay," Brain said. "You just met her. I think she understands."

"She doesn't have anyone," Aazar said. She thought about her own predicament and knew she would've wanted someone there for her.

Brian frowned. "Most of us don't have anyone, Aazar. You shouldn't get stuck on such a small thing. It happens a lot in our community since most of us are first-generation."

"First-generation? I thought that people like us had been around forever."

"Well, yes…and no," Brian said. "There's always been a few of us here and there, but for some reason, our numbers have tripled in the last ten years. No one is sure why."

"Maybe it's something in the water?" Aazar offered.

"Looks like we shouldn't have been worried about the fluoride."

Aazar smiled. They were quiet for a moment again.

"Do you like the resistance?" Aazar asked. "I know they provide a lot for…um…our kind…but do you like it? Does it give you a sense of purpose?"

"I found out my power when I was ten," Brian started. "I was throwing a fit one day and decided to slam my room door. I took it off."

Brian paused for a moment, and Aazar waited for him to continue.

"My parents thought it was a fluke, but I suspected it was something more. Soon after that, during a football game, I almost killed a student during a tackle. They all thought I had just been uncharacteristically rough. It wasn't until I hugged Emily Karlson and broke six of her ribs that people were afraid. After that, no one wanted to hang out with me, and my parents were more than just a little suspicious. I ran away and started getting into bar brawls and fights for cash. I'm wanted for assault and battery in four states."

Brian sighed. "Then I ran into KJ at a truck stop in New England. I started a fight with some jerk, and KJ came over and shocked me. I went down like KJ tased me. The other guy ran away, but KJ helped me up. He told me he knew some people who could help me handle my ability and allow me to live a somewhat normal life, but I had to promise not to hurt anyone on purpose again. Of course, I agreed, and I've been with the resistance since then."

"I don't know if I feel like I matter because of the resistance, but they did give me a fighting chance at normalcy. I haven't seriously injured anyone in quite a while, and when it does happen, no one hates me. They all understand.

They understand it's not something I do on purpose. We all have our flaws, you know?"

Aazar thought about that for a moment. "Do you think they have someone who could help me? With my fire thing?"

"Yeah. We've got quite a few people who can do what you do. I call them Heaters."

Aazar smiled. "Do you have nicknames for everyone's abilities?"

"Oh, yeah!" Brian said, lighting up. "Todd is a Reader. I'm a Hulk." He looked at her. "I'm still working on that one. KJ's an Electric. I call Britney a Pheromone, but there's another name out there for what Britney does. It's inappropriate. I'd rather not tell you if you already don't know."

"How many people are in the resistance?"

"You must come to headquarters one of these days and find out. After Britney recovers, you'll go on the mission with us. You already met Ivan, so it should be pretty easy getting you in."

"A field medic has that much sway?"

Brian openly laughed. "Ivan is second in command of our organization in Broughton."

Aazar blinked. "Really?"

"Yeah," Brian said. "We're not sure if Ivan is his real name, but we'll never know. He's hands-on with us. Ivan goes out into the city to help with people and cases and things like that. He's about non-violence, but we have this new commander, and he's asking for more. We're not sure how long Ivan can keep things from getting out of hand."

"A new commander?"

"Yeah, this guy came out of nowhere. About six months ago, we were told this kid got promoted above everyone and was the new commander for the region."

"A kid?" Aazar asked, surprised.

"Yeah, he can't be much older than you," Brian speculated. "He's about eighteen. Many people were against it at the beginning, but people jumped on board when he started showing his violent ideas. Since he joined, we've been getting more attention in the news. His tactics are kind of reckless and risky, but many people believe that's why it's working."

"How do you feel about this guy?"

"He's a real character. He smiles a lot, but he's cold, you know? Like, you can tell he's always got a plan going on. He scares me."

"I can't believe anything scares you," Aazar said.

Brian smiled. "Yeah, well, you meet the guy and then tell me how you feel. He makes me shiver just thinking about him."

He leaned forward and turned on the television. There was a commercial about the presidential candidate this year. They pictured a man in a nice suit, then a video bashing him in every way possible. Then they showed another man smiling and waving, saying he knew what the state needed.

"I like this guy," Brian said. "He's promising to grant rights to the Variants and stop the discrimination."

"He's not going to do anything." a cracked voice said with an edge in its voice.

Both Aazar and Brian looked at Britney, surprised but relieved.

Chapter Fifteen: Revealed

"You're awake! That was fast." Brian grinned. "And it's good too! No internal bleeding!"

"Did you hear me, you idiot?" Britney spat as she groaned. She was still staring at the ceiling. "That guy isn't going to do anything for the Variants. He's trying to keep us from rioting, so he promises the world. It's what humans do."

"Well, he's better than the other guy; I can tell you that much."

"Oh, please." Britney scoffed. "He's not going to do anything different. They don't care about us and want us to be silent. The first guy will keep us from rioting by lying to us, and the other will do it by locking us up. Either way, we don't get anything."

"I don't think it's that bad yet," Brian said, frowning.

"Of course, it's that bad," Britney snarled. "We're a part of an alliance to overthrow the government. We're forced to become terrorists. That's what this whole revolution is. You don't think you can change things by voting anymore, do you?"

"You don't have to be so mean. Brian helped save your life, you know," Aazar said.

Britney glared at her. Her face softened as she turned to Brian. "I'm sorry, Brian. I don't mean to be mean. I'm just telling you the truth. We're about to break into a medical facility soon. It's gotten too far for petitions and ballot initiatives."

Brian gave her a sad smile and looked back to the television. "But what if he's not lying, Britney?"

"He's lying, Brian."

"But what if he's not?" Brian looked at the screen full of hope. "What if he isn't lying, and you've just given up too soon? What if he does everything, he says he will? What if everyone just wants peace?"

The room was quiet for a moment.

"You must be hungry, Britney," Aazar said. "Would you like me to grab you something?"

"Yeah, that would be awesome. Then I have to get out of here,"

"You're kidding," Brian said, looking at her. "No way, you're leaving. Ivan said you'll be off your feet for a while. I'd be surprised if you could come with us on the mission."

"I just need some food."

"Let's see how you feel after you eat, okay?" Aazar said, pretty sure that the medication would have worn off by then, and she'd be feeling the pain.

"Okay. Thank you," Britney said, staring back at the ceiling.

Aazar went downstairs and straight to the kitchen. As she passed the downstairs study, she saw Mr. Belize typing on the computer with his Bluetooth headset in his ear. He reminded her of Peter. Aazar found leftover soup in the refrigerator. She poured it into a microwaveable container and put it in the microwave. She heated it for two minutes, then pulled the door open before it beeped. She tip-toed back up the stairs, down the hall, and into the guest bedroom.

"Here," Aazar said.

"Thanks," Britney said, sitting up in bed.

Brian yawned. "Okay, well, since you're awake, I think I'm going back home. Contact us if anything happens, okay, Aazar."

"Sure, no problem."

Aazar looked at Britney while she sat up and sipped soup from her spoon. Britney stared at the television as though Aazar wasn't there at all. The room was quiet.

"So, how are you feeling?" Aazar said.

"You don't have to fill these silences," Britney said, never looking away.

Aazar smirked. "I just wanted to know if you were leaving soon or not."

Britney looked down at her soup. "I'll leave, but maybe after a short nap."

Aazar didn't understand why she was being so stubborn. She picked up Britney's cell from her bag. She put Peter's phone number in it.

"I'm going to let you rest. How about you call me if you need anything else?" Aazar hoped she'd sleep through the night and not call because she knew Peter would throw a fit.

"Fine," Britney said, looking back to her meal.

Aazar walked out of the room. She didn't know what Britney's problem was. She had never spoken to her, but up until now, she had assumed she was nice. Now she seemed unreasonably mean. Maybe it was because she had just gotten hit by a car. Aazar decided to give her the benefit of the doubt.

She walked out of the house's back door and down the street. She wasn't sure how things seemed to spiral all the time. A month ago, she worried about whether Avery thought she was pretty. Now she was helping injured Variants and planning revolutions.

Aazar left the neighborhood and headed toward the main street. She didn't want war, but it seemed inevitable. If one side didn't attack, the other would. It was a matter of time. And the Variants looked to be pushed to their limit. She had her own horror story, but she was sure everyone else had them too. Clearly, she was average in the Variant community.

She reached the dirt path she'd seen with Peter earlier and walked straight for it. She loved this strange little forest outside of the Belizes neighborhood. It was the first time she'd been alone in a long time. The path gave way to a clearing, and she stood there for a moment, looking up at the night sky. She wondered what it must have been like a million years ago; to be able to see the stars. She could only see a few now. She frowned at the thought. If they could get the stars back, maybe people might be too busy looking up to fight and kill each other.

Looking down at her hands, she wondered if she could make herself set on fire at will. Everyone else seemed to control their powers, so why not at least try it out?

Closing her eyes and trying to calm her breathing, she wanted to make it happen. Nothing happened at all. She tried to remember how she felt when she caught fire the first few times. She had been furious and scared. She knew she couldn't scare herself on purpose, so she tried to get mad. She thought about her mom hating her, about being on her own. She thought about how her father had betrayed her in the end. It hurt thinking about them at all.

She could feel her face warming in anger. She looked at her hands, and they were ablaze. She smiled, looking at them. As she smiled, they flickered out again. Frowning, she thought about how mad she was again and watched her hands light. She held on to the anger to keep the fire flowing.

"Hey, what are you doing?" A male voice called from across the field.

Startled, her fire went out. She couldn't make him out, but she knew it wasn't anyone she knew. She ran back toward the house. She couldn't believe how stupid she'd been. The fire in her hands lit her face. He could've seen her face. How could she allow herself to be seen?

She didn't stop running until she got to the Belizes neighborhood, keeping to the shadows as much as possible. She was too afraid to turn around, so she decided to speed up whenever she got the urge. She lost breath and realized she was a few houses away from Peter's home. She finally dared to look behind herself. No one had followed her. She slowed down as she turned the corner and tried to catch her breath.

After the door closed behind her, she let herself breathe. She couldn't believe she'd cut it so close. As much as she wanted to visit Peter to tell him what had happened, she thought it would be best to sleep first. She didn't know how he'd react to her being a Variant, but she knew he'd be furious if she knew she'd been caught using her powers outside.

The door to Britney's room was still closed as she'd left it. She opened the door and peeked inside. Britney was sound asleep with the soup bowl in her hands. Aazar walked in, took the bowl from Britney, put it on the desk, and tip-toed out of the room. She would figure out how to tell Peter about her power tomorrow.

***

Aazar exhaled. After pacing back and forth in her room for about an hour, Aazar had gained the courage to go to Peter's room and tell him the truth. She waited for his reaction.

"What a weird cry for attention," Peter said, not looking away from his computer.

"It's not a cry for attention. It's the truth," Aazar repeated. "I'm a Variant. I control fire."

"No, you don't control fire because you can't do it on command," Peter said, still scrolling through the news article he was reading.

"Yes, I can!" Aazar exclaimed, "I mean, I did it last night."

"But you can't do it now."

Aazar didn't want to explain that he made her nervous. She hadn't figured out why, so there was no point in letting him know she was. "I can."

"Well," Peter said, reading an article, "I'm waiting."

Aazar's eyebrow furrowed. "You're not even looking."

"I don't have to. You're not doing anything."

"I could be. You can't even tell."

"If your hands suddenly lit a fire, I'm pretty sure I could tell. Even if I wasn't looking."

"You don't have to be a jerk," Aazar snapped.

"You don't have to be a liar."

"I'm not lying," Aazar said, irritated.

"Mhmm." Peter grabbed the soda can sitting by his computer and took a swig.

"I'm not."

"Good for you."

Aazar was seething. Peter looked at her and fell from his chair. From the floor, he looked at her in horror, eyes wide with shock.

"Holy shit, you're on fucking FIRE!"

Aazar noticed the mild orange hinge around her body for the first time. Embarrassed, she felt herself cool down and watched the orange haze disappear.

"Well, I…I wasn't trying to that time."

Peter forced himself to his feet. He walked up to her and grabbed her hands, turning them back and forth in his own. Aazar blushed despite herself.

"No burns," Peter murmured. He began to grin. "Fucking amazing."

"Thanks," Aazar said awkwardly.

Peter looked at her, and his smile dropped. "All this time, I've been yelling at you, and you could've fried me."

"I don't fry people," Aazar said, irritated.

"Sorry," Peter said. "Just stating the obvious."

There was a brief silence.

"Wait a minute," Peter said. "So, you DID see a guy out last night while you were juggling fireballs?"

"Yes," Aazar said. "And he called to me and walked toward me, so I ran."

"Christ, Aazar."

Peter paced back and forth for a few moments. He began speaking again, "I know you're new at this, but using your powers outside is a risk. What if someone called the cops? What if my family found out? Jesus, they'd have you crucified."

"Talking to Jesus or me?"

"Don't be funny." Peter rolled his eyes. "You're not funny."

"I could be funny."

Peter stared at her.

"It doesn't matter. He didn't call the cops. I don't even know why I told you in the first place now."

"You told me because it's the smart thing to do. We must tell the group about this," Peter said. "They need to know what you can do and that you were spotted. Maybe they can go on a hunt to see if they can find the guy before he spooks and goes to the authorities."

"They already know what I can do."

"WHAT? You told them before you told me!?" Peter asked incredulously.

"It's...complicated," Aazar said. She realized she wasn't sure about telling someone who wasn't a Variant about their ability to sense one another.

She changed the subject. "Anyway, we're not telling them anything about the guy I saw. There's no point. He didn't call the cops or follow me. As I said, I don't even know why I told you. Everything is fine."

Peter stared at her for a moment, contemplating what to do. "Fine," he said when he spoke. "I won't tell for now, but if you see that guy again, we're hunting him down and silencing him."

"I wouldn't know if I saw him again anyway." Aazar sighed. "It was dark, I almost couldn't see him at all, and he was pretty far away."

Peter sighed and flopped back into his chair. "Honestly, I don't know what I'm going to do with you. You're a Variant, and you don't tell me. You play with your fire in public like a moron, get spotted, and can't say who saw you. Amazing."

"Peter, you're not helping,"

"You're not helping yourself! Why would you do that?"

"I don't know. I wanted to learn, okay?"

"Well, why didn't you ask someone in the group?"

Aazar looked at her shoes. "I don't know if I want to join up with those guys yet."

Peter's eyes widened. "Why wouldn't you want to join up with them?"

"They seem a little…hardcore. I don't know if I want to go around blowing up buildings and striking. I'd rather just learn to control my fire and never use it again."

"But you're a Variant, Aazar," Peter said. "Don't you want rights?"

"I have rights as long as I keep my mouth shut."

"That's not what rights are about at all," Peter exclaimed. "You should be able to be who you are without hiding it. It's not fair."

"Life's not fair, Peter," Aazar said, making a point. "If life were fair, I wouldn't be a Variant. I'd still be with my mom and dad, playing in the field instead of living here, getting yelled at by you."

"Your parents are alive!?" Peter asked. "They found out about your powers? That's why you left?"

Aazar sighed, realizing she'd have to tell him everything now. She nodded. "I burned a girl on accident. They're religious, so they didn't take it well. My mother wanted to kill me."

Peter looked shocked.

"My father stopped her," Aazar interjected, "but banished me. They called me a demon. So, I just started walking, and that's when Norma picked me up. I had nowhere else to go, and I didn't want to go to a shelter or anything."

Peter sat back. "That's rough, sorry."

They both sat in silence for a few minutes.

"Look," Peter said, "I know you don't want to, but you should talk to someone in the group about learning how to use your power. They could help you, and it'd be much safer than just going alone."

"Maybe," Aazar said. She knew it would be the safer option, but she wasn't sure about the group yet. They seemed to be going in a different direction than she wanted to at the moment.

Chapter Sixteen: The Glow Up

Aazar left Peter's room and went to find Norma. She needed a little bit of ordinary right now. She was tired of thinking about powers and Variants and the mysterious man.

She knocked on Norma's door.

"Come in," she said.

Norma was lying on her bed face down with her head hidden beneath an orange pillow. She was making sniffling sounds.

"Are you okay?"

Norma didn't move. "He won't text me back, Aazar."

"Who?"

"Why won't he text me back!?" she said, muffled under the pillow.

"Who won't text you back?"

Norma snatched the pillow off her head, threw it to the floor, and sprang up to face Aazar. Her hair was all over the place, and mascara ran down her cheeks. Her lipstick was smudged.

"ADAM!" she wailed. "Aren't I pretty?"

Aazar just stared. "Um…I…"

"Aren't I skinny enough? I mean, I could be a model, for God's sake. People tell me so all the time. So why won't he text me back?"

"Maybe he's busy?"

"Texting doesn't stop just because someone's busy, Aazar. Don't you know anything?"

Aazar shrugged. She hadn't been much of a texter.

"I didn't mean that, Aazar. I'm sorry. I know you're weird and don't like phones, but I'm distraught!" Norma said, starting to cry again. Aazar felt uncomfortable but didn't want to leave Norma alone.

Norma flung herself back onto her bed, staring up at the ceiling as tears slid down the side of her face and onto her comforter. She began speaking again.

"You start to like someone, and then they just ignore you. They pretend to be nice to you in public, but then after you're out of sight, they don't care about you anymore and are seen walking down the street with Mary Buchanan from Spencer High, even though she's not as pretty as you are and isn't that rich and might be a bulimic."

She dissolved into loud crying again. Maybe coming to Norma wasn't the best idea.

Norma grabbed a tissue from her dresser, and a loud, unattractive honk came out when she blew her nose. "He just thinks because Mary can do the splits, she's cooler, but she so isn't." She rechecked her phone, sniffling. "She's just a stupid twig with an eating disorder and no brain. Why would he want someone so stupid?"

Aazar was about to answer when Norma's phone began to buzz. She snatched it up. Her eyes darted back and forth urgently for a moment, then her whole face relaxed, and a grin spread over her face.

"He said he was walking with Mary because they have an assignment together!" Norma smiled. "He said she tried to make a move on him but that she was gross! He even wrote the word 'gross,' see!" She turned the phone in Aazar's direction, and as Aazar leaned in to see it, Norma snatched it away in the excitement and began feverishly texting him back.

Well, that was a roller coaster, she thought. Aazar said in silence, waiting for Norma to finish her reply. She couldn't stand the texting craze. It felt rude to text while other people were around. She felt that if she left right then, Norma wouldn't notice. Just as Aazar stood to leave, Norma's face yanked up toward her.

"Where are you going?"

"I was just going to step out—"

"No, no, don't! Come with me to Adam's pool party tonight. It will be awesome."

"Pool party? It's the end of Fall!?"

Norma rolled her eyes. "No one is going to go swimming, silly! We just take pictures by the pool!"

"Oh, I don't—"

"OH, COME ON, Aazar! You never want to do anything fun. You just want to sit around with Peter and his computer. That is so lame. How about you come with me tonight? Stretch your legs."

"I still don't have a…." Aazar started.

Norma grinned and grabbed a shopping bag from her dirty floor. "I got you covered!"

Aazar took the bag and opened it. There was a shimmering one-piece suit at the bottom of it.

"Well…" Aazar said.

"You could even invite Peter if you want, he probably won't go, but you could ask him. Adam won't mind."

"Okay, I guess so," Aazar said, not seeing a real way out of it. Plus, keeping Norma out of the house and away from Britney was always a good plan.

"Awesome!" Norma said. "Now, let's get ready."

"Now?" Aazar asked. "It's only five."

"Yep, the party's at ten, so it will take about four hours for us to get ready." Norma gestured toward her bathroom.

"What!? Why?"

"You don't think you can go to one of Adam's parties like that, do you? We need to get you in that dress we bought last time we went to the mall, then we need to do your hair which will take forever, then your makeup, and maybe even do your toenails?"

Aazar was starting to dislike this party already. "Well, let me just go down and ask Pete—"

"Not a chance," Norma said. "Not until you're ready. After that, you can ask him."

"What? Doesn't he need five hours to get ready too?"

Norma laughed. "Aazar, you're so funny! He'll only need like twenty minutes. If he goes at all."

"But—"

"Now, come on. You can take your shower before I take mine."

With that, Aazar was shoved into Norma's bathroom and handed a towel.

* * *

About four hours later, Aazar felt like a plucked goose. Her legs and arms had been shaved, and about a third of her eyebrows were gone. She was stuffed in a light blue dress that she almost couldn't breathe in and had heels so high she would be doing a balancing act to walk down the hall without stumbling. Norma had straightened her hair, so it flowed down her back in a dark straight mass. She started biting her lip, then remembered Norma saying it would ruin her lipstick, and she didn't want her to do it over again. It had been annoying enough the first time. She'd argued against false lashes, so Norma had covered her natural lashes with heavy mascara. Her toenails had just finished drying.

"Okay," Norma said, looking at her handiwork. "NOW, you can invite Peter."

Aazar felt ridiculous. She knew Peter would probably laugh at her and slam the door in her face. When she got about three feet from his door, she stood there for a moment. Maybe she could just tell Norma she invited him and that he said no without suffering embarrassment.

A low whistle came from the other end of the hall. She turned around, surprised to see Norma's father. He had a business suit on and looked to be headed out. He was beaming at her.

"Looks like Norma outdid herself this time. You look phenomenal. You'll knock 'em dead tonight."

"Thank you, Mr. Belize."

"Where are you headed?"

"Some pool party thing Norma's friend Adam is throwing."

"Ah, Adam!" Mr. Belize said. "Good man. I play golf with his father at the club on the weekends."

Aazar smiled and nodded.

He looked her over again. "You'd better watch out tonight, little lady. You'll be catching all kinds of guys. But don't bring any of them home. They're probably scumbags."

He bellowed at his own joke. Aazar smiled and pretended to laugh.

"All right, I'm off. You kids have fun," he said. He looked behind her. "Peter, are you going too?"

Aazar turned around so fast that she almost fell over. Peter was staring at her. She blushed.

"I…I…was just about to ask you if you wanted to go," Aazar said.

"Yeah, maybe."

"Good man!" Peter's father said. "You need to get out once and a while and meet some kids. Have a good time!" With that, he passed them through the kitchen and out the door.

Aazar looked at Peter and pulled down the hem of her dress.

"A pool party?" Peter asked as he looked at her. "Who dresses like that to go to a pool party? Who even has a pool party in the all?"

Aazar smiled, looking relieved. "I said the same thing, but Norma said no one would be swimming. You're supposed to have your bathing suit underneath to make people think you MIGHT swim."

"Sounds like a party Norma would be going to."

Aazar felt uncomfortable. "Um…so do you want to go?"

Peter looked at her like he wasn't sure how to feel about what she was asking him.

"I mean, we could laugh at the snobs there, you know. Maybe they'd have some good food or something. It might be fun." Aazar couldn't believe how desperate she sounded.

He looked at her for a moment again. "Sure."

Aazar blinked. "Really?"

"Yeah," he said. "I don't want you going there alone. Norma will split the second she sees Adam." He looked her up and down. "I'm assuming it's a black-tie thing?"

"Black tie?" Aazar questioning.

He smiled at her. "Never mind. I'll be ready in twenty."

He closed the door as Aazar walked back to Norma's room. All of a sudden, she was excited. The whole ordeal seemed to be worth it if Peter was going. She knocked on Norma's door and walked in.

Norma wore a short, orange skin-tight halter dress with a fake diamond necklace, a matching tennis bracelet, and an anklet. Aazar could see the pure white bathing suit underneath, and her earrings matched her dress. She was leaning over her dresser, looking in the mirror as she put on her last false eyelash.

"He said yes!" Aazar said, more excited than she thought.

"Really?" Norma said, dropping the lash. "Shit." She took a moment to replace it. "I KNEW he'd go." She blinked a few times to ensure the lash would stay put. She turned to look at Aazar. "You look amazing, and he's a guy, so I figured…"

Aazar blushed. "You think I look amazing?"

Norma smiled. "Well, you'd better after all the time I spent on you." She turned to the mirror. "Peter always acts like he doesn't like makeup and all of that, but as soon as he sees the finished product, he's got no problem with it. Men, I swear."

Aazar stood in silence as Norma finished getting ready. She listed names of people Aazar should try to talk to and people she should avoid, but Aazar didn't listen. She hadn't planned to speak to anyone if she didn't have to.

A few minutes later, there was a knock on the door. Aazar opened it. It was Peter dressed in a pressed dress suit jacket with no tie. He wore multicolored swim trucks you could see peaking from underneath his suit pants. His unkempt hair was combed back, and he smelled even better than usual. Aazar took a step back. He looked like he belonged in this world. She was so shocked at how easy it was for him to transform. She felt intimidated. He looked past her to Norma.

"Are you kidding? Aren't you ready yet?" Peter growled at her. "Christ, you've been up here for six hours, and you're still applying makeup? You look like a fairy fucking princess. Now let's get the hell out of here,"

Aazar laughed. You could take Peter out of the hoodie, but you couldn't change him.

"Oh, shut up, Peter. God. Why do I invite you anywhere? You're such an ass."

Peter laughed. "You stare at a mirror for half the day putting skin-colored dirt on your face…and I'm the 'ass'?"

Norma glared at him in the mirror for a moment. Then she changed the subject. "Don't you think Aazar looks great? It took me forever, but she looks amazing, right?"

"She looks fine without all that stuff," Peter said, still not looking at Aazar.

"Still, she looks great, right?" Norma pressed, looking at him pointedly in the mirror.

Peter looked down at Aazar, then away again as he shifted his feet. "Well, yeah…I mean, she looks better in it than you do."

Aazar let a smile slip from her lips for a moment. Peter's face went red.

"Can we hurry it up already?" he said, irritated. "Don't want to be late, right?"

"Of course, we do!" Norma said, turning around. She held onto the counter as she put on silver high heels that were even higher than Aazar's. Aazar wondered how she could balance those things. "If we show up on time, we'll be the only ones! We'll show up at around eleven after things get started."

"It's already ten-fifty," Peter said.

"Holy shit! We're late!" Norma said, grabbing her orange club purse and throwing Aazar a matching blue one. She ran to the closet and threw a tie at Peter, who watched it hit his chest and fall to the floor.

"Peter put it on."

"Drop dead."

"Dammit, I don't have time to argue with you," Norma said, exasperated.

"Then don't. Let's go."

Norma sighed and grabbed her keys. "Fine, you win."

They all piled into Norma's car. Aazar sat upfront with Norma while Peter stretched out in the back, despite Norma's pleading. Usually, she let the top down on her convertible, but today they put it up, not wanting to ruin their hair. Norma said she would put it down just before they got to the party so that they'd look cool pulling up. Peter rolled his eyes and groaned as loud as he could. Norma ignored him.

"This is going to be so awesome," Norma said to Aazar, full of excitement. "We're going to have a DJ, and there's going to be alcohol since Adam's parents have a full bar. Plus, everyone's going to be there. The whole football and cheerleading teams, some soccer boys, and even some of the kids in AP."

"That's everyone, huh?" Peter smirked. "What about the mathletes and drama kids?"

"Some of the kids in AP are drama kids, Peter."

"Ah." He rolled his eyes.

"I am not going to allow you to ruin tonight, Peter. I look great. Aazar looks great. You even look decent, and Adam will be there, and Mary will have to eat her heart out when she sees Adam and me together. It will be spectacular."

"Happy we could be here for this historic event."

"SHUT UP, Peter!"

As promised, Norma pulled the roof back on the convertible and slowed down on the street filled with huge houses.

"This kind of stuff is stupid. I don't know why I even bothered to go," Peter grumbled.

"I know why," Norma smirked.

Peter stayed silent.

They pulled into the driveway of a mansion even more impressive than the Belizes. Aazar even had to stare at the expensive cars. Teens were standing on the front lawn holding red solo cups and talking. Everyone was dressed to impress, and Aazar was very happy she allowed Norma to dress her up. Without Norma's guidance, she wouldn't have known what to do with herself.

Some people waved as they stepped out of the car, and others whispered. A boy ran inside. Norma was smiling and waving, with Aazar walking awkwardly behind her. Peter was behind Aazar, sulking. When they reached the door, Adam wore a black suit jacket with matching black swim trunks. He looked irritated. He glared at Peter, and Peter glared back.

"What the fuck is he doing here!?" Adam growled at Norma.

"I…I thought it would be nice for Aazar to have someone else she knew, that's all."

"Your brother's a fucking disgrace."

"I think we have a different idea of what it means to be a disgrace, Muscle head," Peter spat.

Adam pushed Norma and Aazar to the side. Peter stood his ground.

"What did you say to me?"

"I said, you look like you should be exploring your sexuality in Juvie right now instead of being on the football team. Surprised you haven't made it there the way you shove girls around to try and intimidate people."

Adam turned beet red. "Only thing keeping me from knocking your lights out is the threat of Juvie, you fucking ingrate."

Peter made a kissy face at him.

Adam lunged forward, and Norma jumped in front of Peter to stop the fight. "Adam, come on now." She touched his arm. "Just ignore him. You've been drinking. You know Peter." She took a second to glare at her brother. "He'll just be sitting in a corner somewhere soon. You won't notice him."

"I'd better not," Adam said. He then looked at Norma, half-interested. "You look good," he said.

Norma didn't seem to notice the banality of the compliment and beamed. "REALLY!? Thanks, you look great too."

Adam looked at Norma after her compliment and smiled. "Yeah?"

The couple walked inside arm in arm, forgetting about Aazar and Peter. Aazar looked at Peter. He seemed furious.

"Are you okay?" Aazar asked in a gentle tone.

"Come on, let's go inside," he said.

They walked into a massive room with a high ceiling and a chandelier cascading from the second-floor roof. There were brown leather couches and small dining tables everywhere. The kitchen was connected, and you could see the massive amount of pizza boxes and wing dip on the counter.

The bar was to the back, and the kids gathered around it, laughing a little too loud. A pool could be seen through the large glass doors to the rear of the home, but just as Norma said, while there wasn't a single person swimming in it, tons of teens were taking selfies by the pool.

Peter and Aazar found a corner to stand in.

"I'll get us some pizza. What kind do you want?" Peter asked.

"Oh, um…pepperoni?"

"K. Be back in a second."

Aazar stood watching the other kids. She didn't think she belonged anywhere near any of these people. Anyone who wasn't flirting with someone was either looking for someone to flirt with or staring at their cell phones, texting. The music was on, but no one was dancing. She couldn't imagine anyone dancing in the shoes they were wearing. Then as soon as she thought about it, she saw movement from the corner of her eye. A brown-haired boy with a green shirt that said, "Kiss Me I'm Not Irish," and blue jeans with white sneakers. He was making faces and dancing mockingly to the music. There was a small group around him laughing. The boys were cheering him on with their ties loosened and their glasses held high, spilling drops of alcohol here and there. The girls were smiling and giggling behind their hands and purses. Peter came back with the pizza.

"Why didn't that guy have to dress up?" Aazar asked.

"Oh, that's Londonn," Peter said. "That guy gets away with murder. Plus, there's a rumor that he's a Variant."

Aazar blinked. "Really?"

"Yeah, but it isn't true," Peter said. "I think he just says it to get attention. He's always doing something to get attention. Coming to this thing dressed like that, for example."

Aazar thought he looked happier than anyone else at this party, though.

"So, have you thought about it?" Peter asked, taking a bite of pizza.

'About what?" Aazar asked.

"About learning from the group."

"No," Aazar said, annoyed the topic had come up again.

"Aazar," Peter said, swallowing a piece of food, "you need to learn from someone. You can't just wing it."

"Why can't I?" Aazar asked. "As long as I do it in a safer place, I think I can do it on my own."

"Jesus, you're worse than me when it comes to asking for help," Peter said. "Wouldn't you want to learn from someone with the same ability as you?"

"I don't trust those guys as much as you do."

Peter looked away. "I guess I understand."

Aazar was shocked. She never won arguments with Peter. Usually, they just went on and on until one of them left the room. They stood in silence for a moment.

"Aren't you going to get a drink?" Aazar asked.

"Do you want one?" he asked her.

"Oh no, I was just wondering. I thought you drank," she said.

"Not anymore." Peter glared. "Not since the accident, anyway. No one believes it wasn't my fault because I was known to drink, so I've stopped."

Aazar said, "Adam's an asshole."

"Damn right, he's an asshole!" Peter said, smiling. "I was afraid you might like that ass wipe."

"I don't understand how Norma does."

"Me either!" Peter replied. "He's such a jerk. He's always like that, too, don't let Norma fool you with that "slight temper" bullshit. That guy is always shoving his way down the halls looking for trouble. Last year he beat this one kid within an inch of his life. His parent's influence kept him out of Juvie, but if he puts even a scratch on another kid's head, he's going away. I hope he does."

Aazar didn't like the idea of Adam fighting anyone. He seemed too large to even think about being violent to someone else.

Peter stood up all of a sudden. "I've got to take a leak. I'll be back, okay?"

Aazar nodded as Peter walked away. She took a small bite of pizza, not wanting to ruin her makeup. Then she officially decided she hated makeup.

"You'll ne'er finish eatin' like that," a voice with an Australian accent said.

Aazar looked to her side and saw that it was the dancing kid. She couldn't remember his name now.

"I'm sorry, but who are you?"

"Londonn. With two' n's."

"Um…Hey."

"Why you eatin' like that?" Londonn said with a huge grin.

"Like what?"

"Like a bleedin' rabbit? You'll ne'er finish."

"I…I don't want to ruin my makeup." It sounded stupid coming out of her mouth.

Londonn bellowed with laughter. "That's the stupidest thing I ever heard! Fuck the bloody makeup and eat, dammit."

"But…"

"Anyone who matters won't care, darlin'."

Aazar smiled. "I guess you're right." She took a normal bite.

"THERE ya go!" Londonn applauded. "Don't ya feel better already? Don't ya stomach just love getting a real bite in there?"

Aazar laughed.

"Oi, Peter! You look smart this evenin'! Got ya hair brushed and everything! "Londonn said behind her. Peter had just walked up, looking annoyed.

"Hey, Londonn."

"Oh, come on now, the way you said that the girl will think ya don't like me."

"I don't like you, Londonn."

Londonn made a pretend hurt face. "Now, that's not fair, mate. You'll hurt my feelings."

"Hope I do," Peter said.

Londonn looked legitimately upset for a moment, then smiled at Aazar.

"Don't mind him, honey. The kid's always angry for some reason. I'll catch you at school then?"

"School?" Aazar had forgotten about school again.

"Well, you go to our school, don't ya?" Londonn said. "How else would you know, Peter? The bloke doesn't ever go out otherwise."

"Shut the fuck up, Londonn."

Londonn threw both hands up in mock surrender. "All right, all right, no need to get all huffy. I'm off." He dropped his hands and looked back to Aazar. "Hope to see you again soon." He winked and walked off.

"He doesn't seem that bad," Aazar said to Peter.

Peter sighed. "He's not. I just can't stand how happy-go-lucky he always is. Londonn's fine in small doses, but the guy never turns it off. He's never serious about anything."

Aazar smiled. "So, he's the Anti-Peter."

"Oh, shut up, don't you start," Peter said. "This is why I never go out anywhere. People always give me shit."

"Well, it's not so bad, Peter," Aazar said. "Maybe your dad's right. Maybe you should go out more."

"My dad is never right," Peter snarled. "Got it?"

"Well, I only meant—"

"Forget it. I'm going to go outside for a minute. I'll catch up with you later."

Aazar stood by herself as Peter walked away. She felt like she had betrayed him. She looked around at the other kids, but they ignored her. It was probably because they didn't know her social standing. Norma waved to her a few times, but for the most part, Aazar was alone. Londonn had gone back to entertaining a group of kids. She felt her brow begin to sweat and worried about sweating her hair out, making it curly again. She hated thinking about that. Aazar walked outside and saw Peter lying back on a swinging bench alone. He was looking at the sky. His hair was uneven since he'd put his hands underneath his head. One leg dangled off the bench. She watched him for a moment, swinging back and forth. She walked over to him, careful not to trip as her heels sunk into the grass.

"Hey."

"Hey," he said.

"Look, I'm sorry," Aazar started.

"No," Peter said. "I'm sorry."

Aazar waited, not wanting to ruin a moment when Peter would apologize.

"I just hate these kinds of things. The pageantry of it all," he said, still looking at the sky. "This is all new to you, so it's fun, but I've been dealing with black-tie parties and galas my whole life, and it's all just bullshit. We all dress up in uncomfortable stuff to talk to people we want to impress, so they'll give us stuff we don't need. It's just bogus. I forget that it can be fun sometimes."

Aazar smiled. "To be honest, I hate this outfit and my hair."

"You shouldn't hate the outfit. You look great," Peter said, looking at her. "I do kind of miss your curly hair, though."

Aazar blushed. "Well, I hate the shoes, too."

"Then take them off," Peter said as he sat up, making room for her. "Do you want to sit down?"

"I've never wanted to sit down more in my whole life," Aazar said.

And so, she sat with a sigh of relief. She hadn't realized just how much her feet hurt. She took her shoes off and let her toes touch the cool grass as she looked over at Peter. He was smiling at her.

"You're pretty great. You know that?" he said.

"I…I'm okay, I guess."

"No, okay, isn't a good way to describe you. You're great. Really great. I don't mind hanging out with you, even at this place."

"Th-Thanks."

Peter nodded and looked back to the sky. "I'm sorry to ruin this party for you. But I keep thinking about how so many people are suffering, and we're sitting here enjoying ourselves. I feel guilty. What makes me so special, you know? My dad? My mom? Why do I get this life while other people starve or get hit by cars and can't go to the hospital or have to leave their homes because of who they are."

Aazar looked down at her feet. She was starting to understand what he was talking about. Before she had gotten here, everything had been so much harder. Her parents slaved away to get their tiny home. Saving and being economical were the only options for her. Makeup, clothes, and shoes had never been something she even thought about. Now she couldn't eat pizza without someone telling her to do it normally. She had already grown accustomed to the new privileged life she had.

"We'll fix it," she said.

Peter looked at her.

"We'll fix it all. There's no need for people to struggle when other people never have to. There's no need for people to hate others because of who they are. But we'll fix it. I know we can. Just thinking the way we do, we're already fixing it."

Peter smiled. "Yeah."

They both looked up at the night sky in silence for the rest of the night.

Chapter Seventeen: The Old man

The days began to run together after the night of the party. Trips with Norma and Adam to the mall, Lunch with Britney while she rested, evening meet-ups with Peter and the Variants at the café, and even later, fire control practices Aazar had begun for herself in the woods. Somehow during all of it, Mr. Belize had warmed to the idea of Aazar staying around more permanently.

Since she was turning eighteen soon anyway, they filed as temporary foster parents for the remainder of the school year. Aazar was surprised that her parents hadn't contested the filing or called the authorities, but it seemed her parents would rather just pretend she had never existed. She was more relieved about it than she wanted to be.

It was shocking how fast her first day of school went. Norma's parents had gotten Aazar enrolled in the local private high school within a few weeks of her stay. Norma was pleased, able to show her "pet project" to all her friends. Peter was almost militant, telling her different people to avoid and clubs not to join. Aazar began to feel as though she was a spy infiltrating a cult. Norma was the patsy; Peter was her superior officer. The time she spent alone in the forest was beginning to feel like the only time she was allowed to think for herself.

After a long evening meeting with the group, Aazar snuck off to the woods alone. She loved hearing the grass crunch under her feet and the cool fall air blowing through her hair. She listened to the wind howled through the leaves as she reached her clearing. She stood outside and closed her eyes. She'd been coming out there for a while now to practice.

After a deep breath, Aazar thought about being angry. She allowed the anger to flow from her mind, throughout her body, and into her hands. Her hand lit. She opened her eyes and tried to keep her hands lit for as long as she dared. She had learned that holding fire for longer than eight minutes would cause her to burn herself. She had ended up with a minor burn that Peter condemned her about. It was all over her hands but stayed that way for a week. Peter was mad because she had hurt herself, but she was frustrated because she had missed out on a week of practice.

She let the flame go out for a few minutes, then tried again, this time thinking about Adam and Norma's pre-engagement. Her hand went ablaze. She couldn't believe they were going to get married. What horrified her most was the Belizes' total approval. It was more like a business transaction than a marriage proposal. Mr. Belize and Adam's father had announced a merger, then days after, Adam proposed to Norma, and they threw an engagement party. Norma was ecstatic, of course, while Peter's feelings were ignored during the entire discussion.

The flame went out again. As Aazar focused her energy on her parents' abandonment, she heard a noise behind her. She turned around fast. Knowing no one would recognize her in Peter's over-sized hoody and jeans didn't keep her from dashing into a bush. She heard a twig snap and grass rustle as she saw an older man enter the clearing. His weathered brown face seemed to oppose his body, which remained strong and resilient. He moved with swiftness into the clearing, looking this way and that. She saw gray and white hair peeking through his tight curls as she took in his bulging calf muscles and noticed that the man wasn't wearing any shoes. He stood there for a moment and looked around.

"I know you're here." He spoke. He didn't yell it, he almost whispered it, but Aazar heard him like he was standing next to her.

She stood in front of the bush, stunned. The man turned left and right. He closed his eyes and stood not saying anything. He turned in her direction and stepped forward as she pressed against the bush.

"This isn't the best place to practice with your powers, you know," he said with his eyes closed. He took another step forward. "You can see the light from the flames through the trees if you look hard enough from the street. It's not far enough in the woods."

Aazar held her breath and knelt. He took a few more steps in her direction, and she could feel her heart racing. She was frozen on the spot. When he stopped walking, he was close enough to see her if he opened his eyes. His eyelids opened. He looked at her, and Aazar was stunned to see the man was blind.

"Come on now. I know you're here. I can see you."

Aazar found her voice. "But…but you can't."

He smiled. "There are other ways to see other than with one's eyes, child."

Aazar stood and closed the distance between them.

"It's rude to stare." The man said.

Aazar looked away. Then she looked back at him and found herself irritated with him. Who was he to walk up to her like that? She was a Variant.

"I'll set you on fire if you tell anyone." Aazar heard herself threaten. She allowed her hands to glow.

"Ahhhh, you've gotten a little more control since the last time I saw you," the man said, smiling down at her hands. "You mustn't allow yourself to use anger to control your power. Eventually, the anger will control your power and you as well."

Aazar stopped the glow and stared at him.

"How do you know so much?"

He laughed. "I'm an old man."

"You don't move like an old man," Aazar said.

He raised his eyebrows. "No. I don't suppose I do."

Aazar felt the familiar sense. "You're a Variant."

"Ahhhh, it finally hit you," he said. "After a few years, it will strengthen and come along much quicker. I'm surprised you haven't run into more Variants since it was easy to find you here. Then again, I am very old."

Aazar stared at him.

"You channel your power through anger and emotion," he said. "As I've said before, that's very dangerous. I've seen people driven crazy by using their anger to access their powers. I can help you if you'd like. I run a sort of 'school' for Variants farther into the forest. The students there are learning control through meditation and other techniques. Using emotion is easiest, but it isn't the best way."

"No thanks," Aazar said, annoyed. "I've gone this far alone. I can continue."

The man looked at her for a moment, lost in thought, then smiled again.

"Well, if you feel angry all the time, or are drinking more water than normal, or if you just change your mind. Find me."

With that, he turned away from her and walked farther into the woods.

"Find you?" She called to him.

"Find me. The name's Flenoid, by the way." He whispered, but she heard him again as though he was right next to her.

The man disappeared into the forest.

* * *

"Sounds like a creep to me," Peter said after hearing Aazar's story. "But he's right, Aazar, you need to learn from someone. Surely you trust someone from the group before some old geezer in the woods, right?"

"Doesn't matter anyway," Aazar said. "He told me to find him if I changed my mind, but I don't know how to do that. He mentioned something about the familiar sense, but…"

"What are you talking about?" Peter said. "Familiar sense?"

Aazar hesitated a moment, then decided to tell him, "Well, we can feel each other out. Like, we know when one's around."

Peter thought about that for a second.

"So, Londonn isn't a Variant, then?" Peter asked.

"Oh," Aazar said, realizing she hadn't even thought about it when she'd met him. "No. He's not."

"I knew it." Peter smiled at himself. "What a tool. Londonn is a phony. Total joke. Fabrication of the system."

There was a moment of silence.

"Anyway," Peter said, "there's another meet-up tonight. Do you think

Britney will be up for it?"

"I'm pretty sure she will be. She's been itching to leave since she got here. Have you been up to see her?"

"Nah," Peter said. "She's a little…prejudiced against me."

"What? She doesn't like you because of your race?"

"Because I'm not a Variant," Peter said, annoyed. "Clearly."

Aazar thought for a minute. "I guess you could be right. I never got the vibe from her. Then again, I'm a Variant, so…you know."

"Yeah, I know," Peter said. "Anyway, bring her tonight. I'm sure she'll probably want to go and stay with her boyfriend anyway.

That evening, Aazar, Britney, and Peter snuck out and headed toward the café. Britney didn't say a word to either of them. It had been an awkward couple of weeks with Britney there. Norma was starting to suspect that Aazar was an over-eater since she seemed to be eating twice as much as usual, but she couldn't figure out how she didn't gain any weight. She'd been begging Aazar for her secret. Aazar had been surprised that Norma's parents didn't notice an extra person living under their roof. She had been afraid they'd end up in the guest room at one point, but Britney had been allowed to recover with no incident. The maid had visited her mother for a few weeks, so they didn't have to bribe her. Also, they didn't have to worry about Britney causing a fuss in the first place since she spent most of her time in bed staring out the window. She'd only had a handful of visitors, just the doctor, and Todd. Britney pretended that Aazar didn't exist when she placed her meals by her bed.

Britney became a different person when they turned the corner to the café and saw Todd standing outside. She ran into his arms and kissed him passionately. Aazar and Peter walked past them and sat at their usual booth in the Café.

"Good," Peter said, looking out the window at the couple. "Maybe she'll leave now."

"Britney was hit by a car," Aazar said to Peter. "You should give her the benefit of the doubt. It traumatized her."

Todd and Britney came into the café arm in arm. They managed to sit down without letting each other go. After them came Brian, giving Britney a vast grin. Britney stood up and hugged him.

"Britney! You're with us again, it seems."

She smiled. "Yes, of course." She looked to Todd. "I had many reasons to come back."

Peter rolled his eyes. The café door swung open again, revealing KJ, Ivan, and the rest of the group. KJ smiled as he saw Brian kissing Britney's hand.

"Well, it looks like you're feeling much better," Ivan said.

"Thanks to you," said Britney

"Thanks to everyone that helped out. We needed you back, and everyone pitched in to help."

She smiled. Ivan looked around the table. "We're all here then?

Okay, let's begin." He sat down.

The group settled in their seats, leaned forward, and was quiet. They glanced around the room, checking patrons in the café to see if they were eavesdropping. Aazar loved the energy of a group of people conspiring. It felt like a magic blanket was thrown on top of the group, shielding them from the outside world.

"Because of the sensitivity of this mission, command like to add a new member soon," Ivan began, "We have a guy whose ability is instrumental in medical situations, but we need this mission to go off without a hitch. His name is Jake. He'll be here next week so that you can meet him."

"What can he do?" Todd asked, irritated. Aazar figured it was because of some kind of male dominance thing.

"He can destroy atoms," Ivan replied.

Most people at the table blinked in shock. Todd cleared his throat.

"That's rare," KJ said. "I've never met someone who can do it. How difficult."

"What does that mean?" Brian asked. "I've never even heard of that power."

"An atom crusher can destroy things on an atomic level. They can make anything they want to disappear out of existence."

"Whoa, that's intense," Brian said. He whispered to Aazar, "New name: Atom Crusher."

Aazar couldn't believe there were so many crazy powers out there she didn't know about. She worried about the owners of these powers.

Ivan continued, "He removes unwanted masses from people's bodies like cancer, ulcers, cysts, and other things. He's got great control over it. He hasn't had a single casualty doing surgery like he does."

Aazar was relieved he didn't use his ability to destroy and kill people or things. Maybe the resistance wasn't as horrible as she sometimes believed it to be. Movements are made up of all kinds of people, not just people like Todd and Britney.

"What do we need a surgeon for?" Todd asked. "None of us have any lymph nodes we need removing."

"His ability will come in handy when destroying the medical supplies. As a surgeon, He'll be able to identify the correct component. Since his ability is silent, he'll be able to dispose of the component in the most efficient way. You'll be able to walk in and out without anyone knowing you were ever there."

"Can't he just destroy everything in the pharmacy? The place shouldn't be running at all."

"There's no need to destroy all of the supplies, other sick people there have nothing to do with this, and there's no reason to risk their lives. Plus, it would be seen as an act of hate instead of justice. Besides, your brother will use his abilities to short out the entire building, rendering the location useless."

"But wouldn't that kill people too?" Todd asked.

"The building has backup generators that will protect the patients. It will just be a large inconvenience."

"Large inconvenience?" Todd glared at Ivan. "While they torture and kill our own, we just give them a large inconvenience? I say we get our own out and destroy the building."

"Luckily," Ivan said, "I'm in charge, and you're not. You'll carry out the plan as discussed."

Todd sat back in silence.

Ivan changed the subject. "Britney, have you used your abilities since the accident? Have they changed?"

"Power can change?" Peter asked.

"When the body goes through a traumatic event, sometimes the power becomes stronger or weaker. It remains the same most of the time, but after Britney's ordeal, I wouldn't be too surprised if she had a fluctuation."

Britney looked at a guy across the bar. As though he could feel her watching him, he turned in her direction. He stood and began to make his way toward her. She stood up and walked to him. They spoke for a few moments, and he tried to grab her ass. She slapped him and walked away. He blinked a few times and went back to his stool in confusion.

Britney sat down again. "It seems to be working fine."

"If you feel any fluctuation, please let me know. We need you at your best on the day. If we can't get the security guards out of the way, they'll be a big mess."

"I understand," she said while holding Todd's hand again. He stroked it protectively.

Ivan looked at Peter. "And you're sure accessing the computer system won't be a problem."

"Unless they got Larry Page to build it, I'll be fine."

"Great," Ivan said.

"When do you believe we'll get the green light?" KJ asked.

"Within the next few months."

"A few months? Are you kidding? We should do this thing as soon as possible!" Todd exclaimed, "Do you realize how many people die in that facility?"

"I know," Ivan stated. "But we need to be secure politically. Right now, we're not getting the most support in the media. We need to ensure sentiments have changed for the better before engaging in a mission of this significance. Also, I'd like you to get to know Jake better before sending you on a mission with someone new. I must make sure it's a good fit. Some people are more…disagreeable…than others."

Todd's face turned a slight shade of red.

"The next time we meet, I'll bring Jake along. I would've brought him this time, but he had surgery this afternoon."

The meeting adjourned. Ivan chatted with KJ for a few minutes, then headed out. KJ smiled at her and walked over, happy to see her.

"I don't know why, but it feels like I haven't spoken to you in weeks," he said.

"I've been swamped. Norma with her mall trips. Britney with her injuries. Peter with his angry ranting."

He smiled again. "Seems pretty hectic."

"Only every day."

He chuckled. "So, what do you think about having a new member join the group? It means you're not the new one in anymore."

"I still don't consider myself a member of this group yet," Aazar said.

"You let a resistance member stay in your home," KJ mentioned.

"She's just a recruit, not a member," Aazar pointed out. "And it wasn't my home."

He smiled, "You come to every meeting, you met the second in command, and you never told anyone about us." He leaned in and whispered in her ear, "You secretly practice with your power every night…"

She leaned back and stared at him, "How do you know that?"

He laughed again. "I wasn't sure until now. Flenoid told me he met a fire user with the same description as you. He said you were 'laced in anger.' That was the only thing that threw me off because you never seem angry to me."

"I don't like when old men spy on me," she said, irritated. "Or talk about me behind my back."

"Point taken."

"Look, I gotta go."

"Hey," KJ said. She turned to look at him. "You should come and practice with him. He is the best teacher around here. The resistance can do it, but they sometimes don't have the best methods. The resistance focuses on how quickly you can produce power, but Flenoid focuses on how much power you can control safely."

"Same difference."

"Not at all, actually," KJ said. "Just think about it."

"It's all anyone wants me to think about," Aazar mumbled. "Why doesn't anyone want me to think about something normal, like *The Bachelor Season 103*?"

"Do you need someone to tell you why you shouldn't think about The Bachelor?" Peter asked from behind her.

She turned to him and smirked. "Whatever, come on, let's go."

"Aazar," KJ said, "catch up with me once in a while, okay?"

Aazar softened and smiled. "Yeah, okay."

Like Aazar figured, Britney went off with Todd, forgetting all about Peter and Aazar's hospitality without as much as a thank you. As Peter and Aazar headed home, Aazar saw the forest edge from the street. She squinted hard. Aazar realized she could make out the edge of the clearing she practiced in. She sighed in frustration.

Chapter Eighteen: Unpleasant Surprise

When they got home, they were greeted by an unfamiliar sight. Norma was sitting at the kitchen table texting ferociously while Mr. Belize stood in front of the stove with a ridiculous white apron and metallic decals that said, "Storm Trooper Cook." Mrs. Belize was bored at the bar as she watched her husband cook steak on the stove. It was a little unnerving to see the entire family in one room. Mr. Belize turned when they shut the door.

"Peter, Aazar," their father said, turning off the stove, "You're home. Where have you two been?"

"Uh—" Peter started as he looked at Aazar.

"Making out, no less," Norma said, winking from the table.

"Oh, really," Mrs. Belize said with her eyebrows furrowed, sipping a glass of wine. "Peter, I'm not sure if you should be dating anyone after what you've been going through…"

"We're not dating," Peter growled as he sat down at the table. "What the hell are all of you doing down here anyway? Is this an intervention?"

"Peter," Mr. Belize replied as he placed a grilled piece of steak on a plate, "don't say 'hell'."

"We have an announcement to make," Mrs. Belize said with bright eyes. "We thought we'd all have dinner to discuss it. It concerns everyone."

The meal was served. It was steak tenderloin with stewed carrots and mashed potatoes. Not a complex meal, but Aazar was surprised anyone in the family could cook. She'd never recalled seeing the oven even being used. There was always a gala, a brunch, a business dinner, or Chinese if there weren't any events. Mr. Belize looked somewhat happy to be cooking. The bags under his eyes even looked less defined.

"Okay, Let's try some of this," he said with excitement. He bit a piece of steak from his fork.

"Mom, what's this all about? I was supposed to meet up with Adam." Norma said before even putting her fork in her mouth.

"Well, it's—"

"Can we at least enjoy one meal together before discussing business?" Mr. Belize pleaded.

"What kind of business?" Peter said as he pushed his plate to the side. "Your business is never any of ours, haven't you noticed?"

Mrs. Belize took a giant swig of wine as Mr. Belize's jaw clenched. "Well, we're hosting a gala next week."

Peter stood up from the table with his hands balling into fists. "WHAT?"

"A gala!" Norma said, dropping a fork full of food. She sounded excited and panicked at the same time. *"By next week*!? But why? How will we get all the planning done in that time?"

"There was a venue cancellation at the last minute for the 12th Annual Hunger Gala we sponsor, and your father graciously stepped forward, dear," Mrs. Belize said. She stood up and poured herself another glass of wine from the bar.

"I hope someone died," muttered Peter.

"Honestly, Peter!" Mrs. Belize shouted.

"What?" Peter said, folding his arms. "This is crap. Every time you have one of these things, I lose a week's worth of time that I could've been researching just so I can be your gardener, pool guy, concierge, maid, valet…"

"We all help, Aazar," Mrs. Belize said as she made her way back to the table. "He's exaggerating."

"No, I'm not; you're too busy socializing with every human on Earth trying to get an audience. Norma's too busy freaking out about what to wear, so she stands in the mirror hating herself the whole time, and Dad goes to work as usual. Do you think all the grass gets weeded and trash taken out by themselves?"

"Peter, stop being a jerk," Norma said, already looking back at her phone, her food forgotten. "A gala is always a lot of work, but they're worth it in the end. The last time Dad hosted one, he bought that stupid computer you spend your whole life on, so why don't you shut your mouth for once."

"He could've kept the computer," Peter said with his eyes becoming wild, "I'd rather have my time, and that's something you can't BUY back. The most important things are the things you CAN'T buy, Norma. You're too thick to get it."

"Don't call each other names. That's not helping anything," Mrs. Belize said, downing another glass of wine.

"Like you ever want to help in the first place," Peter spat.

Mrs. Belize stared off drunk in the distance. It was clear Peter was right, but she didn't say anything.

"Don't talk to your mother that way." Mr. Belize said as he neglected his own meal for the fight.

Peter gasped. "WOW. Dad's entering the conversation. I must be in trouble now."

Mr. Belize pointed down the hallway, "Go to your room!"

Peter laughed, mocking. "You're joking, right? You make a big deal, sit us all down, and say we need to talk about this, but I need to go to my room as soon as I start talking. Why the hell did you force me to be here anyway? There's nothing to talk about."

"Peter," Aazar whispered.

"No," Peter said, turning back to his father. "You say we're having a family meeting about the gala, but this is a family meeting about indentured servitude."

"Oh Jesus, here we go…" Mrs. Belize said. Norma sighed as loud as she could.

"A meeting about who needs to be where doing what. You want me here, so I'll know when to stop, when to go, who's ass to kiss, who's a drink to fill to the top."

"We all help in the ways we can," Norma said as she looked up at her brother. "You suck at socializing, so you do other things."

"I don't want to help," Peter said. "I don't want to help with this bullshit facade."

"Aren't you being a little—" Aazar started.

"How would you know?" Peter spat. "You haven't been here long enough. Do you think you've seen ass kissery so far? You have no idea how low these people will go to get a couple of extra dollars on their paychecks. It's almost degrading."

"Get out of this house," Mr. Belize yelled, "right now!"

Peter blinked a few times in surprise. "What?"

"You heard me," Mr. Belize bellowed. "I'm DONE with your constant disrespect. Get the hell out of my house, and don't come back until you've learned how to treat your family like human beings."

Peter knocked over his chair in defiance. "Nice dinner." Then he stormed out the front door.

Aazar was frozen as the rest of the table fumed. She wanted to run after Peter, but she wasn't sure if that would be best or not. She didn't feel like getting lashed at, and he seemed to be in the mood for it. She looked at the family. They looked as though they'd all been wounded.

She ate her meal as quietly as possible, afraid that any amount of noise would make the table explode. They all ate in stony silence. Aazar finished her food and lifted her plate as she stood.

"It was a wonderful dinner, Mr. Belize." She said. He nodded and gave a small uncommitted smile as she placed her dish in the sink and headed upstairs to her room. She wondered why they were so quiet. Was it because they were so angry at Peter or because he was right?

* * *

When Aazar woke the following day to loud talking and banging throughout the house, it was like a circus had taken over. She put a robe over her pajamas and walked downstairs. It was not a circus of clowns and animals but of interior designers and hairdressers, as she came to find out as she came downstairs to the kitchen. Aazar went to the kitchen. She was disappointed to see Melissa scrubbing the floor. The small woman jumped when she saw Aazar.

"Hello, I'm sorry, I just need to clean in here."

"It's fine," Aazar stated, feeling she was the one out of place. "I'll see if I can find a snack in Peter's room."

Aazar headed down the hallway toward Peter's room and ducked past Mrs. Belize, looking at streamer patterns with a tall man wearing a multicolored suit. She passed Norma in the dining room, standing in front of a large portable mirror in a stunning gown, holding her hair up as the tailor measured her. When she reached Peter's hallway, she found Peter scrubbing the tub in the bathroom across from his room. She had just realized he was the only person in the family without a personal bathroom. Aazar blinked several times, then felt her cheeks warm as he turned to look at her. She was happy she picked matching pajamas.

"You're here? Cleaning? After all of that yesterday?"

Peter smirked. "I know, right? She's got me cleaning the bathtub. Who the hell uses the bathtub during a gala? Couldn't we just close the shower curtain?"

Bewildered at Peter's sudden compliance, she almost forgot her purpose for being there.

"Hey, do you have anything to eat in your room? Melissa is cleaning the kitchen."

"Oh, yeah," Peter said, picking up the scrub bucket. "There's a power bar on the desk by the computer. I'm supposed to mop the kitchen, but I'm pretty sure Melissa's already doing it. Heaven forbid a speck to be on the floor in Lord Marshall's presence."

"Lord Marshall?"

"My dad's boss."

"Oh."

"See ya." He said, walking out of the bathroom.

Aazar looked into the mirror. She didn't look too bad for just having woken up.

"Aazar!" A shout came from down the hall. It was Mrs. Belize.

Aazar peaked her head out of the bathroom, "Yes?"

"Do you know where Peter is?"

"He just left to mop the kitchen."

"Did he say if he was using the blue disinfectant or the red one?"

"No."

Mrs. Belize gave a loud sigh and threw her hands up in the air. "That's fine. Well, I'm off to lunch with Michele to talk more about streamer colors, so if you see him before I do, tell him to use the blue disinfectant for the floors and show the gardener how I like the lawn. And if he could find a place for the car other than the garage for the week while we have so many people coming by to do things, that would be terrific."

"Okay,"

"Oh, ask him if he could give the garage a quick rinse down by the end of the day too."

"Okay."

"Thanks, Hun!" She started to walk away.

Aazar wondered something. "Mrs. Belize?"

The woman stopped, "Yes, dear?"

"Is there anything you want to tell Norma to do?"

Mrs. Belize waved the notion away, "Oh no, no, Norma won't be useful to anyone until she's finally figured out what to wear."

"Oh," Aazar said, already irritated for Peter. "I understand."

"You should go out and pick something up too. I'm sure you want to look gorgeous for Peter, right?"

"No, I—"

"Have a wonderful day, dear."

She heard Mrs. Belize begin speaking to Melissa as she walked away from the door.

After grabbing the power bar from Peter's room, she returned upstairs to put on clothes. She walked into Norma's room to find her in another gorgeous gown with her hair down behind her. The tailor stood next to her nervously. She turned around after seeing Aazar in the mirror.

"OOH, what do you think," she said, standing up as tall as she could. "Hair up or hair down."

"Either way works."

"Sometimes, Aazar, I swear you're a guy." She pulled her hair up and looked to Aazar again. "Up or down."

Aazar looked at her for longer this time. "Up."

Norma looked in the mirror at herself for confirmation. "Yes, You're right. Up for this one."

Norma looked at herself with confidence for a moment. Then her face began to fall.

"But my face looks fat when my hair is up. I really should wear it down. Get me the green dress again."

"Yes, but ma'am," the tailor said, not moving towards the green dress at all, "the earrings that match that dress get covered by your hair when it's down. And when we put your hair behind your ears, you said it made you feel goofy."

"I know, I know," Norma said, biting her lip in her reflection. "Do you have anything that would look good with my hair down and no earrings?"

The stylist looked her up and down. "Yes…but you'll need a necklace to pull it off."

"How long of a necklace? Too long looks hippy-ish." Norma frowned again.

Aazar interrupted, "I think I'm going to find Peter."

"Sure," Norma said, not seeing her at all as she slipped out of the dress and grabbed the next one.

Aazar couldn't believe how many people were running around the house. A florist was down each hall, adding bright purple and pink flowers everywhere. A guy was cleaning the carpets in the living room, and other people dressed in white polos and black slacks lined up chairs in the backyard. She found Peter in the kitchen with a mop in his hands as he spoke to a panicked Melissa.

"Don't worry," Peter was saying. "I'll cover the dishes. You can focus on the laundry and the bedrooms, okay?"

Melissa relaxed as she went running out of the room.

"It's a madhouse," Aazar said.

"You're telling me." Peter huffed.

"Sir," a man ran up to him with a notebook wide open, "Madame told me to refer to you about the rock placement for the serenity garden?"

"Serenity Garden? Are you serious?" Peter sighed and ran a nervous hand through his hair. He took the notebook from the man and looked it over, allowing the mop to clatter to the floor. "Okay, yeah. She'll probably want it where it was last time. Left of the band area."

"And where would the band area be?" The man asked.

"Hold on," Peter said to Aazar.

Aazar grabbed the mop from the floor. "I'll do this. You go ahead."

"Really?" Peter said.

"Sure, I have nothing else to do anyway,"

He smiled and walked toward the backyard, pointing to the left and talking. Aazar saw him approached by one of the guys fixing the chairs before he'd stepped a foot out of the door.

She couldn't for the life of her understand why Peter had jumped in line. She had to find out the next time she had the chance. She looked at the already clean floor before her and proceeded to mop as she'd promised.

Chapter Nineteen: A Gala Affair

The next few days were more of the same. Mrs. Belize went to a luncheon to discuss further plans, and Aazar relayed them to Peter while Peter groaned and moaned every step of the way. Norma spent most of her time crying off her mascara as she tried dress after skirt after pantsuit and not finding the right one. Mr. Belize was a ghost for most of it. The only time you seemed to see him at the house was to write a check for whatever service was completed.

Aazar and Peter went to sleep every night exhausted. She hadn't had time to ask why he was working so hard for the gala. Aazar was seeing a different side of him. She never saw Peter as one of the upper echelons, but it was like he flipped a switch, and now he was a boy born and raised to be a wealthy socialite. He knew which napkins to use and where the tables needed to be placed. He was knowledgeable in classical music and which dishes would be served in which order. He never talked down to the servers and cleaners, but he didn't befriend them either. He knew his role didn't allow it. Peter still managed to stick his middle finger down his throat in protest every time he caught her eye when no one was looking or complaining about the bourgeoise when he stopped for an apple in the kitchen while she wiped down counters, but for the most part, he was tame. Peter had even skipped a few Variant Meetings to get everything done. She saw that the Belize family lost an asset when Peter quit the capitalist dream.

Aazar was still surprised at how dedicated he seemed about the whole thing, even though he hated it at every turn. When the day arrived, the house looked more like a castle than before. Aazar never felt more uncomfortable when using the restroom or coming into the house with shoes on. They'd worked so hard for everything to look perfect, and Aazar didn't want to be the one who knocked over the wrong $10,000 vase rented for this occasion.

Peter was ready an hour early in a tailored suit. Aazar had been fitted for a dress while Norma cried without cease as she got her Brazilian wax.

Peter and Aazar listened to her wails from his room, the only room uncleaned and still just as trashy as it had been since she'd moved in. If it weren't for Peter's room, Aazar wouldn't have been sure she was in the same house. Another howl from upstairs.

"What an idiot." Peter grimaced. "No one's going to see her vag in a floor gown. Why even do this to herself?"

"Maybe it's for Adam," Aazar joked.

"I never want to think about that guy banging my sister."

They both smiled despite themselves.

"So," Aazar started, "are you ready for this?"

"There is no real 'being ready' for something as asinine as this, but I guess I am."

Aazar was silent for a moment.

"You know, the guy we mean to impress won't even be here on time. Lord Marshall will probably show up around an hour before it's over, already drunk, say some fucked up shit, and then leave."

"Why do you bother to do all of this for them?" Aazar asked.

"They'll give me hell if I don't."

"That never makes you do anything else."

There was a knock at the door.

"Peter?" Mr. Belize said through the door.

Peter stood up and opened it. "Well, look who decided to show up? I haven't seen you in a couple of days. Working late?"

Mr. Belize's face turned red in anger. "Don't start. Your mother wants you outside greeting people with us for half an hour before the party and half an hour after. You know the drill. Come on. Aazar, you will be introduced as our guest, but you only have to be there for the first half an hour if that's okay."

Aazar realized this wasn't a question. "Okay."

"Great." Mr. Belize looked to Peter. "Come on then."

They made their way to the front room. At first, there was an awkward silence as they stood around. Mrs. Belize and Norma straightened their dresses more than once, while Mr. Belize pulled his tie back and forth. Peter had his hands shoved in his pockets while Aazar fiddled with her fingers. Then the doorbell rang, and their body language shifted to stances of confidence and ease. Mrs. Belize glided forward.

"MARTHA!" Mrs. Belize said as she opened the door. "How wonderful you could make it! And first, too!"

Martha smiled. "Well, they said the gala was switched to Mrs. Belize's house, so I just had to see what you did. Are those gardenias?"

"Yes, they are!" Mrs. Belize said.

"So beautiful! A bit bold for this season but so beautiful. To hell with the rules, right?"

Mrs. Belize's smile faded, but it wasn't noticeable.

"And it's so good to see your family again! I'm so glad you're okay after the accident, Peter. Boys and their toys, right?"

Peter plastered on a fake smile and remained silent. It seemed like it was all he could do.

"There are drinks in the parlor if you'd like some," Mrs. Belize said fast.

Martha gave a small laugh. "I'm parched." And she walked to the parlor with her husband.

That was the friendliest greeting of all of them in the half an hour Aazar stood to greet people. It was all she could take. After all the hard work they'd put into making things perfect, everyone seemed to find something wrong with it. And all of them felt the need to bring up Peter's accident.

As soon as her half-hour required greeting time was over, Aazar made her way to the food. She felt herself eating everything in sight, so she didn't have to speak to anyone. There were so many people, and so few of them looked friendly. There was the occasional drunken older man, but people chided them until they'd made their way to the garage to avoid the rest of the party. Several women looked as though they couldn't breathe in their gowns, including Norma, who looked a shade of pink that Aazar wasn't sure was healthy. Peter walked around with his father for most of the evening, smiling and shaking hands. She was impressed at his ability not to snarl or slouch like she was used to seeing him do.

The evening began to settle down as the wine auction began. Peter's father and mother stood on the stage and smiled at the rest of the group. Aazar was surprised when she realized this was the first time she'd seen the couple together, looking happy. She also learned how rehearsed they seemed to her. It was strange what brought some couples together. Mr. Belize raised a glass and tapped it for silence. The crowd gathered around the stage in chairs and waited patiently for his remarks.

"We're ecstatic you could all make it to our wonderful gathering on such short notice of the venue change. We're delighted that we were asked. When I told my wife we'd be hosting, she began preparations, and if it weren't for her, none of this would have been possible."

A modest amount of applause broke out among the crowd. Aazar was irritated that he hadn't mentioned all of Peter's efforts, but when she looked at Peter, she saw him shaking hands with yet another man as he took his seat, unbothered by the speech.

"We've got a 1989 Petrus here for auction, and all of the proceeds will be going to the Belize Foundation Fund for Cancer Research. We'll start the bidding at six thousand dollars."

Aazar's mouth dropped. She couldn't believe people would pay that much for a bottle of wine. Sure, it was for charity, but she was shocked that the people here could afford to bid at such a price but never seemed to give a red cent to those in need living right down the street. She listened as the bids went higher and higher and the wine sold for $30,000. She knew that was more than her father made in a year because he reminded her whenever she had finished all the cereal.

Mr. Belize brought out wine after wine, each selling more than the previous one. The final wine was up for auction, and her head was spinning. The last one sold for $80,000. She knew her father would've had a stroke then and there.

"We have a rare and unique 2015 Chateau Cos d'Estournel from the Boliverto Vineyard of Italy, starting at thirty thousand dollars. Do I have thirty thousand?"

"One million dollars."

The crowd gasped just as Aazar had, and everyone looked to the back of the group to see who would place such an extravagant bid. They saw a short man with a tamed mustache and two gorgeous women much younger than him on his arms. He smiled with a smug look as he gazed up at Mr. Belize on the platform.

"Ah, I see Mr. Marshall is a generous man, any other bids?"

The crowd remained silent as they all kept their eyes on the short man with the beautiful women.

"Sold to Mr. Marshall for one million dollars."

The crowd burst into applause, and Mr. Marshall raised his hands for calm.

"No need for applause, no need," he said.

"That concludes the auction for this evening," Mr. Belize said. "You can now enjoy the dessert platter at the back near the serenity garden."

The crowd dispersed, and the band began playing classical music again.

Peter found Aazar and grabbed her by the hand.

"Do you want to dance?" He smiled at her.

"What?"

"Someone has to start the dance, or no one will go out. Come with me."

Aazar turned red. "I'm a terrible dancer."

"That's okay. I can lead." He held out his hand. "My mom wants me to do it, and if you don't, I'll have to grab some old lady. Can you help me out?"

Aazar smiled at the thought of him dancing with some old lady. Peter read her mind.

"Please don't do this to me," he pleaded.

She took his hand. "Okay, lead the way."

He bowed as he took her hand and guided her to the dance floor. He pulled her close to him by her waist and glided around the dance floor. It was easy to follow him, she realized.

"You lied!" he said as he spun her around. "You can dance!"

"I…" Aazar started. "You're a good leader. I don't feel like I'm doing much." He looked around at the crowd as another couple joined the dance floor. "You move well."

She relaxed and listened to the music while she danced in his arms. She looked at him as he scanned the area. He was so handsome with his hair out of his face and his clothes clean.

"I can't believe you're so good at all of this," she said.

"Well, when you're born rich, they make sure you know their rules. I'm pretty sure you picked up on a few yourself today."

He swung her away for a moment, then brought her in close.

Aazar laughed as she leaned against his chest. "I didn't know Gardenias are banned this season."

"That old bat was wrong anyway. Gardenias are perfect for this time of year," Peter said.

Aazar laughed again. The dance floor began to fill up, but Peter hadn't let her go. He noticed Mr. Marshall making his way to the floor with one of his women in tow.

Peter leaned into Aazar to whisper in her ear and pointed discretely toward Mr. Marshall, "That's Lord Marshall, my father's boss. He'll be wanting to criticize and harass us all soon. Try to speak as little as possible. He doesn't like the idea of people having opinions or thoughts."

"Is he really a Lord?" Aazar asked, feeling stupid and judging by the comical look on Peter's face.

"AH, is that Peter, I see? My, you've grown since the last gala," Mr. Marshall said as he came up to them.

Peter took a moment to look pained before letting her go and turning to Mr. Marshall with a perfect smile.

"It's wonderful for you to attend, sir. My father will be pleased."

"He should be," Mr. Marshall said. "He's lucky he was even chosen for this type of event, given the family history." He gave Peter a nasty look.

"My father shouldn't be blamed for my shortcomings, Sir."

"Is that so?" Mr. Marshall snarled. "Then who is to blame? Your mother, no less?"

"I am, Sir."

"Good lad," Mr. Marshall said, laughing, "you should always take responsibility for your actions. At least your parents bothered to teach you something. I wish they'd taught you how to drive better, don't you?"

Peter forced his smile to remain intact.

"You do realize if you'd turned a little more to the left, my godson would no longer be alive."

"I'm well aware, sir."

"Are you?" Mr. Marshall said. "You've yet to apologize to him for such a blatant disregard for his life. I'd assume you'd get to that as soon as you realized your fault."

"It's been...difficult, sir."

"Difficult admitting your guilt, or difficulty finding your way to my godson's home to ask for forgiveness?" Mr. Marshall asked. "He's dating your sister, so he's around often, isn't he?"

"He doesn't stick around, sir. He takes my sister out."

"To get away from you, no less." Mr. Marshall looked annoyed and seemed to grow tired of harassing Peter. "Where are your parents? I want to congratulate them on their party. They did a wonderful job, all things considered."

"My father is by the punch."

"Phenomenal. Hope to see you again soon?" Mr. Marshall said as he walked toward the punch bowl.

Aazar looked to Peter. He looked genuinely hurt for the first time she'd ever seen him.

"I'm going back to my room."

"Peter..."

Peter stormed off to his room, leaving her standing alone. She followed him. Aazar reached the hallway just before he shut the door. She pushed it open and watched as Peter snatched off his tie and flung it across the room. Aazar felt it might never be seen again in a mess. He kicked off his shoes and turned on his computer. Aazar felt invisible. She was about to leave when he started speaking.

"What a fucking asshole. Just like his fucking godson." Peter fumed. "I wish I had gone a little to the left, then that fucking dick would've been dead, and maybe my dad would've lost his job and had to get a job that he could be proud of rather than suck the dick of that fucking cock."

Aazar remained silent.

"Who the fuck spends that much money on a bottle of wine? Of course, that fucking son of a bitch would, so that he'd look like a fucking saint. Anyone who comes within three feet of the fucker would know who he was in minutes, so I don't even know why he bothers. I wish he'd been in the car that day. Maybe I would've broken his fucking arm and collarbone. Not that that fucking accident was my fault in the first place. Maybe if his godson had his fucking head out of his ass, he would've seen the fucking stop sign and not ruined whatever was left of my rep."

"I thought you didn't care about your rep."

"I could give a fuck about my rep, but my family is who suffers from it. And they care about their reputations. Everyone treats them like shit because of that fucking accident. Because everyone treats them like shit, they fucking treat me like shit. And I don't fucking deserve any of it. Not after I smile and nod at fuckers like Lord Marshall, his grandson, and every other fucking fuck out there tonight. Not after I slave to make sure these shit events come out perfect just so assholes can hate them."

"Why did you do all this work if you feel like this?" Aazar said. "I mean, it doesn't make any sense; you say you hate all of it, but then you do it anyway. Isn't that hypocritical?"

Peter sighed and threw his jacket across the room. "I do it because they're still my family."

Aazar was surprised. She never thought she'd hear that from Peter. She waited for a better explanation.

"They freak out about these kinds of things, and they care about them. I don't want them to be embarrassed, and I don't like it when people use me to hurt them. I don't mind hurting them but fuck anyone else who tries to hurt them. They're still my family. I still give a shit about them, you know."

Aazar realized "give a shit" was as close to 'love' as Peter would get. He unbuttoned the sleeves of his dress shirt and shoved his sleeves up to his elbows, then ran his fingers through his hair.

"I don't know," he said. "They're good people. It's not their fault they're blind, stupid, and part of the problem."

"I think it's their fault they're stupid. Especially since they don't appreciate you," Aazar said.

"Whatever," Peter said. "You appreciate me, right?'

Aazar swallowed. "Well…um…yeah."

"That's fine for now," Peter said. "Come on, let's do more research on the Variant project. I'm weeks behind."

"Won't your parents come looking for you?"

"I did what was required," Peter said in a soft tone. "They won't notice I'm gone now."

With that, Peter began typing on this computer. Aazar pulled out a massive book from underneath a pile of laundry, glad to avoid using a computer.

"You look nice, by the way," Peter said, never looking away from the computer.

Aazar looked up and smiled but said nothing as she opened the book in front of her.

Chapter Twenty: Cobwebs

The doctor paced in front of the table back and forth with his chin in his gloved hand. "There is no doubt about it. She's a Variant."

A bright light beamed down on her as Aazar struggled against the medical table. A nurse put a calming hand on her. The nurse was her mother.

"Hush now," her mother said as she ran her hands through Aazar's hair.

Aazar looked around, panicked. "How did you find me? What are you doing?"

"We've no choice," the doctor said to her mother as he bent under the table to get something. "She'll need to be handled."

"What do you suggest?" Aazar's mother asked, concerned.

"Let me go!" Aazar tried to break the restraints, but nothing worked. "Please, let me go!"

"We'll have to amputate her. We can't have her setting people on fire."

He pulled out a circular saw.

"NO!" Aazar said. "PLEASE, NO." The nurse held her tightly by the shoulders.

"Brace yourself, sweetie," her mother said, smiling and stroking Aazar's hair. "They're getting the demon out."

"NO!" Aazar screamed.

The saw came down.

Aazar screamed and screamed, thrashing around in her bedroom. Her bed was covered in fire, and she continued to yell.

Peter came into the room in a panic. His eyes grew wide as the fire threatened to lick the ceiling.

"SHIT!" he yelled to her. "You're doing it! Aazar, stop!"

As she looked at him with wild eyes, the flames extinguished. The only thing that was destroyed was her comforter. It was nothing but ash as she moved off the bed and dusted the residue from her pajamas.

Norma rubbed her eyes as she came in. "What are you all yelling about—OH MY GOD, what happened!?"

Aazar was frozen in shock. Peter shrugged his shoulders and lied, "Uh… she left a candle on, and it caught her comforter on fire. I put it out. It's fine."

"This is NOT fine!" Norma said, walking into the room and picking pieces of ash from the bed. "That was an original 16th-century comforter from Dad's last trip to China! It's irreplaceable."

"It's just a fucking comforter, at least Aazar *alive*," Peter said.

Norma's face paled. "Oh my god, I'm so sorry, Aazar. Are you okay?"

"I'm fine," was all Aazar could manage.

"I'll get Dad," Norma said.

"It's fine, Norm," Peter said. "He's got work. He won't do anything except get pissed that we woke him."

Norma didn't like being the one in trouble. "Yeah, okay, fine. I'm going back to bed then." She looked at Aazar and the ash-covered bed again. "No more candles, right?"

Aazar still looked at the bed with wide eyes.

"No candles, night, sis," Peter said.

Norma looked at Aazar again but shook her head and went back down the hall.

"What the hell was that!?" Peter grabbed her by the shoulders. "You could've burned the fucking house down!"

"I…I had a nightmare…I wasn't—"

"You have to get this shit under control," Peter said, looking into her eyes. "My parents would flip about a Variant living here, and I'd rather not wake up in flames."

"Yeah, well," Aazar retorted, "me either."

She snatched herself away from him, and Peter smiled. "Sorry. I wasn't trying to—"

"It's fine, whatever," Aazar said as she tried to dust the ash off the bed, wondering how to tell Melissa about the mess.

"I'm not going to tell you what to do…just…get it together, okay?" Peter said.

"I'll figure it out," Aazar said as Peter walked out the door.

* * *

She stood next to the street near the edge of the wood. As much as she wasn't interested in learning about her powers from an old fool in the forest, she couldn't make herself join the resistance to learn, either. She wasn't sure what it was about the resistance that rubbed her the wrong way.

When she reached the middle of the clearing, she tried to remember what Flenoid had said. How would she just know? Then she remembered the familiar feeling she got when she was around Variants. She calmed herself and silenced her mind. All of a sudden, she got a warm feeling from her left side. She headed in that direction.

She'd been walking for a little while before she saw an old shed. She didn't see anyone around. She wondered if the man lived there. She made her way up to the porch, covered in leaves, dust, and spider webs. She had a hard time believing someone lived there at all. She knocked on the dusty wooden door, and it swung open. She felt a warmness in the cabin that didn't seem to match the actual weather.

After living with the Belizes, she got used to extreme cleanliness.

This cabin was giving her the creeps. There seemed to be more spider webs than air, as she coughed and spit them out as she moved forward. She swung her arms back and forth, getting covered in cobwebs as she cleared her way. She was starting to think the warmness she felt was from the giant number of spiders that must live here. She didn't understand how she hadn't seen any yet.

After spitting out what felt like the last of the cobwebs, she looked across the room and saw a desk with a book lying open on it. She walked toward it and touched it. It was so warm that she pulled her hand back in shock. She squinted at the first page and read out loud.

"For someplace safe to be truly special."

All of a sudden, the floor disappeared. Aazar was falling, and just as soon she realized she would break her legs, Aazar slammed face-first onto a hard wooden floor. She glanced around and stood up and stared.

The wooden cabin was now clean and in perfect condition. She saw the same desk and book in front of her. She looked at her clothes and realized she was no longer covered in webs. Aazar glanced around and saw Flenoid drinking a cup of cocoa on the sofa. He smiled when he saw her.

"You came!" he said. "You're a little early for today's lesson, but you're here. That's great."

"What...what just—"

"Oh, it's a very clever cloaking spell, something I had made by a former student. This cabin looks like nothing but an empty, desolate building until the right kind of person speaks over the book. Then you can see what is really in front of you." He stood up and patted her on the back.

"Wait," Aazar said. "So, you've been sitting there the whole time?"

"Yes, I have," he said, smiling.

Aazar blanched. "Did you see me—"

"Cough and sputter all over invisible cobwebs. Yes, I did." He grinned. "Very amusing."

"If the cobwebs weren't real..."

"They were only as real as you believed they were. You must be blocked off from your powers. Most people only see a few, but you seemed to drown in them."

Aazar blushed.

"No matter," he said, gesturing to the cabin's back door as he walked toward it, "By the time we're finished, you'll see the house as it is when you walk up. However, you'll never be able to see who is in it unless you read from the book."

Aazar followed behind him. "But what happens if some random person comes by and reads the book?"

"The book can only be used by Variants. It is the entrance and exit to this cabin."

Flenoid held the back door open for her, but then, there was a thud behind her as the front door closed. She watched a boy with brown hair and glasses walk up to the book. He stood very still, and a blue light rushed over him. He steadied himself and looked around.

"Hello, old Flen." The boy grinned.

"Don't call me that, Dylan." The old man pretended to glare.

"And who's this?" the boy said, looking at Aazar. "She's new."

"I'm Aazar," Aazar said. She smiled and put her hand forward for a handshake.

"What a name!" he said, grabbing her outstretched hand. "Aazar. Fitting."

"What do you mean?"

"Pretty name for a pretty girl," he said.

"Leave the poor girl alone," Flenoid said as he rolled his eyes, "She's only been here for a few seconds."

"Oh really?" Dylan said. "You're new then. Tell me, did you have problems with the cobwebs?"

Aazar blushed as she and Dylan walked through the back door with Flenoid. "I um…"

Dylan laughed. "Ah, yeah, I had a difficult time with them too. The old man thinks it's funny to freak out folks with the cobwebs. You should see regular people when they find this place. They don't even put a foot inside. None of them even notice there are no spiders."

"I noticed there were no spiders," Aazar said with pride.

"Ah, you're brighter than most, it seems."

The backyard was just an empty field of dry grass and local trees. She peered at the ground and noticed small scorch marks in places where grass no longer grew. Aazar watched from the backyard as KJ entered the cabin smoothly. Aazar saw that he didn't trip or bump into anything. She felt uncomfortable looking at him without him knowing. He came out of the back door, and when he spotted her, he smiled.

"You came," he said, walking straight toward her and hugging her. "Brilliant."

"Hey!" Dylan said, annoyed. "You know her already? How?"

"She goes to a lot of the resistance meetings."

"The resistance?" Dylan said, looking at her irritated. "They're not up to any good. They're going to destroy everything. We'll never become electable if we've got terrorist cells."

"They're not terrorists," KJ said.

"Not yet." Dylan glared as he kicked a patch of grass.

"I just went because I needed to meet more people like us." Aazar said, looking back and forth at both boys, "If I hadn't gone, I wouldn't be here."

"Ooh, another one of those 'fate' girls. I'm no longer interested," Dylan announced to no one in particular. He shoved his hands into his pockets.

KJ rolled his eyes. "Anyway, let's get to it. Todd is opting out as usual."

Flenoid frowned as he took a sip of cocoa. "I keep hoping he'll see the light one day."

"Today, isn't it, buddy," Dylan said. "Let's get started."

"All right, fine." Flenoid cleared his throat and placed the cup on the ground beside him as he sat on the sharp grass. "Make a circle. All of you."

They all made a semi-circle around Flenoid. Aazar held back.

"Won't people see us? We're outside of the cabin."

Flenoid smiled. "The cloaking spell stretches to the edge of the clearing. Check for yourself."

Aazar walked to the edge of the clearing and ran into an invisible barrier. She heard Dylan laugh behind her. She placed her hand against the border. It was soft but firm, like a wall made of clear plastic. She felt like she was in an invisible upside-down fishbowl.

"That's why you have to enter and exit through the book. It's like we're here, but we're not here," KJ explained as he shifted on the ground.

"That's amazing," Aazar cooed, sitting beside him.

"Okay, everyone. Let's begin. We'll start with the basics, see how well Aazar gets on, and then I can decide if she needs more work before progressing with the group."

"What?" Aazar said. "You mean I won't be learning with everyone?"

Flenoid crossed his legs on the ground, "They've all been coming here for a long time. I can't keep everyone back just because one person can't keep up."

"I can keep up," Aazar said defensively.

"We'll see," Flenoid said. "Now, everyone, bring your minds to silence."

Aazar saw KJ and Dylan close their eyes. She closed hers as well.

"Now, feel the warmth of your power inside you."

Aazar couldn't feel any warmth other than the feeling she was getting from the others.

"Not like that, Aazar. You must feel it from inside. Clear your mind," Flenoid said.

How did he know she was doing it wrong? She wondered.

"Wondering is not a clear mind, dear."

"How are you doing that?" Aazar said. She opened her eyes and saw that KJ and Dylan were still closed. She thought she saw tiny sparks from KJ's fingertips.

"How I do anything is clear my mind first, Aazar. Feel the power within you." Flenoid said, not opening his eyes.

She sighed and tried to clear her mind. She had a random image of Peter pop into her mind. She shoved it out immediately. She didn't want Flenoid talking about that out loud with everyone. After a while, she felt a stillness come over her. Then she was warm all over.

"Good!" Flenoid said. "Very good. Now channel that energy to your hands, your mind, whatever it takes to access your energy."

Aazar's hands felt warm and tingly.

"Now, open your eyes."

Aazar looked at her hands. They were covered in flames. She gasped, and they went back out. She closed her eyes and moved the warmth to her hands. She opened them, and the flame was there. It stayed steady. She was ecstatic.

"I'm doing it!" she said. "I can't believe I'm doing it!"

She looked around a noticed KJ's hands covered in electricity. It seemed wild and not contained. He bit his lip to control it. Dylan's eyes were solid white and glowing. KJ looked at Aazar and smiled. A random electric spark flew up into the air, slamming against the invisible barrier. He looked away and focused on his hands.

"Good save, KJ," Flenoid said. "Well, done."

"There are a couple of kids coming this way. They're about a mile off, but I'll keep an eye on them," Dylan said.

"Okay, that will be your practice for the day. See if you can see details a little clearer now. Focus on skin and fingernails."

Dylan nodded.

"KJ, can you practice shooting one bolt of electricity at that tree to your left?"

"I don't know I can, yet, Flenoid," KJ said as he shifted to get more comfortable.

"That's what practice is for," Flenoid said, smiling. He looked to Aazar.

"How are you doing?"

Aazar looked at her hands. "I'm doing better than I have the entire time I practiced alone."

"That's because you were tapping your emotional energy instead of your resting energy. You'll start strong but burn out fast when you use your emotions to gain power. But if you tap into your resting energy by cutting your own feelings out, you'll accomplish more," Flenoid said thoughtfully. He picked up his mug and took a swig of cocoa.

Aazar thought about this for a moment. "But if you use your emotions and the resting energy, won't you have more power?"

"That's impossible. You can either be at rest or be emotional. And if you try to do both, the emotional power will take over and you will lose control."

"I don't understand."

"Okay, let's do a test," Flenoid said, standing up. "You already have your power at a point of holding. Try and get upset about something."

Aazar stood up too, as the boys looked at her. She thought of the dream she had the previous night. She watched as her hands grew brighter and brighter. Flenoid stepped back as her flame began to rise and spread. The other two had stopped what they were doing to back away and watch. All of a sudden, Aazar felt anger sweep over her in a way she had never felt before. Why had her mother been the nurse? Her anger grew and grew. She closed her eyes, trying to stop the feelings of betrayal, but they were becoming more prominent, just like the flames.

"Aazar, stop!" Flenoid yelled at her.

The group was standing at the edge of the barrier. Aazar's flames were all around her now, covering most of the grove. She panicked as the fire grew larger.

"Aazar, you must stop!" Flenoid yelled again. "Your anger started this all, but now your fear is making it go out of control!"

"I...I..." Aazar said, panicked. She was going to kill everyone. She was going to kill KJ.

"Close your eyes and breathe!" Flenoid shouted. "Find your calmness. Find the familiar warmth! NOW Aazar. NOW!"

She took a deep breath and closed her eyes. She tried to relax. Then she heard a scream come from the other side. Someone must have gotten hurt! She couldn't focus.

"Aazar," KJ yelled. "Think about Todd!"

Todd? Her mind was confused. Why would I think about Todd? As soon as the thought finished, the flames extinguished.

Dylan collapsed to the floor.

Aazar ran to help him. She had burned Dylan's arm, and it looked severe. As he saw her advancing, he pushed himself up and staggered back.

"Don't! You get away from me!" he screamed at her.

Aazar froze. She'd done it again even though she swore she wouldn't. She'd hurt someone. Flenoid held Dylan's arm in front of him. He began waving his hand back and forth over the burn.

"I didn't know she had so much power. It's rare for anyone to have such a violent power, let alone so much of it." As he slowed his rhythmic waving, the wound began to disappear. "You'll be fine. It was just a flesh wound. It didn't even make it to the muscle."

"I...I'm sorry...I," Aazar started.

"It's fine, Aazar," KJ said. "Accidents happen."

"I'm not practicing here when she's here anymore," Dylan said, staring at Aazar, holding his almost healed arm in fear. "No way. We could've all been killed. You should just teach her how to turn it off. There's no controlling that."

"That's enough," Flenoid said.

Annoyed, Dylan smirked. "You can get turned into barbecue if you want. I'm leaving."

He stroked his arm as he walked back into the cabin. Moments later, they saw him reappear as he walked straight by them without seeing them and through the barrier back into the woods.

"Dylan's a little sensitive," Flenoid said. "He'll be fine."

Aazar looked at her hands; they were normal again, not burning red like before. She turned them back and forth. She looked up at KJ.

"Why did you tell me to think about Todd?"

He said, "Well, I know you don't have any particular feelings about him. Since you were overcome with feelings, I figured thinking about something random you had no feelings about would stop the power."

"And good thing you did, too," Flenoid said. He looked at Aazar and placed a gentle hand on her back. "You must never let your emotions get out of control. I had no idea you harbored such power. If I had, I would've never let you try it out. This was my fault."

"I didn't know, so how could you know," Aazar said with her shoulders slumped.

"If you control your emotions, you will control the power," Flenoid said. "You have a complicated challenge ahead of you. You must not allow yourself to get overly emotional, or you'll hurt someone. You and KJ are more alike than I understood."

KJ looked away and up at the sky. His face dropped as he pointed upward, and Aazar and Flenoid looked up. There was a small burn mark in the sky. She had burned the protective barrier.

Flenoid rubbed his chin. "Now that's astonishing." He stood silent for a moment. "I know we've just begun, but this was very trying for everyone involved. Let's start up again in a few days after things have settled. I don't think KJ objects to working with you…"

"Not at all," KJ said, throwing an arm over her shoulder.

"Good," Flenoid said while still looking at the sky. "Well, I'll see you both soon."

Aazar and KJ walked into the house while Flenoid peered up at the scorch mark. They said the incantation and appeared back in the dirty cabin. It had fewer cobwebs this time.

"What do you see when you look at this room?" Aazar asked.

KJ shrugged. "A couple of dusty desks and chairs. Nothing spectacular."

"You don't see cobwebs?"

"Not anymore," KJ said. "I used to see a few of them, but it's just dust now."

Aazar ducked under the cobwebs she could see while KJ walked right through them like a ghost. Flenoid seemed to disappear from the backyard when they walked into the clearing. Aazar looked up at the sky. There was no burn mark. She stepped closer to KJ as they headed toward the woods.

"Are you okay?" KJ asked.

"I felt like I would never feel anything but anger again," Aazar said, walking into the forest. "It was like this violent, angry thing had replaced me."

"It's not your fault," KJ said. He bumped her hip with affection. "Accidents happen. That's why we have Flenoid. We learn how to control our powers and keep from destroying others. You'll get the hang of it."

Aazar gave a slight smile and nodded as they made their way to the street.

Chapter Twenty One: Mommy Issues

We've gone over it a thousand times now." Britney sighed, resting her head on her fist at the table. "Can we just go home?"

"Babe, I know you've got it." Todd looked at her. "I just don't believe the rest of these guys have it."

The group groaned.

"We've got it," Peter grumbled as he slumped in the booth with his feet on the table.

The group looked at him with raised eyebrows. It wasn't like Peter to show his attitude at the meetings. Realizing his mistake, he took his feet off the table and leaned forward.

"I mean, we all understand how important this is," Peter said softer, "but I think we've gone over it enough times."

The fact that Peter had shown his true colors was the final indicator that this meeting had stretched for too long. They had been at Cafe Moana for an hour, rehearsing the plan over and over. It had been two months, and the project hadn't changed, so everyone was annoyed.

The waitress collected empty coffee cups as the group smiled. When she walked away, the group focused on Todd again. He'd lost his mind. If someone took too long to answer (meaning more than an extended pause), Todd would start the whole scenario from the beginning. He stressed that knowing in what order things were supposed to happen would help the entire group.

KJ looked more irritated than Aazar had ever seen him.

Clearly, the closer to the mission they got, the more upset he became.

After working with him and Flenoid, Aazar knew just how hard it was for KJ to control his power. She knew how stressful it was for him to use it. Having to take out a building with people in it couldn't sit well with him. KJ ground his teeth at Todd, while Todd plastered on a fake smile to shoot toward Peter.

"I don't think anyone thinks it unimportant," Todd said. "I want to hear it through completely at least once. Let's start again."

Before the group could groan, Britney started from the beginning once again.

"I go up to the security guards and flirt with them until they leave their posts to talk to me," Britney said, sighing. Britney was back to her old self again. She seemed nicer to Aazar since she stayed with them, but she was not kinder to Peter. Now that Aazar knew why she tried to keep her distance.

"Good," Todd said. "Next?"

"From the van, I hack into the security feed and change the camera system to a loop of the previous day. I also access the database for the key codes. I give the plans to you," Peter said. "I flash the lights once to let Britney know she can leave."

It was her turn. Before Todd could interrupt, Aazar continued.

"Todd, Brian, Jake, and I dressed as medical professionals, leave the van and use the codes to access the building." She didn't see why they needed her in the mission at all. She feared it was so she could use her abilities to stop someone. Aazar decided a while ago that she would hang back as much as possible. Regardless of what she was designated to do, she knew her real job was to avoid using her powers.

"Okay," Todd said. "Next?"

"I set off a fire alarm in the building to clear personnel and security," Peter said. He'd been working non-stop since the gala to find the fire alarm codes in the system. Aazar knew he'd found them when she heard him whoop for joy in his room while in the kitchen.

"After we hear the alarm, we head to the medicine room," Aazar said. "I stand guard while Todd and Jake go inside." Aazar didn't have any feelings about Jake. He kept to himself at the last few meetings and looked uncomfortable.

There was a pause. Everyone looked at Brian, who piped up, "I stand guard too."

Everyone looked at Todd. He seemed satisfied, and the group breathed a sigh of relief.

"All right," Todd said. "Then?"

Jake cleared his throat. "I will destroy the medical supplies."

Aazar looked at him, wondering what his power looked like in practice. He caught her eye and looked away. She spoke again.

"I lead Jake back to the van, and we wait for further instructions," Aazar said.

"When the medical supplies have been destroyed," Todd spoke. "Brian and I will go to the patient's ward and free the Variants. We will then head back to the van with the patients." This was the essential part of the plan for Todd. Not because he wanted to save lives but because he knew he would get his promotion after freeing these Variants and getting them to join the cause.

"I will be there for backup," Brian said, "in case we run into trouble."

"And finally?" Todd said.

KJ sighed. "Finally, I destroy the electrical system, disabling the entire facility in hopes they can never use it again."

"Great!" Todd said. "So, we've all got it then?"

"Of course, we have it, Todd," KJ said, irritated. "We've had it for the past forty-five minutes."

"Well, if Brian didn't keep forgetting his par—"

"I remember my part," Brian said. "I just kept forgetting where I went in this weird little play you have us reciting. I'm there to back you up. Period. No need for all of this timing crap."

Todd ignored him and looked at the rest of the group. "We do this next week, you guys. Nothing can go wrong. Nothing. This is our first vital mission, and I'm not screwing this up. None of us are screwing this up. You got that?"

Everyone nodded. The new commander had just come into the resistance camp, and he'd been riling up the local chapter. Todd became more aggressive at meetings and began sounding more and more like a zealot. It made Aazar nervous, but she'd already promised everyone involved she would help. Plus, she didn't want to embarrass Peter. KJ sighed again and looked away.

"Do you have a problem with the plan, KJ?" Todd said. "No one's going to die just like you wanted. No one will know what happened until it's far too late. What's your issue now?"

"I starting to believe this isn't the best way to solve things with the others."

Todd rolled his eyes and groaned. "I can't believe I'm hearing this again."

"We should be gathering everyone being destroyed by the system. We should make everyone see that the media and the government are keeping us afraid of each other and unite around that," KJ said. "This attack is just going to make things worse than they already are. Now we'll be terrorists. We'll be what they claim us to be: people to be afraid of."

"They aren't afraid of us, KJ," Todd smirked. "The Normies pretend they're scared, but really, they don't see any real threat about us. They dominate everything, break into our homes, and kill our families. They don't shudder while they murder our kind. They didn't quake in fear when they shot our mother in the face."

Everyone at the table froze. Aazar felt like she'd been splashed with water. What the hell was he talking about? This had gone far beyond an argument about the plan. Everyone looked at KJ, waiting for his response. He took a breath to calm himself as he stood up.

"They kill us because they fear us. Fear drives them to it," KJ said. "Revenge isn't going to help. It never does. What is the point of it if it doesn't change anything? Mom will still be dead, Todd."

Todd pounded the table. "We have to do something!"

"So, do you plan on killing all of them," KJ asked. "Because that will make what you want Genocide."

Todd looked uncomfortable as he glanced at Peter. "No, not all of them. Only the ones that resist us."

"And if Mom's killers don't resist? What then? Will you be satisfied?"

"NO!" Todd boomed. "THEY DESERVE TO DIE. JUST LIKE THOSE

PEOPLE IN THE LAB!"

Aazar looked at the other customers at the dinner, worried they might hear the argument. It looked as though they were all ignoring Todd's random outburst. He looked around, too, and sat back down.

"They know what they were doing," Todd said, growling. "If they didn't want to die at the hand of another, they shouldn't be kidnapping and killing anyone at all!"

"People will apply the same logic to you," KJ said.

"LET THEM," Todd spat. "I'm willing to die for my cause!"

KJ looked at Todd and everyone else at the table.

"Why help at all?" Todd growled. "Why not just walk away?"

"Because you're my brother," KJ said, looking into his hands, "and you need me."

Todd sat there in angry silence. Britney took a deep breath.

"Well, I think that's about as much as anyone can take of this topic right now," she said. "Why don't we call it a day?"

Todd and KJ didn't say anything. So, Britney continued and said, "All right, let's call it quits…Meet here next Tuesday to pick up your uniforms, right, baby?"

Todd still stared with fury at KJ.

"How are we getting those?" Brian asked, trying to change the mood.

"We've got a guy on the inside who can give us extra uniforms," Todd said, still upset.

"Why doesn't he have to come to these meetings?" Aazar asked.

"Because he's not our informant, he's part of the resistance, and his role as an undercover is important," Todd said, annoyed. "Any more questions?"

No one said anything.

"Meet next Tuesday."

KJ grabbed his bag and headed straight for the door. Aazar ran after him. "Hey."

"Hey," he said as he continued walking.

"What was that about?"

KJ slowed down for a moment. He looked at Aazar.

"Our mother was murdered trying to protect us."

"What?" Aazar blinked. "You never told me that."

"It's not a nice story."

Aazar waited as KJ began.

"Todd wanted to run away as soon as he realized my power, but I wanted to stick around. I loved our parents and didn't want to worry them." He let out a small laugh. "I wasn't ready to give up my old life yet."

He paused for a moment to gather his thoughts. "A few weeks after the pool incident, a bunch of people from town came to our house. They started having suspicions and demanded answers. They accused her of hiding a Variant. She said she didn't care and that I was her son, who she loved. They broke in. We ran to the kitchen, and my mother grabbed a large knife and shoved us behind her. She held it out with both hands. I thought it was funny because I was so powerful, and she didn't need to protect me."

She saw his face grow even sadder.

"A man came in with a gun and pointed it at me. Todd later told me that this was when he realized he had powers. He read the man's mind and knew he was going to shoot. So, Todd ran at the guy, and when he did, my mother jumped out in front, and...he shot her."

Aazar covered her mouth in horror.

"Todd dragged me out of the house that night, and we ran away. I had passed out, but Todd could still hear my dreams and said I was screaming in my head."

Aazar stared at him in horrified silence. She'd felt so betrayed by her parents that she never thought about what it would've been like to lose one trying to protect her.

"Is there anything I can do or—"

"No." He looked to Aazar. "No. It's just a lot to remember. Todd hasn't worked through it as well as I thought he had. I didn't know he was still holding on to so much anger after so long."

Aazar thought about her anger at her mother. She knew she would never get over looking down at the barrel of that gun as her father gaped at her. She would never get over being thrown out of her house like an animal. She couldn't even begin to think about how Todd must have been. He was lucky his power wasn't more dangerous.

KJ cleared his throat. "Hey, did you want to—"

A loud slam behind them caused KJ to stop his question. Todd walked out of the café with hands shoved in his pockets. He saw KJ and stormed in the opposite direction as Britney trailed behind him. KJ frowned as Peter burst out of the café doors. He looked up at the sky and stood on the sidewalk with his arms outstretched as though he was embracing the sky.

"FREEDOM!" he bellowed to the clouds. "Man, I feel like Nicole Kidman on divorce day."

"What?" Aazar asked.

"Never mind," said Peter.

"I'll catch you later, okay, Aazar?" KJ said.

"Sure, see you Tuesday," Aazar said.

KJ walked down the street with his hands in his pockets, but his walk was slower and more contemplative than his brothers. Peter jogged up to her with a grin on his face.

"Jesus, we were in there forever!" Peter said, exasperated. He looked at KJ's back. "And all that stuff about KJ and Todd's mom…like…what the hell happened there?"

"It's not a very pretty story," Aazar said, frowning.

"You know it?" Peter rounded on her. "How could you know that?"

"He just told me the gist of it," Aazar said.

"KJ? Really? When?"

"A few minutes ago. Why?" Aazar asked.

"I didn't know you guys were close," Peter said, disappointed.

"We're not that close. We just practice controlling our powers together sometimes." She wondered why Peter was so interested.

"You started going to his guru guy?" Peter said. "Why didn't you tell me this?"

"I don't know," Aazar said. "I didn't think I had to clear everything with you."

This conversation was not going the way he wanted.

"You don't," Peter said, backtracking. "I just…well, I just wanted to know what happened. I mean, someone killed their mo—"

"Peter, I don't think he wants me telling people. It's clearly upsetting."

"But—"

"Aren't you always talking about how gossip is why society is failing?" Aazar said with force.

Peter sighed. "You're right."

They walked for a few moments in silence. Aazar knew Peter meant well. She wasn't sure why she became so defensive of KJ. Maybe Aazar cared more about him than she thought. She decided to clear the tension.

"Gossip is hard to avoid, though."

He perked up again. "It IS! Do you see how easy it is to fall into the trap? This is why nothing gets done. Everyone is watching reality TV because gossiping about other people is more interesting to them than actually doing something worth gossiping about…"

He went on with his rant while Aazar listened, wondering if KJ was okay.

Chapter Twenty Two: The Split

She sat in the clearing with Flenoid and KJ moving fire from one hand to another. To his word, Dylan had not returned since he'd left the training group a few weeks ago. She felt guilty that she'd run a fellow Variant away from a good teacher, but she'd gotten much better at controlling her power and couldn't be worried about some boy who was afraid of her. Aazar wondered how different life would've been if Aazar had known Flenoid before all of this. Would she have been able to maintain an everyday life? Go to school, go home, and warm bath water with her bare hands? She would never know now.

"Concentrate, KJ," Flenoid said, sitting crossed-legged in the field. "You seem distracted."

"I'm sorry," KJ said as he frowned with his eyes closed on the grass.

"There's no reason to apologize, so don't be sorry," Flenoid commented. "Remain still and regain your concentration. Clear your mind."

KJ took a deep breath. Aazar watched him from her own spot on the cool ground. She had never seen him so preoccupied. The mission was only four days away, and he hadn't been able to convince Todd to change tactics. Aazar wondered who this new commander was and why he was putting so much pressure on everyone. It couldn't be good for morale for recruits to be at each other's throats.

"Aazar, Aazar," Flenoid said, "always wondering, never concentrating."

"How are you doing that?" Aazar asked, and as usual, Flenoid smiled and said nothing as he focused his steely grey eyes on the electricity spouting from KJ's fingers.

Aazar wasn't precisely sure what Flenoid's power was. She thought he must have some mind-reading, but that didn't explain his ability to see when he was blind. She'd never met anyone with more than one power, but she was confident that Flenoid had several.

"Hush now," Flenoid said, his eyes moving in her direction. "Keep your mind on your fire. It's almost gone out with all of your pontificating."

Aazar looked down and saw that her flames were no more than flickers at this point. She took a deep breath and watched the flames leap from her hands in perfect circles.

"Fantastic!" Flenoid said, clapping. "Now that you can control the energy within you, you can access energy outside yourself."

"What does that mean?" Aazar asked as she raised an eyebrow.

He touched the ground in front of him. "The earth is full of unused energy that we can tap into if we focus our minds and bodies on channeling it. Please take off your shoes."

It was a strange request, but Aazar knew not to question a direct order from Flenoid. She took her shoes and socks off and placed them near her in the clearing. She felt the cold, wet soil in between each of her toes. She noted that Flenoid never seemed to wear shoes. Was she about to learn why? She sat back down on the ground.

"Now I want you to breathe in, and when you do, I want you to feel the vibrations of the Earth." Flenoid placed his hands in his lap and breathed in as well.

Aazar breathed and tried to focus on the ground beneath her. An ant bit the exposed skin on her ankle, but she didn't notice because of the warm sensation around her feet. She saw a white light coming from the soiled ground and into her feet when she looked down. She inhaled, and as she did, the white light went inside her legs and up to her arms. She was glowing.

"Woah."

KJ stopped his own practice to watch Aazar with a knowing smile.

"Now carefully, *carefully*," Flenoid cautioned as he conducted her with his fingers, "make a small fireball."

Aazar tried to create a ball as big as her fist, but the fireball became the size of her head! She'd never made one that big before.

"Oh my god!" She began to panic, but as soon as she did, the fire and the light went out in the blink of an eye.

She looked around, shocked. She patted herself, looking for scorched clothing and burned hair. "What happened? That was the most exhilarating thing I've ever experienced!"

"You tapped into the earth and used its energy to fuel your power. It's like hooking yourself up to a generator." KJ offered from his patch of grass.

"But why did it go out?" she asked. "Usually, when I freak out, my powers go haywire!"

"To use the earth's energy, you must focus on channeling it. Strong emotions untamed shut you off from the power source unless you are extremely powerful." Flenoid said as he stood up.

"In other words," KJ said, standing up as well, "to use the earth's energy for external purposes, you have to mean it."

"Tapping into the earth is a quick way to recharge your power as well. If I were you, I wouldn't use your powers while channeling, but still a good technique to know if you need a lot at some point." Flenoid explained.

Aazar stood up too, feeling tingling up her thighs that could only mean her legs had fallen asleep. She didn't realize they'd been sitting for so long. She brushed the dirt and the ant off of her pants and began following Flenoid and KJ to the cabin.

"Why didn't you teach me this technique at the beginning?" Aazar asked.

"It's difficult to connect with the energy of the earth when you haven't connected to your own."

The group stopped in their tracks as they watched Todd storm into the clearing. He marched into the cottage in a huff. KJ stood as still as a post. When Todd came to the backyard, his face was full of rage when his eyes met his brothers.

"You told them you thought I was incompetent!" Todd bellowed.

"Todd, relax," KJ started as he put his hands up.

Todd punched him in the jaw. Aazar stepped forward, but Flenoid held her back. "It's not your fight."

KJ wiped the blood from his lip with the back of his hand and stood up. He squared his shoulders and breathed in deep. Aazar realized KJ was trying to keep himself from losing control over his ability. She'd never seen what that looked like outside of herself.

"You're unstable," KJ said. "Look at yourself. You're all over the place."

"Because this plan has to WORK!" Todd exclaimed as he ran both hands through his hair. "I'm stressed out!"

Flenoid seemed to be watching the exchange closely. His glassy eyes darted back and forth into each face.

"Yeah, I know," KJ said, "and it's compromising your ability to make decisions. I told the higher-ups and those in command because I think you're losing control. You're paranoid and always yelling at everyone."

"And you think going behind my back will help me be LESS paranoid!?" Todd yelled as he walked toward KJ. KJ took a step back. Aazar knew he was doing this for Todd's safety, not his own.

"That outburst about Mom at the meeting…it's unhealthy. I think you need to step down and let someone else take over." KJ said with as much calm as he could.

"And who would that be? Hmmm?" Todd exclaimed. "You?"

"Todd…" KJ began. He stepped forward and put a hand on his brother's shoulder, but Todd shook it away.

"Well, they don't want you," Todd sneered, "They want me in charge, but they wanted me to know that there was a RAT in my team!"

"I'm just trying to help you." KJ looked like he was at his wit's end.

"Then do what I ask!" Todd yelled. "Just do what I ask!"

Flenoid walked up to Todd and placed a hand on his back. Todd looked at him with wild eyes.

"Would you like some tea, son?"

"What?"

"Some chamomile tea might do you good." He gestured toward the cottage.

"I don't-I DON'T WANT TEA," Todd said, looking unnerved.

"But it would be nice, wouldn't it? Come on inside."

Todd stepped away. "Don't touch me."

The interaction with Flenoid had been so strange that it had taken the wind out of Todd's sails. He had used KJ's technique, and Aazar was grateful for it. Todd looked back at his brother with less anger.

"I can't believe you would go behind my back. We've been through everything together. Why didn't you just trust me?" Todd pleaded.

"I tried, but you weren't listening," KJ said.

Aazar didn't have any siblings, but she could tell by what she'd seen that the dynamic was challenging.

Todd looked sad for a moment and then smiled. "Well, as I said, your little plan didn't work. I didn't get removed from the mission, but you have."

"What?" KJ said, surprised. Aazar and Flenoid exchanged looks as well. This wouldn't be good for anyone. Todd reveled in their shocked expressions and continued with glee.

"They don't want any cowards working with us. So, you're out."

KJ started toward him, "Todd, this is getting out of control. Can't you see that—"

"No, brother," Todd grinned and pointed a finger at KJ, "it's out of YOUR control. I should've known that you were trying to manipulate me from the beginning."

"You're losing it," KJ growled.

"Don't come back to the apartment!" Todd said. "Figure out somewhere else to live for a while. I don't want to see you!"

"Todd." KJ started. Todd turned on his heel and stomped back into the cottage. KJ followed him, but Todd read from the book and walked out of the clearing without looking back.

KJ stared at his back for a while. This altercation was the second time Aazar had witnessed a terrible fight between them, and KJ looked horrible. Aazar approached cautiously. "Are you okay?"

It took him a moment to answer. "I'll be fine."

"You can stay at my place for the night if you want. I can't see Peter saying no." Aazar offered.

"That's thoughtful of you, but—"

"No 'but'," Aazar said as she placed a hand on his back, "you're coming with me."

KJ smiled, unwilling to argue. "Let's go."

They said goodbye to Flenoid and walked back through the forest quietly. The wind whistled through the trees as their feet crunched the grass underneath them. The sun was almost down, and she could almost make out the outline of the trail to the Belize neighborhood. The crickets began to chirp louder and louder as they walked along, accompanying the sound of breaking twigs and small animals running. Aazar loved walking through the forest at night and was happy she had someone to do it with for once. She couldn't believe KJ wouldn't be going on the mission.

"How are we supposed to do this mission without you?" Aazar asked as they walked in tandem. "Do you think they can find someone to replace you in such a short period?"

He shrugged and shoved his hands in his hoodie pockets. "They must already have someone in mind if they were willing to cut me out." KJ lamented. "I shouldn't have said anything. I should've known those psychos would let him off the reigns. I'm worried about Todd, and I'm afraid of what would happen if he overextended himself."

Aazar looked at him. She could almost make out his blue eyes in the growing dark, "What do you mean?"

"Since he's been trying to amplify his power, he's been hearing more and more voices. He could only grab a few sentences, but now he could hear all the thoughts of anyone within twenty feet of him. Lately, he's been having a difficult time turning it off." He kicked a pebble on the trail, and it bounced and hit a nearby tree.

"Why doesn't he come to Flenoid and learn to control it better?" Aazar asked.

"They had a falling out a while ago. Plus, Todd thinks he has it under control. Todd thinks the more thoughts he hears, the more he understands people," KJ continued shaking his head. "But that's not how thoughts work. Not all thoughts are true. People think of all kinds of things they never do in real life. He's starting to see everyone and everything as a threat."

Aazar thought about that for a moment as the forest became denser around them. Todd must feel so alone right now.

"What can we do?"

KJ sighed. "I don't think there's anything we can do until he's willing to admit he has a problem."

Aazar was silent.

"I'll see if I can get back on the mission tomorrow. I'll talk to the higher-ups and see if I can make my case."

Aazar didn't think that would make much of a difference. She was beginning to be afraid. This mission was starting to look more sinister the closer it got. With Todd losing his mind and KJ gone, she wasn't sure if she wanted to be a part of any of it now, but she couldn't leave Peter to deal with all of this alone.

They traveled through the forest, listening to crickets and other bugs sing in the moonlight. Aazar realized she was alone with KJ for the first time. No buses, no electricians, just them. She enjoyed his quiet and calm demeanor. It almost made things seem like they weren't as crazy as they were.

"You know, the government federally protects these forests," KJ offered.

"Really?" Aazar said as she heard a bird fly overhead.

"Yeah, the rich people didn't want their views to be destroyed, so they made it a national landmark."

"That's hilarious." Aazar laughed.

"It is, isn't it?" KJ smiled and took a deep breath of the forest air. "Rich people accidentally doing a good thing. It happens more than you think."

Aazar thought about the Belizes, and he was right. The family was selfish, wealthy, and ignorant, but they did give a lot of money to charities and the homeless. They'd even greeted her with open arms when she had nowhere to go. Regardless of how little they cared about other people, they still managed to do good things for them.

When they got to the house, KJ stopped.

"This is where I leave you."

"What?" Aazar said, turning to him. "That's out of the question! You need a—"

"Aazar, I can't stay here."

"What do you mean?" Aazar's eyebrows furrowed. She was irritated that he waited until this moment to fight about it.

"I can't stay here…knowing how Peter feels about you."

"Knowing how PETER feels about ME?" Aazar didn't understand. Peter hadn't said anything to Aazar that made her think he had any feelings for her at all. "What do Peter's feelings have to do with you not sleeping on a park bench tonight?"

"You can't tell me you don't know that he loves you, right?"

Aazar blinked and laughed it off. "What!?"

"He's constantly bending over backward to impress you. Ever since he met you, he's been working harder for the resistance to join the ranks. He's very protective of you. He even cleans up for you. So, yeah," KJ shrugged, "he loves you."

Aazar took a minute to think about it. Was that love? Her heart began to beat hard in her chest. KJ smiled as he looked at her. She looked back at him, puzzled.

"But why can't you stay over? Do you think he'll get jealous or something? It's not like there's anything between you and me."

KJ drew in a sharp breath and nodded. "That's true. But I don't want him to get the wrong impression. He needs to be focused, and I don't want to throw it off."

"That's stupid," Aazar said, shaking her head. She grabbed the edge of his sleeve and began to tug at him. "Just come in."

KJ didn't move and tried to hide a smile at Aazar's attempt to force his massive body forward with the corner of his sweatshirt.

He took his hands out of his pockets and placed them on Aazar's arms. "I'll just crash with Brian. He'll be ecstatic."

"Doesn't he live pretty far from here?" Aazar asked.

"It's only two buses. I'll be fine," KJ said as he set his jaw.

She realized she wasn't going to win this fight. She sighed.

"Fine."

"I'll see you around, Aazar," KJ said as he waved and walked back the way he came alone.

Aazar looked back at the vast Belize house and thought about the boy inside. Did Peter love her?

Chapter Twenty Three: All the King's Horses

"Peter, turn that noise down!" Peter's father bellowed from the kitchen.

Peter smirked and turned the music down as he sat back at his computer. It was a couple of hours after KJ had walked home. Aazar sat on Peter's bed in an awkward position, reading a book about new theories of evolution and Variants. She glanced over the pages to peek at Peter. There was no way he was in love with her. He'd never given her any actual hints at something like that. He'd only told her she was pretty twice. They were good friends, sure, but love?

They had been spending a lot of time together. Norma had lost interest in Aazar, and so had the rest of the family. They had gone back to their self-absorbed ways and didn't bother her much. Aazar was grateful, seeing how their attitudes toward life seemed more and more against what Aazar believed.

She still wasn't sure about the resistance. They had recently decided on a name for their group: The Order. Aazar didn't want to engage in violence, and lessons with Flenoid started going well, but she felt she could do more than he allowed her. She was sure channeling energy from the earth was possible while using her own power. He was playing down her abilities.

"You know, if my parents find this book, they'll probably kick you out," Peter said.

"Can't I blame it on you?" Aazar said. "They'd never kick you out."

Peter laughed. "I know, right?" He did his best impression of his mother and squeaked, "Think of the SCANDAL!"

They laughed together. What the group had planned for the medical facility would be a scandal. All of a sudden, Aazar thought about what KJ had said. Was Peter trying too hard to make her laugh? She wished KJ hadn't said anything about it at all.

"Do you think you're ready to do this?" Aazar said. "Going against the law, 'breaking and entering,' and all of that?"

"You're doing it too, remember?"

"Yeah, but I don't have any family or anything like that." Aazar shrugged and tried not to think about her parents. They would've been livid if they knew what she was doing. "Aren't you afraid you'll get your family in trouble?"

Peter paused for a moment. "There are some things you just can't ignore."

"Yeah, I get that," Aazar said.

"They'll be fine, though," Peter said, putting his feet back on the desk in front of him. "They'll just apologize for me and then lock me in my room until I'm thirty-six."

"Or you could just move out," Aazar said.

"Yeah, right. With what job."

"You could find one. At a computer company or something like that."

"You know nothing about the real world. To do that, you need to get a degree. To get a degree, I'd have to get money."

"Are you kidding?" Aazar said. "You know you're rich, right?"

"Yeah, but my dad isn't going to shove any cash toward something like computer school for me."

"What makes you think that?"

"Because he's a dick," Peter stated.

"Oh, come on, Peter," Aazar said. "They love you in their way. They wouldn't just blow you off if you said you wanted to do something for a good job."

"You don't know them," Peter snarled.

"You keep saying that, but it's not true anymore," Aazar said. "I know your parents. They're pretty self-absorbed, but I don't think they'd abandon you. They paid your attorney bills when you got into that accident, right?"

"Well, yeah, but that's because it would've ruined Dad's chances at a promotion if I went to jail. It was still only because it benefited them."

"I think you're wrong."

"Whatever," Peter said. "This conversation isn't going anywhere. I like to talk about ideas and events. Not people. Let's change the subject."

"Peter," Aazar said, "they'd help you."

"Back off, Aazar," Peter spat. "Mom and Dad already told me they did it for their benefit. Mom said I was lucky Dad was up for promotion; otherwise, they'd let me rot in jail. They also informed me that they'd disown me if I ever brought so much shame on the family again. So, I won't be part of the 'family' very soon."

"But Norma isn't tha—"

"Norma is banging the guy who tried to sue me for 'hitting' him, and you think she has a loyal bone in her body? I don't think so."

Aazar sighed. "Fine, forget I said anything."

"Already did," Peter said. He pointed to the computer screen. "Here, check this out."

Aazar looked at the screen. It was a bunch of numbers and letters. "What is this?"

"This is the backdoor of the clinic's programming systems."

Aazar's jaw dropped. "You mean—"

"Yep, I hacked it last night. All I have to do is bring the laptop to the location and hack into their direct Wi-Fi. I'll have control of everything."

"That's pretty amazing." Aazar looked over his shoulder. "Have you told Todd?"

"I'm emailing him now," Peter said, smiling. "I'm so happy I could do it. I was a little worried because it took so long, but it worked out in the end."

"Awesome," Aazar said.

"So, are you ready for this?" Peter asked her.

Aazar thought for a moment. "I don't know. I don't want to hurt anyone, but I don't want to leave those poor people there getting experimented on.

If I were imprisoned, I'd want someone to help me."

"This is going to be a piece of cake," Peter said. "I've got control of the whole system. All you'll have to do is walk in and out."

"I'm not worried."

"You seem worried."

"So do you."

"Whatever."

Peter's door squeaked open. His mother stood on the other side. She looked around the room and covered her nose.

"Peter, this room is disgusting. How do you stay cooped up in here all the time?" She looked at Aazar. "And honestly, dear, how can you stand the smell?"

"What do you want, Mom?" Peter pressed.

"Your father and I are going out. No company. No leaving."

"If you're leaving, why do I have to stay here? It's not like the house is going to watch me."

"Peter, you weren't planning on going anywhere anyway. Just say, 'Okay, Mom,' so I can go, please?" his mom said.

"Look at you, being all frank."

"Peter."

"Okay, Mom," he said in a monotone.

"Thank you. Have a good evening." She closed the door.

Shortly after, the front door closed, and you could hear the car back out of the driveway and accelerate down the street.

"Where did they go?" Aazar asked.

"Does it matter? Let's raid my dad's study for everything he's taken from me this month."

Aazar sighed. Peter's nomophobia hadn't improved in the last few months, and it was starting to worry her. She and Peter headed upstairs. The study was just as it had been all those months ago when Aazar had first moved in. Peter began opening cabinets and drawers. In the array of papers and phone bills, they found Peter's speakers that had been taken away after a loud music day and a pocketknife that was confiscated after the car accident.

They were just about to look for his lighter when they heard the front door close again.

"Shit, that was fast," Peter said. "Come on, let's get out of here."

They turned down the hall and were greeted by Adam, heading straight for Norma's room. Adam gave a sinister smile at the sight of Peter.

"I didn't know you could even leave your room," Adam said. "Maybe you should've stayed there."

"Maybe you should lay off the weights before you look like a blow-up doll," Peter said matter-of-factly.

"You think you're funny, Peter?"

"I wasn't trying to be funny; I was trying to help you," Peter said.

Adam grabbed him by his T-shirt.

"I'm going to smash your face in."

"I feel like I should be scared, but your muscles make you look like a balloon animal."

"Peter," Aazar warned, "cut it out."

Adam's eyes slit at Peter. "Yeah, Peter, better cut it out. You don't want to make this little girl cry do you."

Peter just stared at Adam. Adam put him back down on the floor.

"Thanks," Peter grumbled.

Adam looked angrier than before. "Watch your back."

"Right." Peter rolled his eyes and gave him a sarcastic thumbs up. "No problem."

Adam glared at him and then headed to Norma's room. They heard Norma's squeal of happy surprise when he saw him.

"I don't understand how she can date such a creep," Peter said.

They went back downstairs to Peter's room. He turned on the tiny television he kept on a dresser in his room. The news was on, and they were talking about Variants. A well-dressed female news anchor held a microphone in the face of a resistance fighter. He wore a red shirt with a black bulletproof vest. She realized she'd never seen anyone representing them in the media. The anchor cleared her throat.

"So, you're saying that you are, in fact, a part of the militia group of Variants attacking government buildings."

"Yes. We are The Order, and we are here to bring order and peace to our society," the resistance fighter said.

Aazar leaned in closer.

"I'm sorry, you're calling your group 'The Order?'" the anchor asked.

"We are The Order. We are Variants who have decided we will no longer stand idly by while the Humans exterminate us."

Aazar sat back. "Humans?" she questioned. "I thought we were all humans…"

"He was just exaggerating for effect," Peter reflected. "Wait here. I'm going to grab my lighter from the office."

Aazar nodded as he walked out of the room. She listened to the resistance fighter.

"We will no longer be oppressed. We will rise and stop the genocide of Variants. We tried your laws and your justice system. Now we will create our utopia. You are either with us or against us!"

Aazar swallowed. This was getting worse, and she didn't know if she wanted to associate with The Order. She turned the TV off and looked around Peter's room. She was starting to agree with his mother. He needed to clean in here. She wasn't sure she'd be able to find her book again. She moved a couple of shirts around before hearing a loud series of thumps going down the stairs. Who would be running down the stairs like that? Then she heard Norma's scream.

When Aazar ran out of the room, she saw Peter's body lying at the bottom of the stairs. He didn't move and looked up at the ceiling, unblinking. Norma was running down the stairs screaming. She shook him, and his body rocked back and forth lifelessly.

"WAKE UP!" Norma screamed. "OH MY GOD, PETER, WAKE UP!"

Adam came down the stairs one step at a time, clutching the railing tightly. He looked like he was going to be sick. Aazar walked up to the scene in slow motion.

"P…Peter," Aazar whispered. Peter's eyes looked off into the distance, unmoving. She looked at Adam. "What happened?"

"I don't know. I went to the bathroom and heard the noise. I saw him at the bottom of the stairs when I came out."

"Peter!" Norma wailed again. "Oh my god, Peter!"

"What do we do?" Adam said. "What the hell do we do?"

Aazar was frozen. Then she blinked, ran to the phone on the counter, and dialed 911. They said they were sending people. Maybe he was just unconscious. She brought the phone to Norma.

"Call your parents."

"Oh, my god." Norma rocked back and forth.

"Norma," Aazar said, "call your parents."

"I can't!" Norma wailed. "I just can't!"

"Stop being useless for once and call your parents," Aazar screamed. "NOW!"

Norma took the phone with a shaking hand and walked to the kitchen. Adam followed behind her.

Aazar checked Peter's pulse, but she couldn't find it. His face was looking grayer by the second. "Peter," she whispered as a single tear slipped quietly down her cheek. She shook him. "Peter, don't leave me."

* * *

"His neck snapped the second he hit the floor. It was painless," the paramedic said as he pulled the black sheet over Peter's head. "There was nothing anyone could have done. I'm sorry for your loss."

Peter's mother stood frozen in silence while His father's eyes brimmed with red lines underneath them. He'd been crying in private. Norma wailed in Adam's arms as he rocked her back and forth. Adam's eyes looked as though they would pop out of their sockets. Aazar stared at Peter's fingertip, which was still visible underneath the tarp.

As they wheeled his body into the van and shut the door behind Peter's parents, Aazar was left with Adam and Norma.

"I can't believe this happened," Norma said. "Why did this happen?"

"It was just an accident," Adam said, looking frantic and out of sorts. "Just an accident."

Aazar stared at Adam before leaving them on the lawn and walking into Peter's room. She closed the door behind her and looked around Peter's. It was so quiet. So dirty. She was still waiting for its owner to turn the radio too loud. She wanted to be sad or cry, but she didn't feel anything. She found a pile of clothes on the floor and lay in them until she fell asleep staring at the ceiling.

Chapter Twenty Four: Control

She woke up the next morning wondering why she had slept on the floor in Peter's room. For a split second, she thought he might be in the bathroom, and then she remembered. She remembered everything. She wanted to scream. She couldn't believe her best friend had just fallen down a flight of stairs in his own home. Then she thought about Adam and his story about going to the bathroom. She knew he was lying. Aazar tried hard to give him the benefit of the doubt, but her stomach lurched at the thought.

She peeled herself off the floor and walked out of the room. The family was sitting together in silence at the table. It made her sad that it took Peter's death for them to sit together. They looked up at her when she walked in.

"Aazar, sweetheart," Mrs. Belize said. "I forgot all about you. When you opened that door, I almost thought…I almost."

"I'm sorry."

"No, no," she said. "It's not your fault at all, dear." She looked away. "What am I going to do now? What can I do now?"

They all sat in silence while Mrs. Belize wept. Her crying was an outside expression of what they all felt inside. They looked at their hands. Mr. Belize cleared his throat.

"We'll have to arrange a funeral. Call Mrs. Bernake and ask her who she used when her husband died last year. That was a nice service."

"Peter wouldn't have wanted a service," Aazar said. "He would've thought it was ceremonial garbage."

"Yes," Mr. Belize said. "I know. But we have to do something."

Aazar knew that Peter would've fought back, but she just couldn't. This family needed something to do right now.

"Do you," Mr. Belize started, "do you know any of his friends, people he would've wanted to come?"

"Yeah," Aazar said. "I know a few people."

"I'll invite people from school too," Norma said. "A lot of people liked Peter."

"What are you talking about?" Aazar said. "He hated everyone at school."

"Aazar," Norma began.

"No," she said. "I'm not going to let you invite all your fucking friends for a photo op at Peter's expense."

"Excuse me," Mr. Belize said.

Aazar stared at him. "He didn't like anyone at school.

I knew his friends. I'll make sure they'll show up."

"But my friends are my support system!" Norma said. "I need them to help me through this period of my life!"

"They treated him like shit, Norma!" Aazar yelled.

"Oh, god," Mrs. Belize wailed. "How could we have been so blind."

"Mom, she's exaggerating," Norma said.

"No, I'm not," Aazar said. "They're fucking trash."

"If you're going to continue to speak this way to my family while we grieve, you should leave," Mr. Belize said.

Aazar raised her eyebrows. Peter was right. They would turn on everything he wanted as soon as he was gone. She wanted to spit on the floor, but instead, she nodded and apologized.

"I'm sorry," she said. "I'm just…I just can't believe this is all happening."

They all nodded in understanding. Aazar knew that if she kept going, she would be uninvited to his funeral. She needed to make sure his real friends were there. The only people he liked at all were the Variants. She had to figure out a way to get in contact with them. Peter had always been the one to make contact first. Peter. Peter is dead. She couldn't wrap her mind around the sentence. It felt foreign, like a lie or an unrehearsed joke.

There was a knock at the door.

"It's probably Adam," Norma said. "He said he'd stop by first thing in the morning."

Aazar stood up without warning. "I'll go see what numbers I can find. Excuse me."

She barricaded herself back in Peter's room as she heard Norma's wails start on queue after Adam asked if she was okay.

* * *

"Okay," Flenoid said. "Again."

Aazar tried to calm herself. She breathed in and out. She hadn't been able to access her powers since Peter's death because she felt numb. Peter's face kept flashing in her mind. She couldn't believe how few people he'd known when she tried to get contact information for everyone. She spent so much time with him that she wondered why she was surprised. Surely if he had friends other than those part of the resistance, she would've met them by now. How could she have been so blind? His funeral would be huge regardless, the family had enough people to make it round out without anyone he knew, but she knew Peter would've hated this funeral more than he hated most things. Everything Peter said seemed to be true now that he was gone. Everyone was just full of crap.

"Aazar," Flenoid said, "you have to clear your mind. I know this is hard, but as a training technique, this is a perfect lesson in controlling your power without accessing your emotions."

Aazar sighed and looked at him. "I just don't feel like doing this right now. Can't we just do it next week?"

"You have to be able to control your power regardless of how you're feeling."

"I don't feel anything at all!" she screamed. A slight flicker came from a few of her fingers.

"Look," Flenoid said, "you're becoming unstable. I've told you this before. How you access your power when you learn determines how you'll access it as you age. If you access it by emotion, you will lose control, Aazar. You

229

must focus. Use the power, don't let the power use you."

Aazar retook a deep breath and tried to clear her mind, but her mind wandered to Adam. Her fingers flickered.

"That is not a good sign," Flenoid said. "Who were you thinking of just now?"

"What do you mean?"

"I've never felt your energy like that. It was very violent and angry. You must never access those emotions while working with powers."

He paused a moment. "Perhaps we should work on something else. Get your mind off of your problems right now."

"How?" Aazar said, wondering how much Flenoid could know from just her energy.

"Well," Flenoid said, smiling. "I can teach you how to understand others' energy. You'll be able to know if people are in pain or overjoyed just by feeling their energy."

"So, basically, what you're doing now?"

"We all know how to do this, even normal people," Flenoid said, sitting down in the grass in front of her. "I'll teach you how to expand it with a little more clarity."

Aazar sat with him.

"Now," Flenoid said. "I want you to relax, close your eyes and try to feel the warmth I give off."

Aazar sat on the grass. She felt nothing.

"Think about how far apart we are right now. Feel the temperature of the air around you. Now tell me when you feel the warmth."

Aazar felt the cool air coming from around her. She suddenly felt a warmth near her right knee.

"I feel something."

"Good," Flenoid said. "Now open your eyes."

She opened her eyes and saw that Flenoid held his pinky about a centimeter away from her knee. She looked to Flenoid.

"Notice, you didn't feel me touch you, you felt the warmth given off from my skin, and you knew something was there."

"Right."

"Because of this, I didn't have to touch you for you to know I was there. All humans can usually do this. What I plan to teach you is a heightened awareness of the heat given off by other people. Soon you'll be able to feel them when they are within twelve feet of you. Judging by the temperature they give off, you'll be able to feel temperature changes that affect moods and feelings. When someone has a colder temperature for a few moments, they're scared. When they are warmer, they are happy. Hot means angry. There are all kinds of temperatures between those examples, and you will be able to pick them out like you would a smile or frown."

"That's how you know when we're losing control of our powers and where it's coming from."

"I make a good teacher because I have the best judge of mood. I can tell when a student gets worked up or is homicidal." He looked at her.

"I started to think you could read minds."

Flenoid smiled. "Todd is who you have to worry about with that."

Aazar nodded. "Okay, so how do I enhance it?"

I'll continue this exercise until you find that you can detect when I'm about to move my hand without looking."

"That takes a lot of concentration."

"Yes," Flenoid said. "In some ways, it's easier than clearing your mind. Being aware of the temperature and moving temperatures around you consume your thoughts. It's an overhaul of activity."

Flenoid attempted to touch her again. This time, she detected him at a centimeter again. The next time, Aazar noticed him at two centimeters. By the end of the session, she caught Flenoid's finger from a full inch away.

"That's remarkable!" Flenoid exclaimed. "You might want to think about using this power more than your flames. You're very good at it on your first day. Even I took at least a month to get where you got in two hours."

"Really?" Aazar said.

"Perhaps we should stay away from fire training for a while and focus on this. You could do a lot of good with this," Flenoid said.

* * *

Aazar walked away from the clearing in a good mood. She'd never excelled at anything before. She had never been able to run home with an A-plus report card or win a game in sports. She frowned when she realized that being good at this wasn't something her parents would ever be proud of. It didn't seem fair. Why couldn't she have been like everyone else? Peter's influence on her life made her even less relatable to people than before. He had taught her about politics and materialism and how she could never go back to an everyday existence again. By the time she reached the street, her good mood had vanished. Her fingers flamed.

She mentally made it stop. It worked that time. She sighed. It looked like she was back to the drawing board with her fire control.

"Wow, a little out in the open to be holding fire, don't you think?" an approaching voice said.

KJ was walking up the street toward the clearing. She was so happy to see him. She had to keep herself from running to him. He looked worried. She didn't like him looking at her like a wounded gazelle. After calling everyone in the group about what had happened, she realized calling KJ was the hardest. Her voice had broken, and she had begun to cry. He had tried to comfort her, but she had hung up after. The look on his face proved she hadn't been successful at making him think she was okay.

He stopped in front of her. "How are you feeling?"

"Okay."

He looked back to the clearing. "Just finished with Flenoid?"

"Yeah."

"Any luck?"

Aazar shook her head. "He's decided to teach me sensory powers. He says I'm better at that than my fire control."

KJ was surprised. "Really? I never saw you as an empathic person."

"I'm not."

"You kind of have to be for that kind of power to work," KJ said. "I'm not bad at it, but for him to table your fire for sensory means you could probably do more good with that."

She thought about Adam. "I think I need more aggressive powers. It's a dangerous world."

"You think so?"

Aazar nodded. "There are a lot of people in the world who only respond to aggression."

"But everyone responds to empathy in some way," KJ said. "Shouldn't we start with that?"

Aazar was silent as she looked toward Peter's house. The idea of going back there haunted her. The thought of going up those stairs again made her heartbreak. She didn't understand why the family hadn't decided to sell the house. It was disgusting to stay there after what happened.

"You don't have to stay there if you don't want to," KJ said.

Aazar whirled around. "I'm fine."

"You should let people offer their homes to you before turning them down."

"I thought you were kicked out?" Aazar asked.

"Brian and I still have a little room. You're not that big."

Aazar smiled. "No thanks. It's creepy being there, but..."

"You don't want to let him go," KJ said.

She looked at him. Tears welled in her eyes. "I don't want to let him go."

KJ pulled her gently into his arms and held her. He smelled nice. Peter had always smelled nice too. She felt guilty for wishing he was Peter at that moment.

"You know," Aazar said. "I didn't spark when I saw him lying there."

KJ waited for her to continue.

"I thought that if something emotional happened, I'd catch fire like someone poured a can of gasoline on me. But I didn't. I couldn't understand why until later. It was because I couldn't feel anything. I felt like it was all fake. I wake up every morning thinking it is all a nightmare. But it's not a nightmare. It's my life. And I can't wake up. I'll never wake up."

KJ held her in silence. A few people walked past and gave wondering glances but averted their eyes as they passed. She hated them. They were walking around like Peter hadn't died. Like it didn't matter. Suddenly, KJ shoved her away. His shirt was singed in a few spots.

Aazar looked at his chest in embarrassment as he assessed the damage.

"Don't worry," KJ said. "You didn't get me."

"I'm sorry."

"It's fine. Accidents happen."

Aazar looked back to the house again. She was sure that Peter's death hadn't been an accident.

Chapter Twenty Five: Elephants

"You've got to be out of your mind. We can't go on now!" KJ shouted over the crowded cafe table.

Todd had called an emergency meeting considering Peter's accident. After a moment of silence and a mournful word about Peter, he brought the subject to the mission. They had all assumed he had called the meeting to cancel, but he wanted to go on. KJ was outraged.

Todd looked at him. "We can't leave those people there for another few months while we find a new IT guy. We can use our skills to complete this mission. It won't be as easy as it would've been, but it can still be done. It needs to be done."

"Oh, come on," KJ said. "A little respect from you, maybe? What about the fact that it's the same day as Peter's funeral? Surely you can give the group time to grieve."

"Yeah, I agree," Brian said. "This is a little soon. Plus, you made such a big deal about everything going right, and now you want to do a rush job with only a day worth of planning?"

"Everything is already set up, and this NEEDS to happen." Todd glared at KJ. "The only reason they brought you back on board was Peter's loss. Our guy on the inside of that place already got the uniforms. We already know the security will be lax that day because of scheduling. All that needs to change is that I'll need to read a few minds and get the access codes."

"Draining yourself in the process," KJ said. "And endangering the lives of our team. Not to mention the lives of anyone working there who gets in your way. I don't like this. This is the kind of rushed job that gets people killed. Hasn't there been enough death?"

"Peter falling down a flight of stairs is nothing compared to the lives of those locked in those facilities."

"Peter falling down the stairs is not 'nothing,'" Aazar barked.

Todd looked at her in apology. "Of course, it's not. I wasn't trying to say that. I just meant that these people are getting tortured daily in that place."

"Maybe we should just split the mission into two parts," Britney said. "Destroy the drugs now, get the people out later when we have better IT."

"They'll probably move the people after we raid the place," Todd said.

"Yeah, but we could follow them. See the new location and pick up the people on the next run," Brian said. "Destroying the meds would be easier to do right now. With the security cameras not under our control, sneaking two dozen people out won't be doable."

"I think we should destroy the meds," Aazar spoke up. "I don't think Peter would want us to scrap the whole mission because of him."

KJ sighed as he looked at her, and she tried to avoid his gaze. This was the last thing Peter wanted to do. She was going to see it through.

"All right then," KJ said. "We can destroy the meds this time and plan a rescue at a later date."

"You're not in charge of this group, KJ," Todd snarled. "You didn't want to be, remember."

"Why don't we take a vote," Brian said before the two brothers started to fight. "All in favor of just destroying the drugs to raise your hands."

Brian, Aazar, Britney, and raised their hands.

"All who want to scrap it raise their hand."

KJ and Jake raised their hand.

"All who want to do it all."

Todd looked around at the group as they looked at him. No one raised their hands.

"All right, fine," Todd said, annoyed. "We'll only destroy the drugs. The new plan is this: Britney does her flirt thing to get the guards away from the cameras. Keep them there as long as possible. Aazar, I need you to burn the lock off in the back storeroom. Brian and Jake will follow soon after. I'll listen for the code for the medicine room. Once I get it, we'll all go to the medicine room. Aazar and Brian wait outside the room to ensure there isn't trouble."

Todd paused a moment to think. Sometimes Aazar wondered how Todd was so great at making plans. He always seemed to know what to do when the objective was clear. It was strange to see him rushing something this important at all. Everything about this mission had been planned six months in advance. Aazar thought KJ might be correct, and Todd was losing control of himself. She had no idea why he was so adamant about doing this mission at this very moment, but she didn't question that now. Aazar needed her own escape from Peter's death. She needed her own distractions.

"After the medicine is destroyed, we all exit unnoticed through the backdoor. After KJ sees us leave, he will blow the electricity out. Britney, you'll just leave with the rest of the staff. Once the place is clean, they'll move the prisoners. Brian will follow them to the new location, and we'll make plans from there. Everyone agreed."

The group nodded.

"Great. Let me hear it in order, from the top. Britney, go."

* * *

Aazar stared at the pouring rain from her bedroom window on Peter's funeral day. Peter would've hated the cliché: Everyone dressed in black, heading into a church to mourn his life in the rain. Instead, he would have liked to be thrown on the side of the road in a garbage bag, as he mentioned to her whenever he had a moment to ponder death and the fallacy that was funerals. Aazar smiled, missing his cynical nature.

Everything seemed fake without his blunt truths spraying on everyone like water from an elephant's trunk. Aazar wished she could've hired an elephant to attend the funeral to do just that. That would've been a funeral Peter would've been proud of. Instead, he would get a few words spoken about him by someone who had never met him.

"Are you ready, dear?" Mrs. Belize whispered from the door. She had lost weight, and her eyes were sunken. She had been very quiet since Peter's fall. When she found out, it was as though the news had stolen her voice. Instead of screaming and howling, she immediately went to her room and locked herself in. She was silent, alone in the room for an entire week. This was the second time Aazar had seen her since the fall.

"I am," Aazar said, smiling.

Mrs. Belize nodded and disappeared from the doorway. Aazar glanced back at the rain again, thinking about elephants. She decided to wait a few moments before following her. Mrs. Belize's grief was almost overwhelming now that she had practiced her new power. The better she became at her new ability, the worse the house felt. She could feel Mrs. Belize's pain, Mr. Belize's guilt, and Norma's unevenness.

Norma's energy was bothering her the most. Something was wrong, but Aazar couldn't put her finger on it. Norma seemed like she denied something to herself. At first, Aazar thought it was because Norma denied that Peter had died, but the more she tuned her skills, the more she believed there was more to her denial than just that.

Aazar walked down the stairs. The rest of the family was waiting for her. Mr. Belize was checking his watch, and Mrs. Belize stared at a nearby plant while Norma pulled the edge of her skirt. There was a ring at the door. Norma let go of her shirt and rushed to the door. She swung the door open and saw Adam there. She threw herself in his arms and began sobbing without stopping. Adam patted her back and rocked her back and forth. He glanced up and saw Aazar looking at him. She felt the ice in his aura and knew Adam was to blame for what had happened to Peter. He was radiating so much cold that Aazar shivered. He looked away fast.

"Thank you for coming, Adam," Mr. Belize said, putting his hand out. "I know you and Peter had your differences, but I'm happy you can look past those and be here for Norma."

"I'll always be here for Norma, Mr. Belize," Adam said.

"How kind," Mrs. Belize said in a soft tone.

"Come on down, Aazar," Mr. Belize said solemnly. "It's time."

Aazar came down the stairs and hugged Norma and Mrs. Belize.

Adam looked at her and said, "I'm sorry for your loss."

Was that nervousness she felt from him? She wished she had studied more about her new power.

They headed to the large cathedral about five miles away. It was a church that the family only visited on Christmas and Easter. The usher smiled and handed out pamphlets with Peter's short life story. She wondered who had written the eulogy. She knew it wasn't Norma or herself, so she assumed it was Mr. Belize, considering how upset Mrs. Belize had been. It told of him being a bright boy with a lot of potential and an aptitude for computers. He was so much more than what was printed on this paper. This didn't cover it at all. She felt like whoever wrote this never took anything Peter would've wanted into consideration at all.

People began to file into the church one by one. She looked at the picture they had chosen for Peter. It was a younger photo taken when he was around fourteen and capable of a friendly smile. The young Peter grinned at her, not knowing he wouldn't even see his eighteenth birthday.

"You know," KJ said from behind her, "I keep thinking he'll jump up from behind one of these pews screaming about the falsehood of funerals and death, claiming the whole stunt was nothing but a farce to show how truly phony the human species is."

Aazar gave him a small smile. "Mrs. Belize would start screaming like a banshee, and Mr. Belize would try to strangle him Homer Simpson style."

"A pop culture reference at Peter's funeral?" Brian said as he approached. "Shame on you."

Aazar smiled. "Yeah, he'd be annoyed." Her smile faded.

KJ put his concerned face on. "Are you okay?"

Aazar's bottom lip quivered. "I just can't believe he's gone."

They all stood in silence for a moment.

Todd had just walked in with Britney on his arm. He shook Mr. and Mrs. Belize's hands and gave Norma and Adam a formal nod. He saw the group and headed straight for them with complete urgency.

"I can't believe this many people are mourning Peter," Britney said. "I'm not saying he wasn't a good guy, but he wasn't very social."

"Most of these people are work associates from Mr. Belize's job and a few of Norma's friends. We're the only friends Peter had."

Everyone was silent again. Todd cleared his throat.

"We're to meet up after the funeral at the medical facility. We don't start until everyone is there, so we can't mess around. We've only got a small window of opportunity to get this done."

"Todd," KJ said. "Some respect, please."

"Peter wouldn't want us to screw this up," Aazar chimed in.

Todd nodded to her. "Right. I'll see you all after the funeral."

Everyone took their seats.

* * *

After an hour of a preacher unknown to Peter talking about his short and fruitful life, the ceremony ended. It was difficult listening to them sing bible hymns and try to convert the congregation while pretending it was a celebration of Peter's life. Norma had sobbed incoherently on the pulpit when it was her turn to speak, so no one understood what she'd said. Mr. Belize had just read the eulogy out loud. Aazar thought about speaking, but she realized none of these people cared, and Peter would've been furious. The entire affair felt so false. The only thing that got Aazar through it was KJ holding her hand.

As they filed out of the funeral home, she noticed Adam chatting with a few girls in the cemetery. She led KJ closer to them so she could listen.

"And his funeral was much bigger than this one…" Adam said matter-of-factly.

"Really?" one of the girls responded.

"Oh yeah, it was way better, I mean, this isn't too bad, but I've been to better, you know?"

"What a scum bag," KJ said to her as he listened.

Aazar didn't take her eyes off Adam. "I think he killed him."

Norma came out of the funeral home, and Adam rushed to her side. She sobbed into his chest.

"That's a huge accusation, Aazar," KJ said. "Do you have any proof?"

"Not yet," Aazar said. "But I'll find it. Come on, let's go. Todd is waiting for us."

Chapter Twenty Six: Best Laid Plans

Aazar and the rest of the group huddled in the van as it bumped down the road. They had all changed out of their funeral clothes and had their employee uniforms ready to go. No one had much to say. Peter's funeral had put a real damper on the mission, and they all had second thoughts except Todd. The Order needed this mission to go off as planned. Since the news broadcast, several media outlets have been paying attention to Variants and their actions. This was supposed to declare their intent for the rest of the campaign.

Todd shifted back and forth. KJ took note and looked at Aazar. Brian and Britney sat silent as the grave, and Jake sat up front with the driver, who was also the outfit provider.

"After I get to the medical facility, I'm dropping you guys off, and I'm out of there," the driver said. "The Order is supposed to have someone waiting outside for you after you're finished."

"You mean, there will be a period where we don't have anyone in the alley?" KJ questioned, "What happens if something goes wrong?

"Nothing WILL go wrong," Todd said. "You're catastrophizing."

"You never said anything about having to wait on a ride after we destroy a building," Brian said, nervous.

"That's because it wasn't important," Todd said. "It still isn't. Now focus."

Brain sucked his teeth, irritated, and gazed back out of the window.

Aazar looked at KJ. "I don't think this is a good idea. Everything seems a little too rushed."

KJ shook his head and whispered, "It doesn't matter anymore. We're here.

The best we can do now is make sure nothing goes wrong."

She nodded, but she didn't feel comforted. Finally, the van pulled into the alley, and they all got out. The driver said nothing as he sped off.

Todd looked at them. "Okay, here we go."

KJ made his way to the ladder on the building next door. At the same time, Britney walked out of the alley and into the front of the building.

"How are we supposed to know when she's got them distracted?" Jake asked.

"It's a small enough building. I'm zeroing in on her thoughts…Britney's got three of them looking at her now…there's a receptionist right outside the medicine room and…a guard." He closed his eyes while he tried to concentrate.

"This building has to be at least ten thousand square feet. How are you doing this?" Aazar asked. She knew that he had gone way past a safe limit for himself. She was suddenly happy that he had never learned to channel the energy from the earth.

"I've been practicing…there's another guard by the prisoners…two…" He opened his eyes and almost collapsed. Aazar noticed that his eye color had somehow become more vibrant. Brian rushed to grab him, but he pushed him away.

"I'm fine," he said, looking more nervous than he wanted to. "I'll give her a few minutes, and I'll check again."

Aazar looked up and saw KJ on the top of the building next to them. He had his hands in his pockets and looked down at them. His eyebrows looked furrowed even from there.

"I'm fine!" Todd yelled up to him, reading KJ's mind.

KJ shook his head and looked off at the city.

After a few minutes, Todd closed his eyes and tried to listen again.

"Okay…yes…yes, they are all talking to Britney now. All that's left is the receptionist by the medicine room. She should have a break in a few minutes. Aazar, burn the lock." Todd said. His eyes seemed back to normal. It must have been a trick of the light.

Aazar looked around to see if anyone was looking. Then she put her finger on the lock and focused all her energy on it, but it didn't work. She swore under her breath. She was afraid her powers would act up.

"Come on."

"I'm doing it." She said.

"Well, Hurry UP!"

Irritated, she felt a spark. She knew it was dangerous to access her powers with anger, but it was just quicker. She thought about her suspicions about Adam and was surprised when the lock became soft against her finger. She watched the metal melt as she pushed her finger through it like clay. She calmed herself down, pulled her finger out, and saw a large hole where the lock used to be.

"Fantastic," Todd said. "Let's go."

Todd walked ahead while Aazar, Jake, and Brian walked behind him. It was a typical office building that had been converted into a medical facility. She looked at the picture of a fruit basket that hung from one of the walls. Did they kill and torture people in a place like this? Then Todd gestured for them to stop, and they all froze.

He closed his eyes. "She's right around the corner," he whispered. "She's supposed to check the medicine before each break, and…yes…she's going now…"

They all stood there as quiet as possible, waiting for whatever happened next. Then the group suddenly heard a scream from the other side of the building.

"What the fuck was that?" Brian whispered as he wrung his hands.

Todd still closed his eyes but answered, "That's where they're keeping the prisoners…okay, the nurse is putting in the code…" He mouthed the numbers to himself. "I've got it…SHIT."

"What?" Jake asked in a higher voice than usual.

"Britney…she's getting tired. I think she might lose the interest of one of the guards…we have to go now!"

Todd launched forward, and the others followed.

"Which guard is thinking about walking away?" Aazar asked.

"I'm not sure. I won't know until he decides where he's going next…shit."

"What about the receptionist?"

Todd didn't answer.

"Todd?"

"We have to go now!" He whispered back.

They walked down the hallway until they reached the medicine room. Todd shoved them all down the hall and looked at them, panicked.

"Try and look normal. Say something about the job." He said.

"What!?" Aazar whispered.

"She's coming out." He stopped as the door swung open.

The woman looked at the group as she exited the room. She smiled and turned the corner. They all held their breaths until Todd relaxed.

"She's going to lunch. She didn't suspect. Let's go."

Todd and Jake walked into the medicine room. She and Brian waited nervously outside. It felt like decades before they came out, and when they did, Jake looked exhausted. "It's all gone."

"Okay, let's go…" Todd stopped mid-sentence. He stared down the hallway and back at the group.

"What is it?" Brian asked, afraid.

"The guard who lost interest…He's going on break," Todd said.

"Which guard?" Aazar asked.

"The one that was guarding the prisoners…" He looked at her.

"NO," Aazar said sternly. She didn't have to read his mind to know what he was thinking.

"It would only take a second for you to blow the locks and free the prisoners."

"It's too dangerous," Aazar said. "We said we'd come back later."

"But we won't have to!"

"No way," Jake said. "I'm getting out of here."

Todd turned on him. "If you walk out right now, I'll tell The Order that you abandoned the mission. What do you think they'll do to you for leaving?"

"I did what I came to do," Jake growled. "I'm not getting involved in anything extra."

Todd looked at him. "You'll do it, or I'll tell everyone about your little problem."

Jake looked at him, confused. "I don't know what you're talking about."

Brian began to bounce in place. "Guys, we need to decide something…"

Todd walked close to Jake. "You know which problem."

Then, he stared deep into Jake's eyes, and all of a sudden, fear and resignment came over Jake's face.

"F…F…Fine." Jake said. "Let's…Let's just go."

"No," Aazar said. "What the hell are you doing, Todd?"

"The right thing!" He exclaimed. "Are you really going to leave those people when you could've helped them?"

Aazar hesitated.

"That could be you in there," he said.

Aazar swore.

"Let's go," Todd said, running down the hallway.

Aazar and the rest of the group ran down the hall as fast as they could. When they reached the door, Aazar opened the door with ease. She tapped into her anxiety. Flenoid would've been furious with her, but she pushed him out of her mind.

Aazar and Brian waited outside while Jake and Todd freed the others. She watched as frail men, women, and children walked out of the building. She tried to count how many there were. Suddenly, a guard came around the corner. The procession stopped in its tracks.

Before she knew what was happening, Aazar felt herself stand in front of the prisoners and activate fire in her hands. Brian ran toward the guard at full speed. When he hit the guard, Aazar heard a sickening crack. Todd came back into the hallway.

"The van is here! We can get a few more in if we…" His face fell when he saw the guard. "Britney…"

They looked up and saw all the guards running toward them down the hallway.

"Get them out of here!" Todd yelled at them.

Jake grabbed a little girl by the waist and ran with her. Brian began to punch another guard as Aazar shoved one of them out of her way. He screamed at the flames that engulfed him. He ran into a wall, and the wall caught fire as well.

"We have to go!" Todd said as he shoved the last prisoner through the door.

"But there are still people—"

"We have to go now!" Todd yelled.

Aazar and Brian ran for their lives as the building began to catch fire. When they reached the van, Todd started to wave back and forth at KJ.

"Do it now!" Todd yelled.

KJ looked at him for a moment as he took a deep breath. As he did, Aazar saw the clouds start to form above him and spin violently. The wind increased as he raised his arms.

"Todd!" Aazar yelled. "What about the fire!"

Todd looked at her for a second and then got into the van. She realized what would happen.

"KJ! STOP!" She screamed, but he couldn't hear her.

He brought his arms down, and the lightning struck the building. The electricity amplified the fire, and the building was engulfed in flames. KJ came down from the building and jumped into the van. He lurched toward Todd and began screaming at him.

"WHAT DID YOU DO!" he screamed. "WHAT DID YOU MAKE ME DO!"

The prisoners stared at the screaming man in shock. A few clutched each other.

Todd yelled to the driver, "LET'S GO."

Aazar tried to calm KJ down, but he wouldn't be soothed. He grabbed for Todd again.

"You're a monster!" he yelled. "You're a fucking MONSTER!"

"SO, WHAT!" Todd yelled back. He gestured to all the people in the van. "Look at them! WE saved them!"

"How many people were in that building!?" KJ tried to work out the number.

"Don't think about that," Todd said.

"Oh yeah," Brian said. "Well, what about Britney!?"

Todd looked at his feet. Brian had tears in his eyes.

"We just left her!" Brian exclaimed. "We just fucking left her."

KJ nose flared as he glared at Todd. "I KNEW this was going to get out of control. What the fuck happened in there!?"

"I saw an opportunity to save lives!" Todd said defensively. "We had a window!"

"Yeah, now a bunch of people are dead, Britney's gone, and we've started a fucking WAR," KJ yelled.

"I'll take the blame for it, okay," Todd offered.

"You're damn right you will," KJ hollered. "This is ALL your fault!"

They all got quiet. Jake was shaking his head back and forth while Brian continued to sob. Todd glared out of the window, and KJ stared off catatonic. She wondered if Britney survived the blast. How could everything have gone so wrong? She suddenly wished that Peter was here.

Then, a small hand grabbed hers. Aazar looked down at the little girl whose hair was matted and dirty. Her little arms had needle marks, and her hospital gown was tattered. The girl looked at Aazar and smiled.

When she opened her mouth, her little voice cracked, but Aazar heard the phrase clearly, "Thank you."

* * *

The van drove out of town and into a campsite about twenty miles away. Large tents, RVs, and fifth wheels were parked all over a dirt lot. It would be different living here after living with the Belizes. She realized that she would probably never see that family again. She knew she needed to stay with The Order now. After what she'd done, there was no going back.

Men stood outside of the camp with machine guns and stern expressions. When they drove onto it and parked, the doors were opened by a few militiamen, and they began helping the prisoners into lines for sorting.

Aazar got out, still holding the little girl's hand. When an armed guard came to get her, Aazar held her with a tight grip.

"It's okay," a voice said.

Aazar turned around to see Ivan, the doctor, smiling at her. She smiled back and reluctantly let the girl go.

"Welcome to The Order Base Camp." Ivan offered.

"It's quaint." She said.

"Well, we're just getting started. Our new commander has a lot of ideas for expanding."

"But what about building permits and—"

Ivan stopped her.

"He doesn't have any time for anything like that. He'll be building whatever he wants, whenever he wants."

Aazar swallowed.

"Oh, you don't have to worry," Ivan said. "The commander is a friend to all Variants." He ushered her to a big tent in the middle of the encampment. She looked behind her to see KJ looking at the prisoners, unsure how to feel. She could relate.

"Are you ready to meet the new commander?" Ivan asked.

Aazar blinked. "Don't you need to be promoted or something to—"

"I don't think that will be a problem." Ivan walked faster. "He's requested to see you."

"Me?" Aazar said. "He knows who I am?"

Ivan reached a large tent and opened the flap. He gestured for her to walk inside. She ducked and looked inside. When her eyes adjusted to the darkness, Aazar saw a boy with green eyes and black hair that once ran across town to give her a necklace. She blinked.

"AVERY!?" she exclaimed.

Avery, her crush from her hometown, gave her his usual grin. "Hi, Aazar. I thought I lost you."

Epilogue

very rocked back and forth as he stared out at the public pool from the lifeguard chair. He still had another hour left of his shift as he sighed loudly and adjusted his vintage 1994 Oakland A's hat. Avery bought it for $700 online and wore it as often as he could. It was the most expensive thing in his closet, but it looked worthless. That was what he liked about it: the hat wasn't what it seemed, just like him. Avery shifted again and sucked his teeth in boredom. Being a Newmalton lifeguard was a chore. He only worked there to blow off steam at the end of the day.

After becoming leader of The Order, he'd wanted to make sure he had time to keep up appearances as a regular teen. However, the job bored him, and he often thought about quitting. Avery felt like he was wasting his time. He'd rather be working on training schedules for his recruits than staring at middle-aged women doing water aerobics. A couple of girls in bikinis giggled as they looked in his direction and walked by. He gave them a brilliant smile and pretended not to notice when they gasped and whispered among themselves.

Girls, he thought as he surveyed the pool. Avery never had a problem getting feminine attention. He knew he looked good but wasn't too concerned about that. Not with what he could do. Avery was interested in one thing, and one thing only: growing his army of Variants.

He felt a warm sensation come over him without warning and sat up straight. He knew what it meant. There was another Variant around. His heart raced as he looked at the people in the pool, trying to pinpoint where the feeling came from. Maybe he could recruit them. It was best to talk to them before the government did. Variants often disappeared after a government official came knocking. Avery's green eyes slowly landed on a girl standing outside the pool fence with a blue backpack over her shoulder. *Who is that*, he wondered momentarily. The girl had curly chestnut hair and brown skin. She was slim but not skinny. The girl pushed the hair from her face, and he noticed she was pretty, if not beautiful. He saw a gold necklace hanging from her neck.

Avery had seen her before, he realized. She was in the same grade at school. The girl didn't have many friends and didn't do any after-school activities. She often looked at her shoes and kept her head down as she walked briskly through the halls. Who could tell if a girl was pretty when she rushed everywhere like that? *A Diamond in the rough*, he thought to himself.

The Diamond looked up, and their eyes locked. The familiar warmth spread down his back. *Yes*, he thought, *she was definitely a Variant*. He wondered what that feeling would be like if they touched. After being seen, the Diamond, visibly embarrassed, turned on her heels and continued walking down the street.

From his chair, Avery focused on the necklace, then, with a flick of his wrist, the trinket fell from her neck into the grass, unnoticed by the owner. Avery smiled at his little success. He'd been in control of his powers since he could remember. Telekinesis had helped him out before, and it would help him today. He knew he could summon the necklace from here, but he didn't want to make a spectacle. Instead, Avery climbed down from the lifeguard chair and walked toward the entrance.

Another Variant in Newmalton, he thought excitedly. He never thought he'd find any of them here, but Avery wasn't sure why he was surprised. There were more of them every day. They were bound to infiltrate small towns. This girl could be essential to The Order, he decided. She could hide in a crowd, and that would be important. He wondered what her abilities were. Avery jogged past the front office and looked down the street where he last saw the girl. His Diamond was nowhere in sight. *She's fast*, he thought.

Avery walked toward the pool fence and saw the tiny necklace glittering in the grass beside the pavement. He knelt to pick it up. It was plain, but it was real gold. Avery was glad he'd secured a meeting with her. He needed to make sure he made a good impression.

He opened the locket, and inside, he saw a picture of a man and a little girl, he assumed to be the Diamond, smiling up at him. He smiled back.

"You're mine," he said to the old photograph.

Acknowledgments

Thank you so much to all of you who pledged to the Kickstarter! I couldn't have done any of this without you!

Jamie Davis, Pamela Madrid, Sharon Actitelli, Rio Madrid, Ryan Stanley, Catherine Autrey, Parisa Hajizadeh-Amini, Brandi Elijah, Andrea Davis, Marc Madrid, Allison Ballou, Samantha Chacon,Francesco Tehrani, and Justin Burgess

About the Author

E.C. Madrid is the author of *The Aazar Series*, a dystopian fantasy trilogy exploring power, memory, rebellion, and the cost of belonging. Her work centers morally complex characters navigating systems of control, where survival often demands uncomfortable choices and peace rarely looks like victory.

She is drawn to stories about found family, inner darkness, and the quiet strength it takes to walk away from power. When she isn't writing, E.C. Madrid is building a life rooted in self-reliance, land stewardship, and intentional community in the American Southwest.

Her novels include *The Flickers of Fall*, *Children of the Order*, and *Variant Rising*.

You can connect with me on:
- https://www.ec-madrid.com
- https://x.com/AuthorECMadrid

Also by E.C. Madrid

Children of The Order: Book Two of The Aazar Series

The Order promised purpose. What Aazar found was control. As old allies fracture and secrets surface, she must navigate the ruins of rebellion and the weight of leadership. *Children of the Order* is a haunting journey through loyalty, loss, and the quiet war between who you are and who you're told to be.

Variant Rising: Book Three of The Aazar Series

Aazar thought she'd left The Order behind. On the California Islands, she builds a fragile peace, teaching young Variants control while trying to silence the fire inside her. But when a powerful Legacy offers her a dangerous job—and an attack reveals Avery is still watching—Aazar is pulled back into a war she never finished. As Legacy bloodlines tighten their grip on power and old loyalties fracture, she must decide who she's willing to become. Leader. Weapon. Betrayer. In a world where control is everything, Aazar will either rise… or burn everything down trying.